"ONE OF THE BEST CONTEMPORARY
MYSTERY WRITERS."
Connecticut Post

Praise for JESSICA SPEART's
Rachel Porter Mysteries

"Each of Speart's books is a great read."
Pittsburgh Post-Gazette

"Chills and laughs galore."
James W. Hall

"The author portrays the stark
atmosphere . . . vividly . . . There are plenty
of appealing characters, not the least of
which is Rachel herself."
Publishers Weekly

"Rachel Porter . . . is a very good traveling companion."
Boston Globe

"Jessica Speart is a revitalizing
gust . . . in a stuffy room."
Nevada Barr

JESSICA SPEART

Restless WATERS

A Rachel Porter Mystery

AVON BOOKS
An Imprint of HarperCollinsPublishers

AVON BOOKS
An Imprint of HarperCollins*Publishers*
10 East 53rd Street
New York, New York 10022-5299

Copyright © 2005 by Jessica Speart
ISBN 0-06-055955-1
www.avonmystery.com

First Avon Books paperback printing: August 2005

Avon Trademark Reg. U.S. Pat. Off. and in Other Countries, Marca Registrada, Hecho en U.S.A.
HarperCollins® is a registered trademark of HarperCollins Publishers Inc.

Printed in the U.S.A.

10 9 8 7 6 5 4 3 2 1

Acknowledgments

Thanks to Fred Kraus of the Bishop Museum and Fern Duval of Land and Natural Resources for their insight on invasive species. Thanks to harbormaster William Aila for bringing local issues and Hawaiian legends to life. I'm grateful to Bob Endreson, Steve Hoffman, and Linda Paul for their help. I am also indebted to Peter Knights and Susie Watts of WildAid, Marie Levine of The Shark Research Institute, and Sonja Fordham of The Ocean Conservancy for being so generous with their time and information. Many thanks to Karen Sheehan for her tireless support, to Dave Vaughn for his help on Oahu, and to Carol Fuca.

Most of all, thanks to Carroll Cox, whose devotion and passion for protecting Hawaii's environment and endangered species is nothing less than inspirational.

Restless
WATERS

One

There are days when paradise actually lives up to its overblown billing. This pristine moment in time seemed to be one of them. I floated weightless on a sheen of pure liquid sunlight, the orb's rays dancing on a sea of cobalt blue. The only thing that could have made this instant any better would have been a properly chilled martini.

That obviously did it. I'd pushed too hard and gone over the paradise limit. Within bloody seconds, my vision of Shangri-la was promptly shot to hell.

"Paddle, Porter! Paddle, paddle, paddle! Harder! Don't be such a wuss. Come on. Stand up on your feet and take command of the board!" shouted the self-appointed General Schwarzkopf of Waikiki Beach.

I'd have gladly shot back a few suggestions of my own, were it not for the teenage hotdoggers that contemptuously snickered while rockin' and rollin' on their surfboards around me. Funny what one's fragile ego will make you do. I placed my hands along the sides of the board, pushed hard with my arms, and stood up in one swift move.

Whadda ya know? This was proving to be easier the third time around.

That thought nibbled at the corners of my mind as a wave pulled my feet out from under me and I tumbled about like a single die in search of its mate. "Shaken, not stirred" could have been my motto as the sea proceeded to toss me around like a limp rag doll. Sheer panic grabbed hold of my nerves as seawater rushed into my mouth and boogie-boarded down my throat. But that was nothing compared to Mother Nature's strong hand, which bounced my head along the shallow bottom like a cheap rubber ball.

Damn!

I flinched as something prickly pierced the sole of my foot—probably a jagged piece of coral or a sharp lava rock. But all concern quickly vamoosed with the appearance of a dark shadow looming off to my left.

My heart abruptly kicked into gear, pounding hot and heavy with fear. I fully expected to come face-to-face with a primal monster bearing yellow-flecked eyes and hundreds of lethal knives in its mouth. Most likely a creature that would regard me as its very own version of surf and turf.

A green turtle, doubling as an underwater flying saucer, swam into view not a moment too soon, and I breathed a mental sigh of relief. My elation was reflected in the dazzling kaleidoscope of greens and blues shimmering above me. I quickly made my way toward them, feeling as if my lungs were about to burst. It was time to call it a day as I broke the surface, coughing and gasping for air.

I'd have deserted my surfboard in a New York minute, were it not for the fact that the damn thing was attached to my foot by a leash. The board bobbed about like a wound-up prize fighter, making me wonder just who was in charge of whom, anyway.

I pulled myself on top of the board and began to paddle for shore, wanting nothing more than to plop down at the nearest tiki bar. To hell with hoping to surf the big waves at Waimea Bay and Sunset Beach one day. Though I might be crazy, I wasn't yet certifiable.

Visions of mai tais danced in my head, each decorated with a colorful paper parasol. The image prompted me to paddle even faster. Which is why I'll never understand what compelled me to glance back over my shoulder and again catch sight of something from out of the corner of my eye.

This time I was determined to ignore any imagined monsters. I'd done a good enough job of scaring myself for one day. Only the damn thing refused to go away. Instead, it momentarily disappeared and then resurfaced, as if daring me to take a closer look. Unable to stop, I obeyed.

The next instant, my pulse wildly hammered in my ears, and I held my breath, as if hoping that might help make me invisible. For this was no docile sea turtle, but a glistening dorsal fin that slashed through the water like a sleekly sinister knife. That's when it hit me. Maybe this was what I *had* seen before.

Help! I wanted to shriek at the top of my lungs. Only the scream impotently froze in my throat. It was then I looked back again to discover that my foot was bleeding.

You idiot! That must be what's attracting the thing. Sharks can smell blood from two miles away!

Terror and frustration duked it out as I now began to paddle even faster, all the while knowing there was no outrunning the marine equivalent of a fighter jet.

Maybe so. But I'll be damned if I'm going to become sushi for some alpha predator, I thought, continuing to flail my legs in the water like a couple of frenzied seals.

Instead I prayed to the powers that be, vowing to change my ways if only I were saved. Hell, I'd even learn to cook, clean, and sew if it kept me from becoming shark bait.

My higher power must have gotten a good chuckle out of that one, for the next thing I knew, I was clambering onto the beach, dragging the surfboard me behind like a ball and chain.

"Quick! Get everyone out of the water!" I gasped while collapsing on the sand.

Dolph Trask remained standing where he was, with his sinewy arms wrapped across his chest, and his steel gray hair pulled back in a scrawny ponytail. From down on the ground, I had the perfect view of what could best be described as his chicken legs, each ornately decorated with Polynesian tattoos.

"Well, that certainly was quite an exhibit of skill and grace you put on," my surf instructor calmly observed.

"Didn't you hear what I just said? There's a shark swimming out there. For God's sake, you've got to get everyone back on shore now!" I barked in growing frustration.

But Dolph did nothing more than raise a weathered hand to his brow, as if in imitation of an ancient bronze statue.

"Are you talking about that hyperactive kid jumping around in the water wearing a snorkel and mask?"

"What I'm referring to is the killer fish with the bucket of nails stuck in its mouth!" I angrily snapped.

"Well, all I see is a mini version of Jacques Cousteau swimming with a plastic shark fin held high in his hand."

"No way," I said and pulled myself up, refusing to believe that I'd been fooled.

Damn! Dolph was right. I'd been conned by a wise-ass thirteen-year-old.

"Yeah, boys like that can be a real hazard to your health," he dryly noted.

No fooling. As far as I was concerned, the kid was a walking, talking advertisement for birth control.

"I could have sworn it was a shark," I sputtered in chagrin, tugging at my bikini bottom in an attempt to release a well-lodged sand wedgie.

"Ahh, don't beat yourself up over it," Dolph gruffly responded. "You're probably just a little nervous, what with that guy being pulled out of the water yesterday."

A businessman had been found floating facedown off Pier 32. It wasn't a spot for swimming, but rather a place where commercial fishing boats docked.

Not much had been left of him. What remained was a bloodless mannequin missing both arms, legs, and part of his buttocks. However, there was enough to determine that he'd been attacked by a tiger shark. It was easy to tell by the bite marks. Their distinctive teeth are curved and serrated like tiny hack saws, with a notch to catch and cut through bone and ligament.

I'd once heard a man describe how his wife had been attacked by one. He'd watched in horror as her body was twirled and flipped about. His description had been so vivid that, although I hadn't witnessed the attack firsthand, slo-mo images still continued to play like a horror flick in my brain. It was also why I couldn't help but wonder what a businessman had been doing in the water off Pier 32 in the first place. He certainly hadn't gone in for a swim, and God knows there were far easier ways to commit suicide.

"Well, a shark might not have got you, but a chunk of rock sure did. Better let me clean up that foot and slap a bandage on it," Dolph offered.

I sat and played patient as Dolph reached for his first-aid kit. I'd hired him over the usual buff surfing instructors for a number of reasons. First off, he was seventy-five years old. I'd figured that would make him easier on me. No such luck. Second, none of the tourists used him. But then few realized that Dolph had once been a champion surfer, winning more competitions than anyone could recall.

These days Dolph ran a concession stand on Waikiki

Beach, and proudly held the title of Honolulu's oldest living beachboy. My hope was that next to him, I'd look like a young babe.

"Maybe you should face facts, Porter. You're just not a natural when it comes to riding a surfboard, or swimming in the sea. They'd never have cast you on *Baywatch*," Dolph brashly announced, bursting my balloon.

"Well, you're not exactly David Hasselhoff, yourself," I lamely muttered, knowing full well that Dolph was correct in his assessment.

"That landlubber? Damn straight. I'm about a million times better, even if I am seventy-five years old," Dolph proclaimed, idly running his fingers through his wispy goatee.

"What say we drink to that?" I suggested, and proceeded to limp over to the nearest tiki bar.

While he might no longer have had Hasselhoff's build, Dolph was one smart kahuna. He'd recently organized the Hawaiian Beachboys Union, convincing hotels, bars, and clubs on the strip to kick into their health insurance plan and retirement fund. In return, the bronzed hunks agreed to draw both the older women and bikini-clad babes, whom they flirted with during the day, to those establishments at night. The deal seemed to suit everyone.

I could have closed my eyes and known exactly where I was, as we walked along the beach, by the distinctive smell. It was the aroma of coconut oil emanating from burning flesh intermingled with freshly frappéed piña coladas. The odor was so intensely sweet that it curled my toes and curdled my stomach.

It didn't matter where you were in Waikiki. The strip boasted a wide variety of tourists. There was the usual assortment of surf bunnies and muscles heads, along with couples on package tours garbed in his-and-her Hawaiian shirts. Sprinkled among them were geriatric swingers, with wrinkled legs and white chest hair touting numerous gold chains. These aging Lotharios were constantly on the prowl for young Aloha babes.

Meanwhile, the upper-crust set stayed mainly to themselves, preening at the Royal Hawaiian Hotel. The women kept their bodies swathed from head to toe in the sun, while their husbands lounged in deck chairs like beached whales.

Last, but not least, were the easy-to-spot Japanese couples who had come to be married. The grooms dressed in trousers and tailcoats, while the brides wrapped themselves in voluminous mountains of crisp white tulle and veils.

What each had in common was that they'd all decided to vacation in the Pacific version of Disneyland. More than likely, they'd never leave the one-and-a-half-mile strip, convinced they were partaking in the real Hawaiian experience.

"So where's your better half today?" Dolph asked, as we slipped onto a couple of bar stools. "Surfing the big ones on the North Shore?"

My better half was at the North Shore, all right. But I truly hoped that Santou was resting at home. Jake's back had been acting up lately, and he was still limping and dealing with injuries from his plane crash of nearly a year ago. That was the reason he'd finally decided to take a leave of absence from the FBI. Santou vowed not to return until he was no longer stuck behind a desk in an office. While he was hopeful that would be soon, I wasn't so certain.

"Santou's busy with a new hobby these days," I revealed. "He's gathering up broken surfboards from the beach and painting Hawaiian scenes on their surface. Who knows? He might even try to sell them to tourists."

I was beginning to worry, though I didn't dare say so. Santou loved his work as much as I did mine, and he missed it. This laid-back version of Jake couldn't last much longer. My concern was, what would happen then?

"Sounds to me like he's just plain bored out of his gourd," Dolph responded, cutting to the chase. "Or maybe I'm wrong and he's found his true calling as an artist."

I raised an eyebrow and smiled.

"Tell you what. Have him paint some hula girls playing ukuleles on a couple of those boards and bring 'em over. I betcha I can sell them for him," Dolph offered. "You'd be amazed at what people along the strip will buy. Could be that Jake has found himself a little gold mine. At least I'll be able to say honestly that they were made in Hawaii."

"Thanks. I'll do that," I replied, and reached for my iced tea.

Dolph shot me a look of surprise. "What's this? You're not turning into one of those health nuts, are you?"

He took a swig from his longneck beer and wiped the moisture off his goatee.

"Not a chance," I assured him. "It's just that I have to work tonight."

Have to were the operative words, even though it was really my day off. I'd been here for six months and was already beginning to lose my mind. It hadn't taken me long to discover that paradise isn't always what it's cracked up to be.

That thought was put on the back burner as the sun began to set. We joined the crowd oohing and ahhing as the majestic orange ball dropped into the sea as if on cue. The surf tried to embrace the last light of day, but it slipped away, its pink and gold hues skipping from wave to wave off in the distance.

"I guess it's time to make the donuts," Dolph observed, polishing off his beer before heading off to his nightly work.

I watched as he wasted no time but immediately struck up a conversation with a lonely female tourist. Then I headed off to begin my own evening maneuvers.

I liked to imagine I was Supergirl as I ducked into the nearest hotel bathroom and, chucking my bathing suit, changed back into street clothes. But somehow the vision never quite worked. Perhaps it was the outfit.

I was balancing with one leg in my pants and the other one out when my cell phone rang. That's what I'm talking about. Supergirl would never have had such a problem.

"Hello?" I answered, juggling the phone between my shoulder and ear.

"Is this the Fish and Wildlife office?" a woman loudly queried.

"Yes, it is," I responded from inside the bathroom stall.

What the hell. For all intents and purposes, it could have been.

"Well, this is Hattie Keoki. One of your people is outside my house damaging our property, and we expect you to do something about it."

I couldn't be certain that I'd understood her correctly, due to what sounded like gunshots erupting like fireworks in the background.

"I'm sorry, but I'm afraid I have no idea what you're talking about."

"What I'm talking about is your agent that's here climbing around in our trees and breaking the branches. My husband wants him off our property this instant, or he's going to shoot him," the woman righteously informed me.

"Yes, I can hear that," I responded as another round of gunfire broke out.

The only problem was there *was* no other U.S. Fish and Wildlife agent here on Oahu besides myself and my three-hundred-pound boss. And I damn well couldn't imagine Norman Pryor trying to shimmy his way up a tree.

"Can you tell me exactly why this person is in your yard?" I questioned, curious as to what sort of wacko would choose to impersonate a Fish and Wildlife agent.

"Well, for pity's sake. I should think *you* would know that," she huffed. "He rang our doorbell, showed his ID, and said he was here to catch some of those pesky alien species we're always hearing so much about. We were happy to give him permission, but he never said a word concerning property damage."

"Do you happen to recall the name on the ID badge?" I queried.

"Let's see. I believe it said I. M. Kuhl."

And that hadn't made her suspicious?

"Why don't you give me your address?" I suggested.

"We're at 1171 Poloke Place, just off Tantalus Drive."

Well, whadda ya know? It was right around the area that I'd planned to scope out tonight.

"All right. I'll be there as soon as I can. In the meantime, would you ask your husband to please stop shooting?"

"Absolutely not," Hattie Keoki adamantly asserted. "He's going to pin your agent down and hold him hostage until we're reimbursed for all damages."

"In that case, I have to tell you that the man on your property is an imposter."

"What do you mean by that?" she suspiciously questioned.

"He's not one of our agents," I replied.

There was a moment of silence, and then Hattie Keoki rapidly clucked her tongue like a pissed-off chicken.

"Ooooh. That's bad. My husband is gonna be plenty mad when he hears about this."

Hopefully not enough to make him haul out any heavier artillery.

Two

I hung up, stuffed my wet bathing suit into a plastic bag, and then headed for the parking garage to rescue my Ford Explorer. Sliding inside, I buckled my seat belt and threw the Explorer into reverse.

"Damn, damn, damn!" I cursed, having managed to sideswipe the concrete column next to my vehicle.

I leaned out the window and took a look. What I saw wasn't good. Shocking pink paint that had been scraped off the column now ran down the length of my Ford. Oh well. People would either think it was an eccentric design, or that I was one hell of a badass driver.

Exiting the garage, I joined what was possibly the worst traffic on the planet. It stretched in one long conga line up and down the strip. The upside was that it gave me plenty of time to contemplate why I'd been sent to Hawaii to begin with.

At first, I'd had a hard time figuring it out. After all, this was the land of Jack Lord and Magnum P.I. It had seemed like a plum assignment. I liked to think that I was finally being rewarded for all my hard work. But any such illusion was promptly dispelled by my new boss, who'd called me into his office and immediately laid down the law.

"Nothing ever happens here. There's no smuggling, no poaching. Only penny-ante stuff. Don't sweat it—enjoy yourself. Just kick back, relax, and keep your mouth shut."

Forget *The Stepford Wives*. Norm Pryor's assignment was apparently to mold me into the perfect Stepford Agent.

"What am I supposed to do then?" I'd inquired.

"Go to the airport, check in with the inspectors, and keep busy with paperwork," had been his response.

In other words, I was to be the equivalent of a Wal-Mart greeter, doing no more than sitting in the office and answering telephones. Considering that my territory included all of Guam, Saipan, American Samoa, Midway Island, and the state of Hawaii, surely *something* illegal had to be going on.

So far, all I'd discovered was a massive invasion of reptiles and amphibians. Alien to Hawaii, the voracious creatures were turning the state's environment upside down. They were the equivalent of snakes in the Garden of Eden, wiping out nearly all of the native wildlife. Even more frustrating was that these aliens weren't arriving here under their own steam power.

There are no naturally occurring reptiles or terrestrial amphibians in Hawaii; no snakes, iguanas, toads, or salamanders of any kind. Yet suddenly monitor lizards, veiled chameleons, and frogs were appearing everywhere. They were being smuggled into the state, along with rosy boa snakes, piranhas, and crocodiles.

As if that weren't enough, they were then turned loose in the mountains and forests. The reason for this? In order to breed and colonize. From what I could gather, the master plan was to round up their offspring and ship them back to wholesalers on the mainland. Once there, the critters were most likely dispensed to large pet store chains such as Animal World and Reptiles 'R Us. Good for kids, along with amphibian and reptile lovers, perhaps. But definitely bad news for Hawaii. The result was that millions of years of evolution were being decimated in one fell swoop.

Hawaii's web of life was shaped by isolation. The island chain is the most geographically secluded place in the world. It's twenty-five hundred miles away from the nearest land mass; too distant for any animal, amphibian, or reptile to swim to and survive. The upshot is that it took eons for each species of flora and fauna to arrive.

Seeds hitched a ride by clinging to birds' feathers, while insect eggs were carried inside pieces of driftwood, or blown along by the wind. They evolved to fill thousands of niches upon landing in Hawaii. The resulting species are so unique that they're found nowhere else in the world.

Many plants need no thorns since they're living in paradise. Some bird species have lost their ability to fly. The adaptation made perfect sense: There were no predators on the ground and, therefore, little reason to flee. I suppose that's what happens when you get used to dwelling in Eden. You eventually let down your guard. Instead, these species became mutually interdependent in a powerful show of cooperation. The downside is that it's created a disastrous domino effect. Paradise left the door wide open for aggressive outsiders against whom they have no defense. The result has been nothing less than an ecological meltdown, which has turned Hawaii into the extinction capital of the world.

Hawaii is now home to one third of all endangered species in the U.S.—not to mention nearly fifty of which disappeared during the first twenty years of the Endangered Species Act. This has led scientists to label the islands a zone of mass extinction; an archipelago of the "living dead." Replacing those once unique creatures are now cats, pigs, and chameleons, in what has amounted to the McDonaldization of Hawaii.

Crossing the Ala Wai Canal, I left behind the crowded beach and tropical ticky-tack of Waikiki to enter Honolulu, where half the island's population resides. Its outskirts are lined with squat, colorless buildings, their facades as tired as worn-out fringe. The local poor live inside these two-and three-story barracks, bringing true meaning to the words "poverty in paradise." I zigzagged through the traffic, feeling relieved as I finally turned *mauka,* toward the mountains, and began to drive inland.

Ahead stood the Ko'olau Mountains, their peaks reaching like fingers for the sky. A tsunami of lights twinkled on their ridges at night, as if they were fallen stars that had come to reside inside people's houses.

I steered onto a narrow road and began the climb toward Mt. Tantalus. The foliage grew increasingly lush and green with each twist and turn. I headed deeper into the rain forest, leaving the urban jungle behind. Pavement was replaced by elephant-ear taro, stands of bamboo, pepper trees, and ficus. Trumpet-flower vines curled up along the tops of telephone poles to strangle the surrounding trees, whose limbs barely seemed to mind, seduced by their beautiful yellow blossoms.

I entered an old, exclusive neighborhood where the privileged class lives. One of these swank, mountainside homes had formerly belonged to Ferdinand and Imelda Marcos. Two concrete lions silently roared, as if to warn me away from their gate. I paid little heed, too besotted by the heady perfume of ginger and jasmine flowers that filled my Ford. Their aroma must have worked like a drug, for only at the very last moment did I catch sight of a large animal that raced across the road.

I abruptly slammed on the brakes, barely able to believe my eyes. If I hadn't known better, I would have sworn it was some kind of mutant cat measuring at least four feet in length. The cocoa brown feline became illuminated in my headlights and then quickly disappeared back into the darkness.

I sat with my hands trembling on the steering wheel, wondering if I'd imagined the creature, or if it had actually been real. The only other explanation was that something had been slipped into my iced tea at the tiki bar.

I released the brake and continued on, vowing to pay closer attention to the road this time. The Ford agreed, its brights acting as searchlights, as we wound our way nearly to the top before turning onto Poloke Place. Hattie Keoki's residence was the last house on the block.

I parked in the driveway and walked across the grass to the entrance of the sprawling ranch. Hattie Keoki opened the door before I even had a chance to knock, having been impatiently waiting for me.

A wiry woman in her late fifties, Mrs. Keoki wore wire-rim glasses and sported steel gray hair the color of a Brillo pad. She held her hands curled beneath her chin, like the paws of a nervous squirrel, as she carefully studied my ID.

"You better get out there and do something quick. My husband is tracking down your rogue agent and swears he's gonna shoot him in the rear," she said, curtly handing my identification back to me.

"As I told you before, he's not one of our agents," I calmly tried to explain.

"We don't really care. He had a Fish and Wildlife badge, and my husband said that's enough to make you people responsible," she loudly exclaimed, as though I were deaf.

I didn't bother to argue, but instead took off toward the sound of gunshots, not wanting to waste any more time.

Tree limbs lay like fallen soldiers in the backyard. I crossed through their war zone and continued on, heading into the jungle. There was almost no need for a flashlight to guide the way. A moon the size of a truck tire hung big and heavy in the sky, its light shining down on a veritable fruit basket of guava, banana, and mountain apple trees.

I took a deep breath and nearly passed out, growing dizzy on air that was thick with eucalyptus mixed with the underlying stench of decay. Fortunately, I didn't have to worry about getting lost. I just followed the freshly broken path toward the sound of bullets.

Stands of tall bamboo creaked and groaned as they swayed back and forth. They seemed to sing, as if announcing my presence. The moon played along, its beams flickering through their fronds in a game of hide-and-seek. Even the ground joined in, having turned spongy as Jell-O after last night's rainfall.

The dark sticky mud clung thick as molasses to the bottom of my shoes. It oozed and sucked at my feet, as if determined to hold me in place. I paid little heed, far too busy ducking and dodging philodendron leaves the size of dinner plates, which sprang up all around me. It was almost enough to make me believe that I'd landed in a remake of the movie *Jurassic Park*.

I didn't watch where I was going and tripped over a root, its girth as thick as a wrestler's thigh. At the same time, a strident screech tore through the dark, sending my blood pressure soaring.

KOKEEEEEEEEEEE!

The sound, loud as a car alarm, ripped apart the fabric of the night.

It was produced by a two-inch tree frog, no larger than a quarter. A beloved mascot in Puerto Rico, where the coqui frog's likeness adorns everything from glasses to ashtrays, it's been condemned in Hawaii as an uninvited pest. The love-starved male's piercing cries grew in number until there was an amphibian chorus reaching ninety decibels. I hurried deeper into the rain forest, my surroundings having turned into a child's eerie fairy tale.

The jungle sprang to life as the spidery arms of a banyan tree now wrapped themselves around me, its long bony fingers plucking at my legs, my hair, my face. Caught in its web, I frantically tried to escape, only to have my feet break through a dense layer of matting. I sank down through its roots. It was as though the banyan were trying to eat me alive.

I was about to let loose a cry when a flicker of light in the trees up ahead caught my attention. Pulling myself free, I began to quietly slink toward it. What I spied was a different kind of bird from any I'd ever seen before.

This one had long, blond Rasta braids that were badly in need of shampoo. Attached to the braids was a teenage Caucasian boy. He sat, perched on a branch, wearing baggy jeans and a T-shirt, with Maori tattoos on his limbs and a flashlight lodged in his mouth. Ooh, yeah. He clearly looked like your typical Fish and Wildlife agent, otherwise known as the ever-so-clever Mr. I. M. Kuhl.

I silently observed as he navigated a long pole with a hook on the end. He guided it with expert precision along the tip of a skinny branch above him. Then I spotted his target: a prehistoric-looking creature with a bony shark fin crest atop its head, four pencil-thin legs, and a supple prehensile tail.

A mind-boggling two-and-a-half feet in length, the reptile shone bright turquoise green in the moonlight. I recognized it even from where I hid. The critter was none other than a veiled chameleon, which originated in Yemen and Saudi Arabia.

The bad news was that not only can it snare birds in midair, but females will lay up to thirty eggs twice a year. In other words, this horny chameleon spelled big trouble for the remainder of Hawaii's native creatures.

The kid skillfully finagled the pole so that the reptile was forced to step onto its end. Then he gingerly lowered the lizard, dumping it into a sack next to him, as it loudly hissed in objection.

I walked over to where two more bags lay beside a skateboard on the ground. Rasta Boy must have heard my footsteps, for he whipped the flashlight from his mouth and aimed it at me.

"Hey, leave those things alone! That's my private property," he angrily protested.

"Not anymore, they're not," I replied, and picked up the sacks. "You'd better come down here now. We need to talk."

"Damn straight about that," he seethed, sounding much like the captive chameleon.

Rasta Boy tied the burlap bag around his waist and carefully made his way to the ground. Then he once again removed the flashlight from his mouth, as though it were some kind of cork.

"I don't know who the hell you are, but this territory is already staked out, and my boss doesn't take kindly to trespassers. So if you're smart, you'll give me back my things and get the hell outta here, bitch."

Rasta Boy tried to grab the bags from my hand, but I twisted sideways, neatly cutting him off.

"And if *you're* smart, you'll shut up and listen. I'm with law enforcement," I told him.

"Yeah, yeah," he jeered, clearly unimpressed. "Big fucking deal. I got ID too. So what?"

The moonlight glittered along eight little hoops that ran the length of his ear, perfectly matching the front gold tooth in his mouth. Wouldn't you know? He already out-did me in the jewelry department.

"Listen, you idiot. I'm not fooling around. I'm a special agent with the U.S. Fish and Wildlife Service."

Rasta Boy showed all the respect he apparently felt I was due by flinging himself at me through the air.

If the kid was going to fight, he needed to learn better moves. I raised my knee and jammed it into his stomach as hard as I could, taking care not to hurt the chameleons. He yelped and doubled over, wrapping his arms around his waist.

I was about to open the sacks and take a peek inside, only to be surprised as he recovered and smacked me hard across the face with his open palm.

I don't know which stunned me more: the fact that I'd been caught off-guard, or that my skin burned as if I'd been stung by a hive of angry bees. Rasta Boy took full advantage of the moment to grab the sacks from my hands and start to run.

You little shit, I thought, watching his dingy hair fly through the air like links of uncooked sausages.

I was damned if I'd let him escape. I began to chase him in an all-out race. But what I'd forgotten about was my foot. The cut from my earlier swim began to pound in time with my face. Even worse, I now found myself slipping and sliding on what seemed to be an endless patch of mud. It was all Rasta Boy needed to make headway.

Come on, come on, come on, I silently urged, willing myself to speed up.

Though I managed to increase my stride, it still wasn't

quite enough. I was left with no other choice but to steal Rasta Boy's earlier move. Hitting a particularly good stretch of mud, I coasted along on it as fast as I could. Then I flung out my arms and hurled myself at him.

Success! I grabbed on to his braids and jerked hard, bringing him to a stop. Only he wasn't yet ready to give up. My fake agent twisted around and attempted to punch me.

I quickly feinted to the left, pivoted on my heel, and thrust a hand against his chin with all my weight. Thank God, Krav Maga, the self-defense system I'd been trained in, had become second nature. I didn't have to think, just react, as he was thrown up against a tree and temporarily knocked out. But our skirmish had attracted another problem. Gunshots now began to erupt uncomfortably close by.

"Hold your fire, Mr. Keoki," I called out to my unseen assailant. "Everything's all right. I'm a federal agent."

However, it didn't get the response for which I had hoped.

"Yeah, I've heard that line before and I'm not falling for it again," came his snappy retort from somewhere in the darkness. "I'm going to teach you a lesson, and that's not to show up on my property anymore."

Great. Just what I needed to deal with—another obstinate, pissed-off citizen.

"The boy that came to your door was an imposter. He's here with me now, and the situation's under control. Stop shooting and I'll show you my badge," I tried to reason.

"I've already seen one too many of those tonight. Why should yours be any different?" he responded, punctuating it with more gunfire.

My foot throbbed, my face hurt, and I wasn't in the mood for all this. In addition to which, I was hungry and tired. That's when bad things can happen to distracted agents. It was time to bring this lunacy to an end. I pulled out my .38 and quickly fired two rounds into the air.

"I'll tell you only once more that I'm a federal agent. Your wife called and asked for my help. Now throw down your gun and come out where I can see you. Otherwise, my target won't be the sky next time, and I warn you that I'm an excellent shot."

A man in his sixties with the torso of a walrus, powerfully built arms, and two double chins walked through the foliage and came into view. His clipped gray hair was coarse as a scrub brush, his face so tight and round that not a wrinkle showed on his skin. The problem was that Walter Keoki maintained a tight grip on his rifle.

"I'm not kidding, Mr. Keoki. Throw your weapon down right now!" I advised, aiming my .38 at him. "If you don't, I'll be left with no choice but to shoot."

Walter Keoki stared at me for a moment, and then slowly did as instructed.

"All right. Now I'm going to reach into my pocket and take out my badge."

I did so, along with my ID, and tossed both items to him.

Mr. Keoki carefully examined them. "They look different from what that other fellow had," he grudgingly admitted. "But you can't blame me for thinking you were a trespasser. After all, what kind of federal agent travels around with a skateboard and a couple of bags of lizards?" he inquired, pointing to the articles at my feet. "Besides, I don't see anyone else here with you."

Damn!

I quickly whirled around, but Rasta Boy was gone, along with the sack he'd been holding. Mr. I. M. Kuhl had proven true to his moniker, coolly slipping away during all the shooting.

"So, is this what you call having the situation under control?" Walter Keoki questioned, beginning to stand a little taller. "And there's still the problem of damage that's been done to my property. Somebody's going to have to pay for that."

I wondered if the lizards inside the sacks had any idea of how much trouble they'd already caused. And if so, did they care at all? Probably about as much as their captor did I figured. I silently vowed that he hadn't seen the last of me yet.

I followed Walter Keoki back to his house, where his wife was busy talking up a storm on the phone.

"Here. Your boss is on the line and wants to speak to you," she said, thrusting the receiver into my hand.

"Porter? I expect to see you in the office first thing tomorrow morning," Norman Pryor darkly intoned.

I gazed at Mrs. Keoki, wondering how the hell she'd managed to get me in trouble so quickly. Norm Pryor's phone number was unlisted, as was that of every other law enforcement agent.

"I'll be there," I replied and hung up.

Hattie Keoki shot me a triumphant look. "You should remember that it's people like us that pay your salary," she lectured, before turning to face her husband. Loudly clucking her tongue, she slapped him in the stomach, and took his rifle away. "And no more fooling around with guns for you, unless I say it's okay."

I grabbed the skateboard and bags of goodies, no longer wanting to play. Instead I walked out of the house and down the driveway. All I wanted to do right now was go home. But I couldn't resist first taking a peek inside the sacks.

Holy leaping lizards! The first bag held a pair of protected Egyptian spiny tails that were roughly thirty inches long and weighed a couple of pounds.

Their clublike tails had large, pointed, sharp scales that

could be whipped around to beat an attacker. Hawaii was far, far away from their desert home. It made me wonder if my lizard-catching friend had planned to set them loose in the hope that they'd survive and breed.

The second bag contained a panther chameleon as colorful as a rainbow on acid. Each of its turreted eyes turned in a different direction. One stared at its surroundings, while the other rolled up to examine me. It must have thought I was one hell of a big bird, for a tongue, twice the length of its body, catapulted out and headed straight for my mouth. I quickly shut the bag to avoid an interspecies kiss. As much as I like wildlife, I did have my limits.

While it was nice to know that I had a smidgen of animal magnetism, I doubted that it would help me in the morning. I started my SUV and took off, certain of one thing: The illegal ranching of lizards on Oahu was a much more highly organized trade than anyone would ever have thought.

Three

I heard the pounding of the waves before I actually saw them. There was a good reason for that. These were the winter monsters capable of swelling up to sixty feet in height. They roll in from the Gulf of Alaska having traveled two thousand miles, gaining strength along the way.

I held my breath and swore I could feel them rumble, the ground trembling as they broke. Salt sprays trailed behind them like a legion of lacy wedding veils, their vapors carried on the air, covering the road in a light mist. It was a gentle reminder that the North Shore couldn't have been further from the bustling streets of Honolulu and from Waikiki Beach.

There are no high-rise buildings, no acres of pavement, and rather than a freeway, only a two-lane road runs along the coast. Three stoplights are all that regulate its thirty-mile stretch. Of course, in just one of those miles are over a dozen surf shops. But then, what else could one expect? This is the surfing capital of the world, a place boasting surf breaks with names such as Avalanche, Monster Mash, Gas Chambers, and Banzai Pipeline. Even the Beach Boys paid tribute to the North Shore in one of their songs, "Surfin' U.S.A."

This was where I was living these days—in Haleiwa, to be more precise, a quirky little plantation town dotted with old clapboard buildings and creaky wooden sidewalks. The highly eclectic population consists of surfers, artists, ex-military, former mercenaries, skateboarding dudes, and multi-ethnic families that have lived here for generations. Throw into the mix the mysterious rich who reside up in the hills, living in multi-million-dollar mansions, mostly paid for with cash.

This was the kind of place where one could purchase a handmade surfboard for ten thousand dollars. If that didn't suit your fancy, cheaper wares were continually being hawked from thatch-roofed stands and off the backs of pickup trucks.

Tourists wandered through, but they generally didn't stop. Rather, they circumnavigated the island in their rental cars or stared out the windows of tour buses. The crowds that did come were those that watched or participated in surfing contests during the winter months. And even they stayed for only a few days before returning back home.

I turned onto a narrow dirt road and headed for a driveway marked by an upright surfboard. For some reason, it always reminded me of a tombstone waiting to be inscribed. I parked the Ford and walked toward an old beach house that was badly in need of a paint job. Its faded blue exterior looked as if it had been dipped in saltwater-blue tears that had long since dried.

The only things that gave the place life were the potted plants lining both sides of the well-worn stairs. Each step sagged beneath my feet, as though caught in the midst of a tired yawn. I did my best not to trip over the ragged hodgepodge of sneakers, shoes, and flip-flops that haphazardly led up to the doorway. Instead, I added my own boots to the collection, all the while being watched closely by Tag-along.

The marmalade-colored cat mewed in rebuke, as if to scold me for coming home late. I placed the skateboard down on the porch, and the feline anxiously sniffed at the burlap bags in my hand.

"Trust me, Tag-along. You don't want to tangle with those things. The spiny tails in there could probably rip your head off. What are you doing outside, anyway?"

I shooed Tag-along indoors, knowing full well that he could cause as much damage to the native birds as the uninvited reptiles on the island. Tag-along had come with the house, as had his owner and our current roommate. I tried to take solace in the fact that at least one of them was under my partial control.

I followed the cat through the screen door, my bare feet padding on the sandy wooden floor. It took a moment for my nose to adjust to all the mosquito punks about the house, their aroma spread by the overhead ceiling fans. I called out, but neither Kevin nor Santou appeared to be anywhere around. That was all right. I had a pretty good idea where to find them. Besides, the chameleons needed to be cared for.

With that in mind, I dragged a potted ficus tree from its appointed post in the kitchen all the way down the hall. A few deft moves and the plant was inside the bathroom. Another couple of grunts and groans and it was hoisted into the tub. Once there, I misted each leaf, removed the Eqyptian spiny tails from their bag, and placed them on its branches. Then I repeated the procedure with a second plant and set the panther chameleon on it.

"Nighty night and sweet dreams," I said, closing the bathroom door tightly behind me.

Then I headed outside and walked down the beach, careful to avoid any sharp rocks that might further slice open my feet. Soon two lava lamps came into view. Their flames flickered in conjunction with a grille that sprang to life, as Jake stoked its fire. The warm yellow light revealed Santou's distinctive features, ever so softly smudging the sharp line of his nose while playing hide-and-seek among his nest of tousled black curls. Even now, my pulse sped up at the sight.

Sitting in a beach chair beside him was a man whose hair had been bleached flaxen white by the sun. He apparently didn't care, for the sun's rays had also etched a web of deep squint lines around his eyes. Their color was lockbox gray, the same as that of the sea after a storm.

The men appeared to be so deeply engrossed in conversation that neither took notice of me. It was the black-and-white pit bull by their side that gave my presence away. Fifty pounds of pure muscle jumped up and began to charge in my direction. Fortunately, Spam had a whole lot more creampuff than Cujo in him.

Jake had stumbled upon the pooch shortly after we'd moved to Haleiwa. The dog had appeared to be abandoned and bedraggled. His ribs had poked through his skin, he'd walked with a limp, and his eyes had been lackluster and sad. Since that time, Spam had been nursed back to health until he was stocky and strong. Perhaps a little too much so.

These days he boasted powerful jaws and a thick muscular neck that held up a head the size of a brick. Spam's cropped ears stood straight at attention like two little horns, while his whip of a tail tapered to a sharp exclamation point. His devilish appearance cleverly belied his sweet nature.

However, if there was ever a candidate for doggy Valium, Spam certainly had to be it. He had the odd habit of accelerating to full speed and bashing head first into whatever stood in his path. At the moment, that turned out to be me. Spam came close to knocking me off my feet as he excitedly jumped up and began to lick my face. And just like most men, he hated to take no for an answer.

"Spam, that's enough. Down!" Santou called out to him. The dog immediately left me and trotted back to his master.

"Hey, chere. Where have you been? We were just about to start dinner without you."

Walking over, I leaned down, and gave Santou a kiss, figuring we should share equally in Spam's sloppy affection. Kevin said nothing, but continued to drink his beer slowly as he gazed off into the distance.

Kevin O'Rourke was a buddy from Santou's past, a ghost that had flitted in and out of his life—one that I'd only recently met. From what I had gathered, they'd known each other years ago in New Orleans. After that, Kevin's background became suspiciously murky.

I'd been told that he'd served in the military, and then had traveled the world. Maybe so. But as far as I was concerned he'd picked some mighty unusual places to visit. Hot spots such as Afghanistan, El Salvador, Lebanon, Iraq, and the Philippines. In other words, he wasn't your average tourist. The only personal item on display in his room was a photo that obviously had been taken years ago. It showed a much younger Kevin in front of a hut, beneath a sign that read SCHOOL FOR JUNGLE SURVIVAL TRAINING. My guess was that it hadn't been a course offered by Club Med.

Though he liked to brag about the numerous languages he spoke, Kevin would never reveal what they were, or exactly how many. I'd have gladly written the guy off as a con artist and jerk. However, Santou wouldn't let me. Instead I could only assume that he'd either been with the CIA or had worked as a paid mercenary—neither of which he or Santou would confirm or deny. The only things I knew for certain was that Kevin was now "retired" and that he annoyed me immensely.

I also wasn't convinced that he was the best influence on Jake. Or maybe I was jealous of the growing amount of time they spent together. The problem was that the housing market on Oahu was both exorbitant and tight. That gave us little choice. If we were to rent, we'd have to reside with at least four other people in a reality version of the old TV series *Friends*.

Our problem was solved in an odd twist of fate. Kevin's girlfriend had decided to split for greener pastures just as we'd arrived. Kevin had a great place and wanted to share expenses. We needed somewhere to live, and the price was right. It was a match made in renter's heaven—otherwise known as how to make do in Hawaii.

"Today was great, chere. Kevin brought me some beat-up surfboards, and I've been learning a new airbrush technique with cut-out stencils. Wait till you see what I've done. Remind me to show you the boards later on."

Kevin's major passion these days was surfing the big waves. He supported his habit by crafting primo hand-made surfboards. It had been his idea for Jake to paint the torn-up boards that they found.

"How was your day, chere?" Santou politely inquired.

I didn't dare tell them about my disastrous surf lesson. Not unless I wanted to become the butt of one of Kevin's running jokes.

"Same old, same old," I blithely responded. "I spent the time catching up on paperwork."

"Oh yeah? Then you must have had one hell of a big pile. Are you certain that it was really paperwork you were doing?" Kevin casually questioned.

I nailed him with a sidelong glance.

Kevin's girlfriend had cheated on him. It wasn't terribly difficult to understand why. As a result, he was now suspicious of every woman he met. I also didn't know how much Santou had told him about our own past problems. It was at times like this I wondered if Kevin was trying to drive a wedge between Jake and myself.

"I took a drive up along Tantalus after sunset," I replied, casting him an icy glare. "It seems some joker is running around the area passing himself off as a Fish and Wildlife agent."

"Why in the world would he want to do that?" Jake asked in surprise.

I was unsure from his tone whether to take it as an innocent question or an insult.

"In order to gain access to private property. I imagine from there he's heading back into the rain forest and collecting illegal reptiles at night," I replied.

"What in hell for?" Jake continued.

"My guess is he's probably selling them. I have a hunch that reptiles are being smuggled and released in the wild to colonize and breed. After that, their offspring are most likely gathered and pipelined to dealers on the mainland where they're sold for big bucks."

"In other words, some lowlives are treating Hawaii as their own private terrarium," Kevin summed up.

"Exactly," I agreed.

I'd once heard that everything grows like gangbusters in this place. All one had to do was plant an item, count to ten, and jump out of the way.

"Personally, I think that's pretty damn clever of them," Kevin added with a smirk.

"Why am I not surprised by that?" I shot back.

"Now, now, children, let's play nice," Santou intervened, having become used to our rivalry. "So chere, did you catch anyone?"

"I spotted a kid with blond Rasta braids and Maori tattoos, but he got away," I grudgingly admitted. "However, he did leave a few things behind. I managed to get my hands on his skateboard and two bags of protected reptiles, a pair of which originally came from Egypt."

"Sounds like white surfer trash to me," Kevin mused, taking another sip of his beer.

"What makes you say that?" I asked, figuring any information would be worthwhile.

Kevin blinked, as if in silent acknowledgement. "Let's just say it has to do with the Rasta braids and tattoos. My money's on a punk that's drifting between trying to be Bob Marley and going native. Then there's the skateboard, of course. That's always a dead giveaway."

There it was: the smarmy undertone that made me want to slap him. Instead I bit my tongue, aware that Kevin tended to be right on the mark.

"It's probably one of those little surfer wannabes who dreams of getting in tight with the big boys and riding the monster waves up here," he concluded.

"You're talking about the kids that are continually breaking into cars and stealing what they can to support their surf habit?" I tried to clarify.

"Yeah. That, and to buy drugs. You've seen them around. They're the scumbags that skateboard all over town when the waves aren't up. You know. The ones who smoke crack when they have the money and huff glue when they don't. Their sole means of support seems to be committing all the petty crimes in the area."

See, that was the thing. I couldn't imagine kids like that would have the smarts to connect with big-league pet dealers on the mainland. In addition to which they'd need the know-how to run an underground business. No, there had to be someone else in the mix; a mastermind behind the scheme.

I sat on a log and thought about it, only to become transfixed by the waves that steadily pounded the sand beneath me.

Ba bump, ba bump, ba bump.

It was almost as if the beach had developed a beating heart.

We were the sole occupants on this paper white strip of sand, except for a stand of tall ironwood trees. Garlands of sea grape encircled their base, insouciant as children playing a game of ring-around-a-rosy. From there the vines languorously stretched and spread out, decoratively lining the shorefront.

I leaned back and took a deep breath, wanting nothing more than to float on the beguiling scent of the sea and the night air. Instead my senses were overwhelmed by the delicious aroma of mahi mahi, cooking on the grill. The smell filled my nose, causing my stomach to rumble and my mouth to water.

A whisper of breeze rustled my hair, its warm breath caressing my back in a seductive dance. I willingly gave myself over, my toes digging deep into the sand. Spam came over to nestle against my leg, burying his damp nose in my calf, as I rested my hand on his fur. If I'd had one wish, it would have been to freeze-frame this moment forever.

My mind continued to wander until Santou removed the fish from the grill and divvied it up on our plates. That, along with the enticement of fresh corn and cold macaroni salad, helped bring me back to reality. I opened a bottle of cold beer and listened to it fizzle. A ghost wind blew from off the Ko'olau Mountains, as if the island were exhaling behind us.

"You know those reptiles that I mentioned having caught?" I asked between bites of corn.

Both men nodded as they continued to eat.

"I just want to give you fair warning. They're stashed in the bathtub. I'll take them in to work with me tomorrow morning."

"No problem, chere." Santou chuckled. "I've been living with you long enough to know its always best to look twice before stepping into things at home, or slipping under the covers."

"Sounds as if you lead a charmed life," Kevin softly sniped.

"You bet I do," Santou said, and drew me close.

There he was, my knight in shining armor. I'd come to realize it was a tacit agreement between couples. You were always there to protect each other's backs. I also knew that one good turn deserved another.

"How about showing me those surfboards you painted today?" I suggested, once dinner was over.

"Absolutely," Santou agreed, sounding pleased.

We walked to a shed behind the house that served as Kevin's workshop. Inside were sawhorses, tools, and drying hardwoods, along with finished surfboards that hung from the walls and the rafters. Each had been polished to a glistening finish and was a beautiful work of art.

Jake reached under a table and pulled out two of his own creations. One surfboard was adorned with a Hawaiian girl strumming a ukulele, while the other bore the likeness of a shark. An involuntary shiver rolled down my spine at the remembrance of today's excitement. I ignored that board, and focused my attention on the babe in the grass skirt.

"Dolph thinks he can sell your boards if you paint them with these kinds of images," I relayed, wondering how hard it would be to shake ones hips and strum an instrument at the same time.

"Sounds terrific. In that case, maybe I'll find myself a couple of models," Santou suggested with a sly smile.

"Like hell you will. The only one that will be modeling for you is me," I advised, trying to figure out where to get a grass skirt and grab a couple of hula lessons.

Santou laughed at my response. "You've got a deal, chere. How about you show me a few of those moves tonight?"

"I'll do my best," I replied, quickly offering a prayer to the goddess of hula.

"That's good enough for me," Jake eagerly agreed.

We headed inside the house, leaving Kevin alone to contemplate the sea.

Four

Dawn woke me early the next morning. Shades of rose and fuchsia lazily stretched their limbs across the water before ascending to turn the sky an incandescent pink.

I rolled over and Santou pulled me toward him. I snuggled there for a moment, luxuriating in the breeze of the ceiling fan and the caress of his hand on my body. Then I gently brushed away a curl and kissed his forehead.

"I have to get up," I whispered, and reluctantly began to drag myself from under the covers.

However, Santou didn't let me go very far.

"Not so fast," he protested, and firmly drew me back into bed.

I gave in, held captive by the rhythm of his heart against my skin, as if it were pulsating for the both of us.

"I think you should find a line of work that has better hours," he murmured, his breath seductively warm in my ear.

"Oh yeah? Then perhaps you'd like to pay me to model as a hula girl for your surfboards," I lightly bantered.

"If I do that, we'll have just about enough money to crash in two hammocks on the beach," Jake drowsily responded.

"Exactly," I confirmed with a throaty laugh. "Which is why one of us needs to get up."

I tore myself away as Spam continued to snore up a storm on the other side of the bed.

I ambled into the bathroom to be greeted by the three lizards, who eyed me suspiciously. They were probably wondering what I was up to now, and where in hell their breakfast was.

"It's coming," I promised, and carefully placed them back inside their traveling sacks.

Then I showered, quickly got dressed, and the lizards and I hit the road.

My Ford soared past fields of red earth carpeted with long green strips of pineapple. Farther down the two-lane stretch stood an array of little wooden houses all in a row. Each was perched on stilts, as though it were a shore bird. Their corrugated tin roofs blazed bright as silver dollars under the morning sun. This was where Del Monte housed their field hands. A few waved to the passing cars as they marched off to work.

I traveled the saddle between the Ko'olau Mountains and the Waianae Range, making surprisingly good time. That is, until I hit the H-2 freeway and came to a dead stop. My vehicle was promptly swallowed up in a line of bumper-to-bumper traffic. There was no need to turn on the radio and listen to Howard Stern or Rush Limbaugh in order to be entertained. Just like every day, the usual crazy mix of drivers was all around me.

There were the Japanese, who adamantly believed they were on the wrong side of the road, while vacationing New Yorkers cut off other cars and flashed them the finger. Marshall Islanders drove their vehicles as though they were on water buffaloes, and Filipinos honked their horns in order to say hello. That angered the Koreans, who took it as an insult, and threatened to kill them. Rounding it off were the usual number of junkies, high on crystal meth and crack cocaine, that were ensconced in stolen vehicles. Worse yet, they were the only ones driving properly on the road.

I got off the H-2 freeway and made my way to the Fish and Wildlife office in downtown Honolulu. Before going up, however, I stopped for my morning dose of coffee. One Venti latte, along with two biscotti, and I was ready to face the world. I walked out the door of the local Starbucks, better known as the American embassy among government employees, and entered the federal building.

The elevator slowly creaked up seven flights. My footsteps echoed as I trod down the hallway. The Fish and Wildlife door was still locked, a clear sign that Norm Pryor had yet to arrive. Using my own my key, I opened the door and walked inside. I'd been assigned the smaller of two offices, in which the prior agent had thoughtfully left behind a poster.

It was of Donald Duck holding a tropical drink and wearing sunglasses while twisting around in a beach chair. What he saw obviously gave him a fright. There were seven bullet holes lodged in the wall directly behind his head. I couldn't have come up with anything better, myself. It conveyed everything that needed to be said.

The other memento he'd left was a note, attached to the computer, which read *This place is Apocalypse Now without the war.*

I was still trying to figure out what that meant.

My boss meandered in at 8:30 A.M. sharp. He was rarely too early and rarely too late, but usually right on time. It was a trick I had yet to learn. What I had discerned was that he liked to think of himself as a cross between Dennis Hopper and Rachel Carson. Probably because he rode a Harley hog, and pretended to be an environmentalist. Truth be told, he was closer to the older

version of Marlon Brando or Jaba the Hut. Norm Pryor
tipped the scale at close to two hundred eighty pounds. At
least he was smart enough to dress accordingly.

Today he was a model of tropical fashion attired in a
colorful Hawaiian shirt, loose camo pants, and white
leather moccasins without socks. A pair of soft pursed lips
were set in a puff-pastry face, and his eyes blinked at me
with the slightest hint of recognition. A hard-core bureau-
crat, he'd left a cushy position in D.C. and come to
Hawaii for one simple purpose: to add "resident agent in
charge" to his resume.

Fieldwork was a necessary element when it came to
climbing Fish and Wildlife's career ladder. However,
Pryor's enthusiasm for hands-on experience had lasted all
of one day. It ended abruptly after checking out a complaint that someone was housing an illegal piranha. Pryor
discovered it was true by sticking his hand inside the
aquarium and nearly having his thumb bitten off. The result was that he no longer had use of it.

"I thought we had an understanding, Porter," he
growled, sticking his head in my doorway. "You don't stir
up trouble, and I don't make you do more paperwork than
is absolutely necessary."

I lifted one of the burlap bags from the floor and
handed it to him.

"You might want to take a look inside and see what's
running around up on Tantalus these days."

Norm Pryor snuck a peek and nearly had a coronary.

"Don't ever just hand me something like that! What in
the hell are those things, anyway?" he asked, quickly closing the bag.

"A pair of Egyptian spiny tails. There's a panther
chameleon in the other sack," I said, offering to show it
to him.

"I'll take your word for it," he responded, thrusting the bag back into my hands. "Maybe a zoo will take them."

Okay, so perhaps not warning him hadn't been very smart. Still, I'd expected a different reaction.

"Don't you think we should keep them in a cage in the evidence room?" I suggested.

"What the hell for?" Pryor snapped.

It was then I saw the piece of pastry he held, and realized I'd probably put him off his breakfast.

"Well, there's a good chance that someone has started a breeding colony in the wild," I explained. "I nearly nabbed a guy with a veiled chameleon on Tantalus last night. We'll need these lizards in order to build a case."

"Don't be ridiculous, Porter. They're probably just someone's pets that got loose. I know these things are illegal, but we can't arrest every kid on the island that gets hold of one. Besides, it's puny stuff not worth our time."

"I really think there's more to it than that," I insisted. "The kid was passing himself off as a Fish and Wildlife agent. He also seemed to know exactly where to find these chameleons, and what he was after. I have a hunch they're being bred here on Oahu and shipped over to be sold on the mainland."

Pryor's stomach must have felt better. He took a bite of his gooey cherry Danish.

"You really are one for conspiracy theories, aren't you?" he scoffed, licking a strand of jelly from his lips. "This is a small place without much action. I'd have thought you'd realize by now that people make up crazy stories and start to believe them. You can't let yourself get sucked into that kind of thing. For chrissakes, some nut even called here the other day claiming that a cougar was running around loose in the mountains."

"I think he might be right," I remarked, recalling the large cat that had crossed my path on the road last night.

"Then you're becoming as nutty as the rest of the islanders. Tell you what, Porter. You prove to me that there's a cougar up in those mountains and I'll eat its scat," Pryor vowed.

Jaba the Hut was on. His challenge was too good to turn down.

"In the meantime, I don't appreciate receiving calls from irate congressmen at night, whose neighbors are bitching about my agent," Pryor huffed. "You know perfectly well that word about this incident will eventually filter back to D.C., and neither of us needs to deal with that kind of controversy."

Pryor was right about one thing. Oahu was a small place with very powerful politics, where almost anyone could bark and get my boss on my back. Oahu was proving to be my most contentious posting so far. Call me crazy, but when it came to Hawaii, the federal government morphed into a giant complaint counter to which everybody seemed to have twenty-four-hour access.

"If you want to do something useful, I suggest that you head over to the airport and try to get your stats up. That's an endeavor that will make us both look good."

It hadn't taken me long to learn how that game was played.

A Customs agent would zero in on a tourist coming into the state with something they probably didn't realize was illegal—say a sperm whale tooth pendant, or leaving with a piece of coral. Fish and Wildlife would then be called in to make the seizure. In turn, Fish and Wildlife was expected to bring the National Marine Fisheries Service in on the case. That way, all three agencies were able to generate *mucho* paperwork.

It amounted to the age-old ploy of, *I'll scratch your*

back with my tourist today if you scratch mine with yours tomorrow. The tactic successfully made all three agencies appear to be busy without ever doing much in the way of real work.

I carried the two sacks of chameleons into the evidence room and placed them in a screened cage, along with a plant from my desk. They examined their new temporary home as I sprayed everything well with a mister.

Fortunately, there were still some live crickets inside an egg crate kept on hand for just such emergencies. I threw a handful of calcium powder into a small plastic bag and, gathering up the crickets, placed them in there as well. A few quick shakes and the bugs looked as though they'd just been through a snowstorm. Then I released the crickets inside the cage, and the lizards promptly set to work.

One by one, their tongues lashed out at the insects with the lightning-fast speed of a whip. A suction cup on the end of each tongue fastened onto its prey, and snapped the cricket into the lizard's waiting jaws. The reptiles then slowly began to munch, methodically chomping up and down.

More than anything, they resembled a bunch of senile old men who'd not only forgotten to stick in their dentures, but also couldn't quite remember that they still had food in their mouths. Eventually, all the little cricket legs and antennas disappeared from between their lips. The lizards looked so benign that it was almost hard to believe these same creatures were ruining the environment of Hawaii.

Having fed them, I then took off for the airport, aware that anything was better than spending the rest of my day at work with Pryor.

I followed Ala Moana Boulevard as it hugged the southern coastline, passing the Aloha Towers and blocks filled with fancy shopping strips. It was as the road transformed into Nimitz Boulevard that Honolulu gradually became seedier. Sam Choy's Restaurant flew past, as did Hilo Hattie's, with its bargain-basement Hawaiian shirts and cans of chocolate-covered macadamia nuts. Soon I was driving through a section filled with industry and down-and-dirty commercial fishing boats, an area that few tourists rarely ever visited.

Without thinking, I abruptly veered off the route to the airport and turned onto Alakawa Road. It seemed to happen of its own accord. There was little choice but to follow the whim of my Ford.

The next moment, I was drawn toward a world far different from any dreamt of in Waikiki: the area by the piers. It was then I remembered. This was where that businessman had mysteriously gone for a swim and been attacked by a shark.

From here, I was able to spot three enormous Japanese ships in the distance, lined up along the harbor. All were stocking up on provisions, food, and fuel, along with changing their crews. I'd always known Honolulu was a vital port, but hadn't realized it was so important to both domestic and foreign vessels. Then again, it made sense. Hawaii is the crossroads of the Pacific.

I focused my attention back to the dock I was on, and slowly made my way down along its piers. Each was filled with an array of longliners that had recently come in, their decks still reeking of fish guts and blood. These are the boats that traverse the ocean year-round, catching swordfish and tuna. Of equal interest was how longliners had earned their name.

Each boat sets lines laden with thousands of baited hooks. These nets extend for up to sixty miles. Though they're after specific target species, their "bycatch" is huge. The long flippers of endangered sea turtles become entangled in them, as do dolphins and marine mammals,

causing the creatures to drown. Meanwhile petrels, albatross, and other sea birds end up impaled on their hooks,
in what amounts to an indiscriminate killing frenzy. It's
the reason that leatherback sea turtles are now just ten
years away from extinction.

Barechested men, doing maintenance work on their
boats, stopped and stared as I drove by. I took little notice
of them, or the sound of their tablesaws, my interest solely
on the fishing equipment on board.

A large pink spool sat mounted on each longliner's
stern. Coiled around its reel was at least a mile's worth of
monofilament fishing line. Next to it was a box overflow-
ing with large buoys, usually referred to as "titty balls"
by the crew. A basket filled to the brim with lethal steel
hooks sat nearby.

Different contingents make up the island's longliner
fishing fleet. It comprises boats from Hawaii, Alaska, and
the West Coast, as well as those belonging to the Vietnamese, Taiwanese, and Koreans.

The boom in Hawaii's longline fishing industry began
back in 1987. It started for the most basic of reasons. East
Coast longliners had trashed their own territory, causing
populations of fish to plummet. As a result, the laws became stricter. The fishermen's response was, "Screw it.
There are no regulations in Hawaii. Let's go there."

But they weren't the only ones to sail west. The same
thing happened on the Gulf Coast, where overfishing
caused the entire ecosystem to crash. The ocean bottom
became so toxic that the shrimp were no longer edible.

To make matters worse, the Gulf Fleet included Vietnamese fishermen that had moved to America and been
given low-interest loans to pay for their boats. The government didn't intend to see them default and fail. So the
fishermen were told, "Go to Hawaii, where it's still wide-
open cherry-picking season."

I'd recently heard rumors that highly endangered black-footed and short-tailed albatross were being caught in longliner nets. Though I'd asked Pryor for permission to take action, my request had been adamantly denied.

"It's not within our jurisdiction," he'd said, polishing off a Krispy Kreme donut. "When it comes to Hawaii, anything that takes place on the water belongs to the National Marine Fisheries Service."

"Yeah, except there's one problem with that. It's not NMFS's job to manage birds," I'd replied.

"You're right," Pryor had responded between bites. "You want to know something else? I don't care. You're to deal only with those species that can be reached without getting on a boat."

The catch-22 was that it didn't leave me with a hell of a lot to do in Hawaii.

I leaned my head out the SUV window and took a deep whiff. The briny sea air tickled my nose and the sun reflected off the windshield, skipping along my skin, as its warmth penetrated deep into my bones. I allowed myself to daydream that I was suddenly my own boss and could do as I wish.

Sun light, sun bright. I wish I may, I wish I might kick Fish and Wildlife's butt and make them do what's right.

The response to my wish came in the form of a catcall.

"Come back on this boat again, asshole, and you'll live to regret it!"

I wondered if someone was possibly talking to me. Quickly looking around, I spied a native Hawaiian in his mid-twenties getting off a longliner that had just docked. The young man was husky, yet tall, had wavy black hair, high cheekbones, and wide, almond-shaped eyes. A knapsack was thrown over his shoulder.

"You and your lousy people," another voice now began to scornfully taunt. "Any place your ancestors took a dump on this island is so goddamn sacred that we're not supposed to fish in the water or build on the land. You lost the war years ago. It's about time you got over it."

"What war are you talking about? You lowlife *haoles* took Hawaii from us, just like you take everything else," the young man shot back, while spinning around.

I cringed, knowing that *haole* was slang for "Caucasian," and in this case had been used as an insult.

The quick move caused him to lose his balance and nearly fall into the water. He caught himself only at the very last moment.

The fishermen that had jeered at him now began to howl with laughter. Though more derisions were hurled, the young man wisely remained silent. His gait swayed from side to side as he walked, as if he were still on board the rocking boat.

I turned down the pier and pulled my Ford up beside him. From up close, I could see that he'd been dealing with more than just insults. Bruises were scattered about on his face and arms.

"Are you all right?" I asked.

I wondered what the fight was really about. Hawaii is one of the most racially tolerant places in the world, making this incident all the more unusual.

He never stopped walking as he turned his head toward me. His eyes narrowed suspiciously, and his lips remained tightly compressed.

"Who are you?" he asked, in a strained voice.

"My name is Rachel Porter and I'm a special agent with the U.S. Fish and Wildlife Service. I heard some of what went on back there," I said, motioning to the boat. "Do you need any help?"

He no longer looked at me, but focused his eyes dead ahead.

"Yeah, plenty. Only there's not a damn thing you can

do about it," he said, and broke into a sprint, heading toward Alakawa Road.

I gazed back at the longliner, where some of the crew
members continued to glare at him. I now saw that they
were a mixed group of whites, Filipino, and Chinese. It
was a small representation of Hawaii's ethnic stew.

One man stuck his tongue out and lewdly wiggled it at
me. It was clearly time to move on. Whatever had taken
place would have to remain a private matter.

I watched for the Hawaiian native as I drove back along
Alakawa Road. However, he must have been an extremely
fast runner; he'd mysteriously disappeared, as if he'd
never existed at all.

Swinging back onto Nimitz Boulevard, I thought little
more of it while continuing to the airport. Along the way,
my Ford passed even more unsightly industry, coupled
with an explosion of car dealerships.

I arrived at Honolulu International Airport and wandered among the fast-food restaurants, gift shops, and lei
stands as throngs of tourists bustled about. They wasted
no time but jumped into cabs and headed for Waikiki to
enjoy sun and fun, laced with booze cruises, sexy hula
shows, and luaus.

This was the commercial face of Hawaii, where the
Aloha spirit is packaged and marketed. Money would be
surgically removed from each visitor's wallet over the next
several days, after which they'd be sent home with a smile,
having been properly done up.

Was it any wonder that Hawaii prayed to the god of
tourism? It's the state's biggest industry, raking in a cool
eleven billion dollars a year, and the rate continues to esca-
late. The process has evolved from a fine art into a science.

I felt like a scam artist myself as I prowled about, waiting to pounce on unsuspecting visitors. Was this what I'd
signed up for upon joining Fish and Wildlife? No longer

was I breaking up smuggling rings and tracking down poachers. Instead I was reduced to pissing off tourists by taking their trinkets and making their children cry.

It was someone else's turn today to be the bad guy. I watched as an airport official relieved a teenage boy of a chunk of lava rock protruding from his knapsack. It's believed if you take a piece from Hawaii that you'll be cursed with bad luck until the rock is finally returned. There must have been some validity to the superstition. The kid's bad luck had already begun.

I hung out for a few more hours and then decided to call it a day.

Tempting as it was to head back up to Tantalus, it was still far too early for anyone to be out catching lizards. Besides, it would be best to let things cool down awhile. With that in mind, I decided to check out an area on the North Shore for alien critters later that night. I took the scenic route home, being that I had plenty of time.

My Explorer looped around past Diamond Head, named by British sailors who'd believed its volcanic glass rock to be diamonds. Come to think of it, they hadn't been far off the mark. The houses surrounding it were worth a fortune these days.

I continued on to Pali Lookout where King Kamehameha had driven native warriors off its steep cliffs. Eight hundred skulls were later found on the ground. All that was to be found there these days was an influx of tourists—most of whom probably believed Kamehameha to be a Hawaiian dish.

I was beginning to feel something in common with those vanquished warriors. I suspected I'd been sent to Hawaii as a means of being disposed of. Talk about feeling isolated. I was stuck on an island in the middle of nowhere. Los Angeles was 2,557 miles to the east; Tokyo, 3,847 miles to the west. And those were the two closest places around. I could have been hit by a meteor and no one would have known it. A nagging voice inside my head said that was exactly the way my superiors in D.C. wanted to keep things.

The Ko'olau Mountains changed as I drove farther north. Their gentle slopes gradually morphed into fairytale mountains topped with fluted towers and minarets.

This was the rainy windward coast. It lived up to its name as dark clouds began to gather, like a convergence of Mafia bosses, and settle against the cliffs. I barely had time to close my windows before the sky erupted.

This was no sneaky rain, so fine as to barely be seen. Heavy drops poured down with a vengeance. It rains here so often that Hawaiians have a name for every type of shower imaginable. This one was *paka ua,* the kind that makes noise when it splatters. The torrent huffed and puffed. I struggled to see through my windshield as enormous pellets pounded the hood of my Ford. Ever so slowly, the storm subsided until it turned into *kehau*, a gentle rain that floats in the air.

It ghosted down the cliffs, creating a mist that transformed the land into a Chinese watercolor. I stared in wonder as threadlike strands bloomed into waterfalls, each a cascade of shimmering quicksilver. Moisture settled like glistening confetti on the surrounding greenery, and a double rainbow arced against the canvas of sky.

I was tempted to stop and search for a pot of gold at its end. Only something equally tantalizing spurred me on: the promise of shrimp and garlic. The rain was over by the time I reached my destination, Giovanni's White Shrimp Truck.

Veering off the road, I parked beneath a banana tree. Its branches drooped so low that they hit my rooftop, their fronds heavy with raindrops. The truck itself was covered with enough graffiti to make one believe it had either done duty in New York City or that Jackson Pollack had used it as a backdrop for one of his paintings.

I ordered the hot and spicy shrimp, peeled off a shell, and popped one in my mouth. A volcano exploded inside me and tears streamed down my face. I quickly knocked back a can of Coke, took a deep breath, and then proceeded to devour the rest. By the time I was through, I'd used up nearly all the napkins in the place. It had been the perfect meal.

Having paid homage to Giovanni's, I proceeded home, where the usual assortment of flip-flops and sneakers cluttered the front steps. I played a game of Hopscotch, picking my way through the minefield of all the scattered footwear.

Tag-along stood waiting behind the screen door, where she broke into a yowl as I approached. I walked inside and quickly realized that Spam was nowhere around. Otherwise, he'd have been careening down the hall by now, in a headlong dash. It also meant that Santou and Kevin weren't here.

The marmalade hairball continued to shriek like a banshee as she brushed against my leg. Good thing I understood "Cat-onese," and knew exactly what she demanded. Scrounging through the pantry, I pulled out the last packet of Tender Vittles, tore it open, and poured it into her bowl. The cat daintily flipped out a nugget, ate it, and walked away. I should have been so lucky as to have her self-control.

I figured that if Santou wasn't here, he'd be out back painting his surfboards. I walked over to the shack and peeked inside only to find that neither he nor Kevin was at work. It struck me as odd at first. But then I realized that Jake wouldn't have expected me home this early.

I started to stroll along the beach, wondering where they could be. My first clue was all the cars that were parked along the road. Then I saw that a crowd had gathered. Santou was probably among them. I kicked off my shoes, relishing the sand that squished between my toes, as I headed to where an impromptu surfing contest was already in progress.

A group of riders sat on their boards, bobbing like corks, waiting for the perfect wave. Had I checked Kevin's answering machine today, I'd most likely have heard his surf report and known where to find them.

Kevin was among those fanatics that eat, breathe, and sleep the waves. There was no question but that he was a gung-ho maniac. I'd viewed his scars from past surfing injuries. He showed them off as proudly as though they were medals. In fact, it was only when Kevin spoke about surfing that he actually seemed happy.

I had little time to ponder his psyche further, as the surfers were up on their feet, an impressive swell having risen on the horizon. It rolled and began to peel in a wave that I'd heard described as a "rice bowl." I looked again at the riders and spotted Kevin, with his shock of white hair.

Only experts surf the North Shore at this time of year—or those that are crazy. Kevin was definitely a little of both. Still, I had to hand it to the guy. He certainly looked like a pro, gracefully flying down a mountain of liquid glass. For the first time, surfing struck me as a dance between a wave and its rider.

"Cool bananas!" a surfer called out, and flashed the "hang loose" sign as Kevin rode the wave all the way in.

However, another surfer wasn't so lucky. A woman gasped as the man was jerked off his board and swallowed in a thick, grinding barrel of water. It was as if the wave had specifically chosen this rider to be its next victim. A guy on a Jet Ski quickly sprang into action and rescued him.

I continued to search the crowd for Santou, but couldn't find him anywhere. Though I wasn't sure why, my anxiety steadily began to build. I blamed it on his plane crash, the memory of which still haunted me, coming and going at will.

I grew restless and wandered down along the beach when a big brown mound caught my eye. It was Spam dozing in the sand, sprawled out like a giant frankfurter. There was no doubt that Jake had to be close by.

A shout from the crowd drew my attention back to the water, where a surfer was coasting through a tube so huge that a Winnebago could have driven through it. I watched in admiration as he finished, and the next surfer took his place in line. It was then that my heart ground to a halt and panic grabbed me by the throat. Santou sat with his legs wrapped around a surfboard, looking like a rodeo rider.

My mind turned blank and my body grew numb. Only when a siren screeched in my head was I jerked from my stupor.

He couldn't possibly be this crazy, I tried to reason with myself.

But then, what in hell was Jake doing out in the water? Granted, his physical therapist had said that swimming would be good. Even some light surfing might be all right. But this was suicidal!

A cavernous wall of blue broke over the jagged reef, and my stomach clenched in a knot. Jake could end up with a fractured skull, or a lacerated leg. That was, if he didn't kill himself altogether. Then another thought hit me. What if he injured his back again and became paralyzed?

An enormous breaker rushed in, sounding like a freight train. It punished the sand and made the ground tremble as it lapped at my toes. The swell curled its lip and sneered at me, as if having read my thoughts.

You have no control over the situation. Don't you remember? The ocean isn't your jurisdiction.

I did the only thing possible. I frantically waved my arms in a desperate attempt to get Santou's attention. Only it was too late. He was already up on his feet and careening down a wall of fluid thunder. I held my breath, too afraid to watch, yet unable to pull my gaze away.

For one long second, time froze and he looked like a Hawaiian god. His feet were perfectly placed on the board, and his arms spread wide, as though they were wings. It was a moment of sheer elation as he leaned forward and rode the wave, one in which nothing else mattered but the pulse-pounding present.

My adrenaline paid no heed to my fear, but sailed the crest, with Santou, as the wave feathered and curved into a gigantic arch.

Come on, come on. You can do it, my heart sang out, ignoring my frazzled nerves.

And I truly believed that Jake could—until the ocean suddenly turned against him. There was nothing specific that gave it away, only the rumble I felt.

Maybe the water was angry because Santou had misread its mood and grown too cocky, or maybe it was a warning never to tempt the hand of fate. In any case, my palms became cold and clammy, as if aware that something bad was about to happen.

The following moment, Jake slammed into a concrete wall of surf.

I stared in horror as he somersaulted and his body was wildly tossed about. It was followed by an explosion of white water that pulled him beneath the waves.

I heard myself scream, but the cry was drowned out by the thunderous roar of the ocean. The next sound to be heard was the thrum of a Jet Ski shooting to life and carving its way through the breakers.

The salt air jabbed at my throat, as sharp as hundreds of tiny ice picks. The pain didn't stop until Jake bobbed back up and was pulled out of danger's way. Even then the waves bellowed and chased the Jet Ski to shore, as if loathe to give him up.

I ran over to where they landed, traversing nearly thirty yards in one second flat. I prayed with all my might that Santou would be all right. It was only after I discovered he was still in one piece that I was tempted to smack the hell out of him.

"Are you out of your goddamn mind?" I seethed, all the while wondering if I could strangle the man without making a scene.

Santou appeared to be momentarily contrite. Then his male ego kicked in and took over.

"What are you doing out here, anyway? You shouldn't even be home yet," he countered.

"No shit," I fumed. "What else are you doing that I'm not supposed to know about?"

It was a toss-up as to who I wanted to pummel first—him or Kevin.

"For chrissake, chere. Calm down, will you?" he asked, looking around in embarrassment. "I know you're concerned. But take a deep breath and try to put this whole thing in perspective."

I looked at him, totally dumbfounded.

"Perspective, huh? Let's see. That would have to include the fact that you're on leave of absence from the FBI due to a bad back. Or have I got that wrong? Maybe you're planning to spend the rest of your life painting surfboards instead."

Santou looked at me, and I knew I was winning the war—until Kevin sauntered over and began his "now you're one of the gang" spiel.

"Hey, nice going there, buddy," he said, patting Jake on the back. "A few more rides like that and you might earn some badges of honor to match mine," he bragged, pointing to one of his scars.

What a jerk! The last thing I needed was to have him reinforce Jake's high-risk behavior.

"Don't you remember, Kevin? He's already has his own badges. Or, have you already forgotten about his near fatal plane crash?" I snapped.

"Whoa! Call off the dogs, Jake," he joked. "And I'm not talking about Spam."

"Very funny. Then I guess you're also planning to take care of Santou after he cripples himself from one of those stunts," I shot back.

Kevin's lips twitched in amusement. "Jeez. What's your problem anyway, Rach? Is it that time of the month or something?"

That did it. Kevin had just sliced, diced, and hung himself.

"You know what? I think you'd be perfectly happy if Santou never went back to work. That way, you'd have someone to play with all day. I don't know what your deal is, Kevin. Other than that you're a selfish prick. My guess is you were probably a dud at whatever your job was, and would like it if Jake dropped out, too."

"All right, chere. That's enough," Santou sharply reprimanded. "Time out, the both of you."

Time out? What the hell did he think this was? Some sort of game being played?

And then I realized that I'd hit upon it. I was dealing with two overgrown kids.

"Fine. You want to kill yourself? Go right ahead. Just

do it quickly," I said, preparing to walk away. "Come on, Spam. Let's get out of here."

Damn! Wouldn't you know? The dog didn't budge. Instead, he chose to remain with those of his own gender.

Five

I turned on my heels and stormed down the beach, cursing the male mentality and all things macho. I was so pissed that I jumped in my Ford and drove straight to the nearest cafe.

It took a burger topped with a slice of grilled Maui onion and a hunk of avocado to help me calm down. What the heck? Why stop there? I also ordered a side of French fries, knowing it would make me feel better. Kevin may have won this round, but the battle had just begun. He didn't know what I was capable of doing when it came to the man I loved.

By now it was late enough to start my search for invasive species. I put all thoughts of today's surfing incident aside, and climbed back into my SUV. Then I drove along the water's edge, following the Kam Highway, past stands piled high with pineapples and coconuts. The sun was just beginning to set as I reached Shark's Cove.

Pupukea Road rose steeply as it wound along the mountain. I turned inland, and slowly followed its trail. The foliage grew increasingly dense and lush all around me, as if overgrown vines were about to swallow my vehicle. Equally strong was the distinct sense of dusk that hung in the air. Fiddlehead ferns drowsily nodded their noggins, while willowy leaves drooped around the reddish trunks of eucalyptus trees for the night.

I was once again leaving civilization to enter the world of the rain forest. Only this time, there was no accompanying sound of gunfire—just an overwhelming sense of silence.

A small dirt road branched off to the right, and I automatically took it. The only thing in sight were two Java sparrows perched in a tree. The markings on their black caps, white cheeks, and bright orange beaks were absolutely perfect. It was as if someone had painstakingly painted each bird, careful not to go outside the lines. The pair looked at me and then, spreading their wings, flew away.

Oahu's oldest *heiau*, or temple, came into view a few yards farther on. Parking my Ford, I got out and walked toward its black volcanic walls. The stones surrounded an upper and lower terrace the size of two football fields. Next to it stood a double-tiered wooden platform on which native Hawaiians still left various offerings.

Human sacrifice had been performed in the past at this site, in order to appease the war god Ku. The only things left these days were bananas, mangoes, and oranges. I hoped those would be enough to please him.

I was thinking about that as I walked to the edge of the bluff, and looked out over Waimea Bay. The last vestige of sun had disappeared, and the moon now cast a silvery path that shimmered like a trail of coins on the water. The breakers rhythmically crashed against the shore, rippling in a succession of deeper and darker blacks as they traveled back out to sea.

I sat on a rock, only to quickly jump up as two doves abruptly shot out of the grass. I laughed nervously and told myself that it was nothing. Then my leg brushed against a sensitiva plant and its leaves closed, exposing their prickly thorns. Part of me took it as a bad omen, while my logical side said I was merely being silly. Maybe so, but something didn't feel quite right.

The air grew cool as night wrapped its cloak around the mountains, and the stones came to life, vibrating with a mystical force. I scarcely breathed, not daring to move, afraid of what might happen, not wanting to take a chance of breaking the spell.

Tap, tap, tap!

The staccato sound echoed in the dark, bringing the mountains, sea, and sky converging in on me. My nerves sprang into action, my pulse raced, and chicken skin ran down my arms. I'd heard that in Hawaii, tapping stones was a way of communicating with the dead.

I swiftly looked around, terrified of what I might find, yet knowing it would be far worse to be caught off guard.

Waimea Valley stretched like a gloved hand behind me, an impenetrable curtain of darkness falling on either side. It was only upon glancing at the ridge to my right that I caught a pinprick of light snaking through the thick jumble of forest.

It's believed that *menehune,* the magical little people, built these temples, forced to complete their task in a single night. Either they were hard at work on a construction project, or someone was sneaking around jacklighting critters. I moved stealthily toward the area, determined to find out.

Roots grabbed at my feet, and vines clutched my legs in an attempt to steer me off course. But I'd have none of it, ready to kick ass after butting heads with Pryor and Kevin, both on the same day. I continued on, pushing my way past banana trees with leaves the size of small motor boats. I was grateful this wasn't the South American jungle. Otherwise, I might have been stuck dealing with tarantulas.

I made headway, one belabored step at a time, until I finally drew close enough to see what I was up against.

Well, whadda ya know? It was Rasta Boy sitting in a tree, with his jeans sliding precariously low down his rear end.

I waited patiently as he caught a veiled chameleon, much the same way as he had the night before. It confirmed exactly what I most feared. There was more than one colony of the lizards here on Oahu.

I remained concealed in the bushes, as Rasta Boy dumped the chameleon in a sack and made his way down the tree. Then I sprang out of my lair and pounced on him.

"What the hell?" he sputtered and began to frantically flail about, having been grabbed unawares.

I managed to hang on as he spun around like a deranged stallion. It was only when he slammed against a tree that I finally fell.

"For chrissakes, it's *you* again?" he angrily exclaimed, glaring down at me.

He turned to run off, but I quickly reached out and grabbed on to his pants. My reward was to catch a glimpse of a pimply full moon that I would have preferred not to have seen. Rasta Boy solved that predicament by pulling them up and irately shaking me loose. However, he wasn't fast enough. I scrambled to my feet and lunged, my fingers clamping on to his braids. If the kid had any brains, he'd eventually figure out the dilemma and get a haircut.

"What's your problem, bitch?" he growled, twisting this way and that.

"You are," I said and smacked him across the head, as he tried to break my hold. "That's not a nice way to begin a conversation."

"Ouch! What's wrong with you? What the hell did you do that for?" he grumbled.

"It's this condition I have that's known as 'don't piss me off.' I tend to act like a bitch when I'm called one. So what have you got inside the bag tonight, Timmy?" I asked, curling my fingers tighter around his braids.

"What's with the Timmy crap? That's a pussy name," my tattooed friend complained.

"All right, then. If you don't like Timmy, what should I call you?" I inquired, keeping a strong grip on him.

"Why the hell should I tell you?" he spat.

"Okay. Be that way. See what I care," I replied, and slipped my hand into his front pants pocket.

"Hey, hey! What do you think you're doing? Diving in for a free feel?"

That's the thing about some men. They truly believe themselves to be the proprietors of extra special goodies.

"I hate to break it to you, but it doesn't feel like there's much down there in the way of bells and whistles," I remarked, and pulled out a wallet.

It was an expensive red leather clutch with decorative white piping and a fancy steel buckle. Either this belonged to a woman, or Timmy had a feminine side to him.

I opened the wallet and found a driver's license that identified Ms. Cynthia Corcoran as its true owner.

"Hmm. It looks like you've been a busy boy tonight, Timmy. Or would you prefer that I call you Cynthia?"

"Cynthia? Oh yeah. She's a friend of mine," he languidly replied.

"Really? Then why don't you tell me her last name?"

"She never mentioned it. We like to communicate in nonverbal ways, if you know what I mean," he said, with a smack of his lips.

"I'll bet. My guess is this wallet has been reported as

stolen by now. Which means, the police will know where she's staying on the island."

This time he kept his mouth shut, and held my gaze.

"All right, then. Here's the deal. I'm going to give you a choice. I can either get this wallet back to Ms. Corcoran, myself. Or you can accompany me, and we'll let her decide what to do with you.

Rasta Boy mulled over both options as the moonlight danced on his gold hoop earrings, as it had the other night.

"What do you want from me?" he finally inquired.

I was seriously tempted to ask for his jeweler.

"First, tell me your name."

He choked, as if a hairball were stuck in his throat. Then he looked me up and down in disdain, and slowly smacked his lips again.

"Dwayne Brewer."

"There. That wasn't so hard now, was it? I'm Rachel Porter."

"Rachel Porter the bitch, you mean," he snarled.

I smacked him across the head once again. If nothing else, he'd learn some manners by the time we were through.

"Just so you know, it sucks meeting you," Dwayne said in a sulk.

"And here I thought we were becoming fast friends," I pleasantly countered. "Do you have any ID to prove you're who you say you are?"

He began to reach into his other front pocket, and I quickly latched on to his hand.

"I'll do the honors," I informed him.

"Sure. Anything to get another squeeze of the family jewels." He smirked. "You know, I could bring you up on sexual harassment charges."

I took a good look at the scraggly kid standing next to me. Not only was he dirty, but Dwayne had enough body odor to knock out an entire courtroom.

"Trust me. That would be a hard sell," I said, and pulled out a billfold.

Inside was a photo ID badge for "Special Agent I. M. Kuhl." It showed Rasta Boy looking suave as ever, with his braids rolled and pinned to each side of his head like a deranged version of Heidi. Behind the badge was a driver's license for one Dwayne Brewer. I noted his address. How convenient. Brewer lived next door, in the town of Waialua. Other than that, there was ten dollars in cash in his wallet.

"Okay. Now what say we have a little chat?"

"What about?" he asked suspiciously.

I didn't respond, but pulled the sack from his hands, turned on my flashlight, and took a peek inside. Whoa! Tonight's catch was Madagascar geckos, along with the veiled chameleon. These little beauties could fetch up to two thousand bucks apiece on the mainland. Dwayne should have been better dressed with the kind of money he was apparently raking in.

"About how I'm going to throw your ass in jail," I responded, placing the bag on the ground.

Dwayne broke into a hack and spit out a lugie. "That's total bullshit. I haven't done anything wrong."

"You mean, other than steal people's wallets and pass yourself off as a federal agent?"

"Haven't you heard? Impersonation is the highest form of flattery," he smarmily retorted.

Oy veh. The kid was a wiseass on top of everything.

"That's just for starters," I informed him. "The real topper is something that's going to send you to prison for years. You might have heard of it—a little crime known as interstate trafficking. I have proof that you're smuggling illegal reptiles to pet stores on the mainland and, in return, getting big bucks."

In this case, I had no problem with stretching the truth.

"Yeah? So what?" Dwayne responded, sounding totally unfazed. "The way I see it, I'm helping everyone out. The state wants all these alien critters off the island, right? Well, I'm doing my part by catching the little suckers. So what, if I make a few bucks in the bargain? I deserve it for my time and expertise. Besides, do you know what a pain in the ass it is to deal with shipping companies these days? And what do I get in return? A little thanks from anyone for my trouble? No. Instead you threaten to arrest me. Well, you know what? Go ahead. Make my day."

Dwayne swung his braids about as though he were the Hawaiian version of Clint Eastwood.

"I can hardly wait to get into court and give my defense," he continued, building up a head of steam. "By the time I'm through, you'll be lucky if you still have a job. The judge will think you're a certified idiot for having ever bothered me in the first place."

The kid was smarter than I'd originally given him credit for—but not smart enough.

"There's only one problem with your scenario," I informed the little weasel.

"What's that?" he gloated, looking mighty pleased with himself.

"You're also responsible for the illegal importation of reptiles into the state, with the intent of setting up colonies to breed and sell them. That's a big no-no."

"Uh-uh! No way are you pinning that shit on me. My job is just to catch these things," Dwayne blurted out.

I silently thanked him for verifying my hunch. I no longer had a doubt that some mainland dealer was in cahoots with a couple of locals here on the island. I had to admit, it was a clever plan to save big bucks. Captive breeding could be an expensive and frustrating experience, with possibly little to show for it. This way, freight was the major cost.

"It makes no difference to me whether you're the one that's bringing the reptiles in, or shipping them out," I informed him. "I guess that also means you haven't yet heard about the new state law that was passed."

Dwayne warily looked at me.

"Legislators have made breeding and trafficking in reptiles a federal offense. That means prison time in the state of Hawaii."

Dwayne's legs began to buckle under my little white lie. I roughly jerked him back up.

"Face it. Your friends set you up to take the rap and be their patsy. They must be real good buddies of yours, huh? After all, you're the schmuck who's out here at night doing all the legwork, dodging property owner's potshots, and taking the risk of getting caught. It's a pretty sweet deal from their angle. They make the big bucks and you do the time. In a sense, you're pretty much their little slave boy," I needled, hoping to soften him up. "It's good for you that I understand how these things work. Who knows? Maybe I can arrange it so that you don't end up in too much trouble."

"Oh yeah? And how would you do that?" he asked, his voice suddenly sounding a good octave higher.

"Well, there's no getting around the fact that somebody will be going to prison. But it doesn't necessarily have to be you. Do you follow?" I questioned, keeping my tone nonchalant.

I could feel Dwayne's legs quiver like two jelly rolls as I continued to hold him up.

"I think I need a beer," he weakly suggested.

"You've got to be kidding," I responded, with a laugh. "What do you expect me to do? Take you to a bar?"

"There's a six-pack in that sack over there," Dwayne said, nodding toward a paper bag that I hadn't noticed before.

I took no chances, but pulled out my handcuffs and manacled my new best friend to a tree branch.

"I bet you have some fun with these things, huh?" he feebly joked.

But I could tell he was beginning to fold.

"Yeah. In fact, I'm having fun with them right now."

Then walking over, I picked up the bag, and pulled out a carton of Tsing Tao beer. A fancy red ribbon was attached to its handle, along with a handwritten note.

Lau, We miss you. Here's a little something for you to enjoy in the afterlife. Much love, your Ginger.

What a guy, what a guy. The creep had obviously stolen the six-pack from off of some poor man's grave in a Chinese cemetery.

I handed him a warm bottle and he pried the cap off, using his gold front tooth as an opener. Dwayne wasted no time but downed half of the beer in a single slug.

"You know what would hit the spot with this? How about some moo shu pork and a couple of eggrolls?" he bantered, apparently feeling much better.

"I have another idea. Let's cut the crap and get down to business," I proposed, as he lifted the bottle and took another gulp. A trickle of beer ran down his chin and onto his throat. "Why don't you tell me who's running this operation?"

"Yeah, right," Dwayne said with a snort, sending a stream of liquid shooting out his nose. "One lousy brewski and you expect me to get on my back and spread my legs like some kind of whore? What do you think I am? Stupid or something?"

"As a matter of fact, yes," I said, unable to get the image of Dwayne on his back out of my head. "Tell me this. What are you being paid for your efforts? It's obviously not enough. For chrissakes, you can't even afford to buy your own beer."

Dwayne dropped the empty bottle on the ground and let loose a burp. "Bullshit. It just so happens I make out pretty damn good. Not only that, but I also work on my own schedule. How many people do you know who would kill for something like that? But since you're being so damn nosy, I'll tell you what I get paid. Five dollars a pop for each lizard. Add those puppies up and it's not bad for a night's work, huh?"

I didn't know which amazed me more. The fact that he'd said it with a straight face, or that he was so damn stupid.

"You're putting me on, right?" I asked in astonishment.

"No. I told you the money was good," the kid boasted.

"For God's sakes, that's pathetic! You're being totally ripped off," I revealed.

Jeez, I didn't even like the guy and I felt sorry for him.

"What the hell are you talking about?" he demanded, and angrily rattled the handcuffs.

"You're out here putting your butt on the line and for what? Do you have any idea what your boss is getting for just one of those geckos in that bag?"

"He told me they go for about twenty bucks," Dwayne retorted, stubbornly jutting out his chin.

"And I suppose you never checked it out, just to make certain he was telling the truth?" I quizzed.

"No. Why should I? He's a good guy," he replied.

But a note of uncertainty had crept into his voice.

"Then let me fill you in on just how honest he is. Each of those geckos can go for up to two thousand dollars a piece."

Or so I'd been told. In any case, I wasn't about to downplay their price.

"Holy shit!" the kid sputtered, his body sagging heavily against the tree.

"That's right. As I said before, you're completely disposable. Like it or not, you're the fall guy, Dwayne," I said, rubbing it in. "So, what do you think of your friend now?"

His face contorted from a look of shock into one of rage.

"I'm gonna kill the son of a bitch!" he exploded.

"Here's something else you should realize. I can make your life a living hell, if I so choose. Do you have any idea what the penalty is for being caught with just three of those reptiles, or a breedable pair of chameleons?" I questioned.

Dwayne shook his head, never taking his eyes off me.

"Up to two hundred thousand dollars in fines," I revealed, telling the truth. "That's what you're looking at right now."

Dwayne's mouth fell open, and his wrist hung limply within the handcuff.

"I don't have that kind of money!" he whined.

"But that's not the worst of your problems. I'm sure you don't want to spend three years of your life in prison. After all, you're a good-looking guy. That means you'll probably wind up being somebody's bitch," I added, figuring that was a nice final touch.

"I'll do anything you ask. Just don't send me away to jail!" the kid wailed, half in tears.

I looked at him and bit my lip, as if thinking it over.

"All right, then. Here's what I want you to do. Set up a meeting for me with your boss. Only you can't tell him that I'm a federal agent. Instead, make him believe I'm an interested buyer," I proposed.

The initial shock must have worn off, because Dwayne suddenly turned cagey.

"Yeah, okay. I could do that. But there are some things that I first have to take into consideration," he coyly responded, and gazed into space.

"Such as?" I questioned, waiting to hear the catch.

"Well, what's in it for me?" Dwayne asked, with crystal clear logic.

"You mean, besides a get-out-of-jail card?" I reminded him.

"That's great, but I've still got my future to think of," he responded.

Evidently a beer was in his immediate future. He motioned to the six-pack with his free hand, and I gave him a second brew. Another thing in his not-so-distant future was a dental bill, as he once again pried the cap off with his teeth.

"If I'm not gonna catch lizards, then I'm gonna have to do something else with my life," he reasoned, ever the skateboarding philosopher.

"What did you have in mind?" I inquired, fairly confident he wouldn't ask to become a rocket scientist.

"Well, I've always wanted to be a beachboy in Waikiki," he confided.

I looked at him in disbelief. "A beachboy?"

"Yeah, you know. Sort of a combination of Baywatch hunk and American Gigolo. The trick is to use the talents you've got. Think about it. There are lots of lonely women with plenty of dough that come to Waikiki on vacation. I'm the perfect guy to make them feel like hot babes again. Talent like mine deserves to be well compensated. So, what do you say? Got any strings you can pull for me?"

I figured any woman that fell for his charms probably deserved what she got.

"As a matter of fact, I do. Dolph Trask is a friend of mine," I disclosed.

"Get outta here! No shit! That dude's legendary."

"Well, I'll give you an introduction. But first you have to keep your end of the bargain. Have we got a deal?"

"To hang with Dolph Trask? Absolutely. That's wicked cool," Dwayne said, his gold tooth gleaming in the dark.

"All right, then. Just don't pull anything funny. Or I'll see to it that you share a cell with the biggest, meanest bubba around," I advised, and unlocked the handcuffs.

Dwayne massaged his wrist. "Yeah, yeah. Don't sweat the small stuff."

I wrote down my cell phone number and handed it to him. "Here. Call me on this line."

"Okay, babe," he agreed, and took the paper from me.

Funny how quickly I've switched from being a bitch to being a babe, I thought, while picking up the bag of geckos by his feet.

"Hey, wait a minute! I'm gonna need those things. Otherwise, my boss will be super pissed," he protested.

The guy was probably right. More important, I didn't want to screw up a possible meeting.

"All right, but this is the last batch of reptiles that you catch for now. And I expect to hear from you by tomorrow," I advised, turning on my flashlight to leave.

"Yeah, yeah. Got it," Dwayne muttered, and reached for the bag, his hand penetrating the pool of light.

The beam revealed nails that were bitten down to the quick. But it was his fingertips that captured my interest. They were blistered and burnt—a sure sign that he was spending far too much time clutching hold of a hot "ice pipe." No wonder he was happy with five bucks a lizard. It was just enough to provide him with a steady flow of crystal meth.

"Remember, I'm trusting you on this," I warned, more aware than ever that I was dealing with a loose cannon. "Don't screw up on me. Otherwise, I swear to God, I'll hunt you down and put you away in a place where no one will ever find you."

Dwayne nodded, swung the bag over his shoulder, and split.

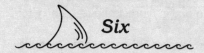 **Six**

I walked back to my SUV and was on my way down the mountain when my cell phone rang. It couldn't possibly be Dwayne this soon. Hopefully, it was Santou calling to make up.

"Hello?" I answered, ready for the first words that I heard to be "I'm sorry."

Instead, I was startled to hear an unfamiliar male voice.

"Hi. This is Sammy Kalahiki, the guy that you spoke with on Pier 32 this afternoon."

So much had happened since then, that I had to stop and think for a moment.

"Remember? You asked if I needed help?"

Right. The Hawaiian guy that was being hassled by the fishing crew.

"Yes. I remember." I was puzzled as to why he was calling now. This was the same guy who had run away from me.

"Well, I've decided that I do."

"What? Need help?" I asked, still somewhat confused. My sole intention had been to give him a lift off the docks.

"Sorry, but you do realize that I'm a Fish and Wildlife agent, don't you? It's probably best that you call the police, if you're in some kind of trouble."

"They're not going to help me," Kalahiki said in a bitter tone. "Apparently, no one is. Forget about it. Sorry to have bothered you."

Shit. I was a complete sucker when it came to guilt trips.

"No, wait a minute. Don't hang up. I just wanted to make sure that you realized who you're speaking to," I quickly backpedaled.

"Don't worry. I know who you are. That's why I'm calling," he grimly responded.

I didn't know whether to feel flattered or take it as a warning.

"Then you have the advantage. So tell me, who are you?"

"As I said before, my name is Sammy Kalahiki. But far more important is what I do."

"Which is?" I asked, taking the bait.

"I'm an observer with the National Marine Fisheries Service," he said, as if that should provide clue enough as to the reason for his call.

I knew bits and pieces about the Observer Program, but not a hell of a lot.

It first began in 1990, when word leaked out that endangered sea turtles were being killed big-time in longliner fishing nets. An environmental group sued, threatening to bring the Hawaiian fishing industry to a halt. The National Marine Fisheries Service quickly stepped in and responded, "Cool your jets. We've got everything under control." And so the Observer Program was born.

Now twenty-seven kids, fresh out of college, are hired and assigned to individually go out on twenty percent of the boats for two- to six-week fishing trips at a time. Their stated purpose is to report any turtle interactions, as well as monitor the fishing industry's impact on other endangered, threatened, and protected species. But in reality, what they do is a very different task. They're instructed to measure every single fish that's pulled on board, and collect its life history data for management purposes. The chore keeps them extremely busy and on the back of the deck, away from the nets. It benefits both the fishermen and the National Marine Fisheries Service. The observers rarely have time to stir up any trouble.

"Okay. You're an observer. I got it. So, what's the problem?" I asked.

"I don't want to talk about it over the phone," Kalahiki responded mysteriously.

Great. Just what I needed: a prima donna. "Why not?"

"Because for all I know, someone could be listening in. I take it that you're probably on a cell phone right now. Am I correct?"

"Yes," I admitted, feeling slightly peeved.

"Well, I don't consider those to be very secure," Kalahiki stated. "Besides, this is a sensitive matter that should be discussed in person."

I automatically ruled out meeting at the office. My boss would intervene if he caught wind that something was going on.

"Okay, then. How about if we rendezvous at Zippy's Coffee Shop down on Nimitz Boulevard?" I suggested, figuring that should be central enough for both of us.

"Uh-uh. It could be big trouble for me if we're seen together. It's got to be somewhere out of the way. What say we hook up at Ka'ena Point around eight o'clock tomorrow morning?"

Kalahiki was obviously serious about keeping our meeting private. Ka'ena Point is the northwesternmost tip of Oahu; a narrow peninsula that protrudes from the Waianae Mountain Range, and is windswept and desolate as hell. It comprises an eight-mile gap in the main road, which encircles ninety percent of the island. In fact, the only way to reach Ka'ena Point is to hike in on foot.

"I'll be at the big coral rock that's along the water's edge. Don't worry. You can't miss it," he instructed.

Kalahiki certainly was into playing cloak-and-dagger games.

"All right. I'll see you there tomorrow," I reluctantly agreed, wondering what could be so confidential as to require my slogging through sand dunes and scrub.

On the other hand, my curiosity was definitely piqued. I just hoped that the hike out to nowhere proved to be worthwhile.

I swung the Ford into the driveway, having arrived home in record time. I walked up the steps to where Spam and Tag-along jockeyed behind the screen door to greet me. Spam didn't play coy, but jumped up and licked me full on the lips. What the heck. I figured it was better to have a pit bull like me than not. Meanwhile, Tag-along showed her affection by rubbing up and leaving a swathe of marmalade-colored fur on my pants. Had I been wearing shorts, it would have looked as though I never shaved my legs.

I heard the television and walked into the living room, where Kevin lay sprawled on the couch, drinking a beer and watching the day's sports. Santou didn't seem to be anywhere around.

"Is Jake home?" I asked, wondering how to possibly make more money so that we could get our own place.

"Nope. He went out," Kevin replied, never taking his eyes off the screen. "He said he needed some down time."

I took that to be guy code for "He went to a bar by himself."

Then Kevin placed a hand behind his head and slowly

turned his gray eyes toward me. "You know Rach, you really need to back off a bit. Santou's going through a tough time right now, what with leaving the FBI. You've got to understand, this is a transitional period for him. It's a tough adjustment to make."

All I could think was, *What a total schmuck.*

"First off, he didn't *leave* the FBI. He's taken leave until his back gets better," I corrected. "And secondly, I understand perfectly well what's going on. That's why I'm watching out for him. It's something couples do when they care about each other. By the way, that little feat in the ocean today wasn't so smart. Jake could have seriously injured himself."

"So what do you want him to do then? Sit around all day and twiddle his thumbs?" Kevin challenged.

"That's about all he'll be able to do after becoming paralyzed from following your dumb-ass example of being the big man," I bristled, just warming up.

Kevin regarded me in silence before he quietly responded. "Am I really that bad?"

His abrupt change in tactic effectively threw me off guard.

"It's hard to say," I replied, suddenly feeling like a defensive uptight bitch. "Especially since I have no idea as to who the hell you really are."

Kevin continued to study me, and then gradually nodded. "I'm someone who's trying to forget a painful past and live for today. Is that so hard to understand? Come on. Haven't you begun to wonder why there are so many ex–Special Forces guys, former mercenaries, and sky jumpers living in Haleiwa? Surely, you've noticed."

I *had* found it to be rather odd.

"It's because we still feel the need to push ourselves to the edge," Kevin said, not waiting for my response.

"What do you mean?" I questioned, in an effort to keep him talking. I'd rarely heard Kevin string more than five words together, and wanted to take full advantage of it.

Kevin rubbed his eyes so hard that loose saddlebags of skin formed beneath his fists.

"It's like those retired cops you hear about. You know, the ones that take to playing Russian Roulette. They do it in order to confront their demons and get a good night's sleep. Well, it's pretty much the same thing with us. Only here, it's a different game. We move to Haleiwa in order to surf and face down the monster waves. It's how we get our daily dose of adrenaline. That's what Jake is coming to terms with now."

"Yeah, but there's more to it than just acquiring an adrenaline rush," I responded, having begun to calm down. "I've noticed that some surfers seem to attain an inner peace. It's almost as if they live to be at one with the waves."

"You're right," Kevin agreed. "Surfing allows us to let go of our worries and, for a few moments, be in a zone of perfect focus. It's as if we've reached a state of Zen." He shrugged and took a sip of his beer. "I guess you could say that a big wave is something akin to a spiritual entity for me."

I was now beginning to understand why Santou was so drawn to surfing. At the same time, Kevin had opened the door just enough for me to find out a little more about him. He'd mentioned something in particular that intrigued me.

"Special Forces, huh? I crossed paths with someone that said he'd been with Special Forces while on my job in Montana. I believe he served in Desert Storm. The guy was a Blackfoot Indian by the name of Nathan, or Michael, or something," I said, pretending to search my memory.

"You must mean Matthew Running," Kevin swiftly responded.

I was surprised to find that the sound of his name still sent shock waves through me. I'd tried so hard to forget about the man. Only it had proven to be impossible.

Matthew Running was the tribal game officer for the Blackfeet Reservation of Montana. We'd worked together on a case, only to become involved in much more than just wildlife. Our fleeting affair had nearly ended my relationship with Santou.

"Yeah, I've heard of him," he continued.

"That's it? You've just heard of him?" I lightly pressed. Kevin would have probably been in Special Forces around the same time. If so, there's no way that he wouldn't have known Matthew.

I could almost feel Kevin weighing how much to tell me. The ghost of a memory seemed to flash across his eyes.

"Let's just say we worked together for a while, and he was one of the best. Running served alongside a close friend that he'd grown up with, a buddy of his who was killed in action."

That clinched it. Kevin really had known Matthew Running.

A shiver kissed the back of my neck and I glanced around, half expecting to find Matthew standing there. My heart sank a little to discover I was wrong.

"So, did I pass your test?" Kevin slyly questioned, bringing me back to reality.

"You're doing better than before," I grudgingly conceded. However, I still wasn't ready to totally trust him. "Listen, you're right. I admit that I'm protective of Jake. But we've been through a lot these past few years. Don't take this the wrong way, but I'm not about to let him be pulled back into any bad habits."

"And that's what you're afraid will happen if he hangs with me?" Kevin queried.

I nodded wordlessly.

Kevin opened a cooler on the floor, pulled out a beer, and tossed it to me.

"I may be a lot of things, both good and bad. But I'm loyal as hell to my friends. And I can swear this much to you. Santou won't be doing any drugs while I'm around," Kevin said, his voice low and intense.

I sipped my beer and said nothing, still not completely satisfied.

Kevin looked at me and sighed. "Yeah, okay. And I'll also make sure that he doesn't take on any more monster waves," he promised. "What do you say? Truce?"

I took a deep breath, and slowly let go of some of my animosity.

"Truce," I agreed.

Only then did we clink our beer bottles together.

I was in bed with the sheets pulled around my head, my body buffeted by a cool breeze coming in off the trade winds. The ceiling fan languidly whirled above, softly purring, as if luring the current to hitch a ride on its blades. The drone of deep rhythmic breathing provided a backdrop of bass, its sound broken only by an occasional dreamlike whimper. It was Spam, fast asleep by my side, his head nestled on Jake's pillow.

I remained awake until Santou tiptoed into the room at about 2 A.M. He gently nudged the dog down along the foot of the bed, and then crawled under the covers beside me. A ray of moonlight traipsed among his curls, its reflection lightly grazing his cheek. The man looked so vulnerable that I thought my heart would break. Jake reached over and pulled me toward him. I rested my head on his shoulder and knew that any disagreement between us had long since passed.

"I'm sorry if I scared you out there today," he simply said.

I ran my fingers through his tangle of hair, splintering the moonbeam into a shower of luminous drops. Santou was home, and I could finally relax.

I'd grown to accept the fact that Jake was the antidote to all the darkness that tried to encroach upon me. He was that essential part of myself that was otherwise missing. Santou had made me believe love was not only worth fighting for, but that it was also worth taking a leap of faith. He was my heart, my breath, my soul mate.

"I'm sorry, too," I admitted. "I just can't bear the thought of anything happening to you."

"Don't worry, chere. I'm here and don't plan on going anywhere without you," he swore in a husky whisper.

Then his fingers began to meticulously explore my body. Each touch was an electrical charge that wantonly probed every curve and valley, constantly finding new territory, until my entire being thrummed in response. It was only then, when I thought I couldn't possibly stand any more, that Santou further explored with his lips and tongue, driving me over the threshold into sheer ecstasy. I let myself fall, unconcerned about a safety net. I didn't need one as long as Jake was with me.

Seven

I woke early the next morning, stretched, and snuggled close to Santou as he snored in blissful peace. Then I lightly kissed his cheek and rolled out of bed. Spam wagged his tail, circled three times, and lay down beside him.

I quickly showered and dressed, after which Tag-along and I ate breakfast together. She dined on a meal of Friskies Classic Seafood Entrée, while I made do with a stale cherry Pop-Tart. By then it was time to call my boss and leave a message at work.

I carefully worded my excuse so that it didn't sound quite like an emergency, yet had more urgency to it than if I'd merely overslept. The gist of it was that I had something to do and would be in late. Then I hopped in my Ford and took off down the road, heading toward Ka'ena Point.

I drove west, past the sleepy town of Waialua, with its overgrown cane fields and sugar mill that stood closed and rusting. From there it was an easy jaunt on Farrington Highway. This portion was a dead-end spur of country road that ran between miles of unpopulated beach and mountains covered with scrub brush.

I lowered the window and took a deep whiff. The sweet perfume of plumeria flowers rushed in. Their scent intermingled with overripe fruit that had fallen to the ground and was rotting. The few horse farms and houses that dotted the area slowly began to disappear. Soon the only thing to be seen was an endless chorus line of waves, topped off by sea birds soaring on the wind.

I looked up and caught sight of a frigate bird out on patrol. The avian stealth bomber was easy to identify, with its seven-foot wing span and long scissored tail. Nicknamed the "man-of-war," it reminded me more of a feathered version of Johnny Depp. The aerial pirate lived by its wits, craftily harassing other birds until they disgorged their food. Then the marauder zoomed in to snatch it from them in midair.

I'd been told never to point at one, or it would bring bad luck. Others believed that death was impending if three frigates flew over a house at once. I spotted a second bird winging toward me now and sped up, not wanting to tempt fate.

Farrington Highway soon began to fizzle out. It went from asphalt, to gravel, to dirt. Before long, even this disintegrated into a rock-strewn path scored with deep ruts. I continued on past the first gate, the point at which most other vehicles tend to give up. I drove until I could go no farther. The trail was finally blocked by a forbidding barrier of gigantic boulders that cut off even the most determined of drivers.

I was left with little choice but to park and lock my Explorer. I looked around, but no other cars were in sight. Either Sammy Kalahiki hadn't yet arrived, or he was hiking in from the other side. Grabbing my bag and a bottle of water, I scrambled over the rocks to enter Ka'ena Point.

The first thing that struck me was the utter sense of isolation. It was as if time had purposely passed the area by. Other than the wind and waves, there wasn't a sound. The Waianae Range loomed to my left, standing guard like a silent sentinel, while off to the right were gently rolling sand dunes. Spits of gnarled lava extended from under their skirted edges, the rocks protruding like long, arthritic fingers to stab sharply at the sea. Beyond lay the entire expanse of the brilliant blue Pacific.

The sun beat white hot overhead, hanging heavy as an orb of concrete in the sky. The intense heat had chased away the clouds and scoured the air, leaving the firmament so searingly clear that it hurt my eyes.

I followed the narrow dirt path, taking extra special care not to step upon any plants in this native Garden of Eden. Dotting the dunes were beautiful beach morning glories, their vines entwined with white-blossomed naupaka. Legend had it that a young woman tore a blossom in half, believing her lover to be unfaithful. The flowers now grew in the shape of a broken heart. Nearby stood a rare akoko plant, its cool green leaves caressing the delicate petals of a golden ilima, the official flower of Oahu.

Ka'ena Point is also home to Laysan albatross, which make their nests on the ground. A number of the birds were sitting on them now. Most of them paid little attention to me, while others were engaged in ritual courtship. I watched as the males bowed and strutted, whistling and braying, reminding me of guys on the make in a bar.

A few birds seemed curious about the unusual creature that was walking around, apparently wondering what some tall redhead was doing in their habitat. They took to flight, soaring avian gliders with eighty-five-inch wing spans. One came so close as to nearly touch my cheek. Then it crash-landed, tumbling to a stop, in an exhibition of why it's also called a "gooney bird." The albatross picked itself up and waddled over to its mate, where they gently touched beaks.

It was then I spotted something strange poking from beneath a bush. I walked over and carefully lifted a branch to discover a Havahart trap. A wooden plank had been placed on its top. Snared inside was a protected golden plover with a smooth black breast, tawny feathers, and great long legs.

The trap had probably been set by a state agent in hopes of snagging a mongoose intent on destroying albatross eggs. The mongoose was yet another destructive invasive species—one for which the United States government could be thanked. It was the Department of Agriculture that had brought them over to Hawaii in 1883 in the first place. The plan had been to set them loose on rats that were ravaging sugarcane fields and costing the planters money. There was just one little hitch. Rats are nocturnal, while mongoose are active during the day. So instead, the mongoose took to preying upon native ground-nesting birds.

The golden plover seemed to grow impatient and began to chirp loudly, as if to say, *Snap out of it and get me the hell out of here already.*

I quickly complied and tripped open the door. The bird didn't hesitate, but hopped out and took off as I continued on my way.

I soon spied a large coral rock commanding a prime view of the ocean. This had to be the boulder that Sammy had mentioned. There was no other one quite like it.

I worked my way over and leaned against its pock-marked surface, grateful for the coolness that seeped into my back. The sun was now high enough to punish whatever didn't take cover. From the looks of things, that appeared to be mainly me.

I nearly polished off my bottle of water, while hoping that Sammy would soon show up. Until then, there was little to do but gaze out over the horizon.

At first, I thought I was experiencing a heat-induced illusion. A cloud of smoke appeared to rise about twenty feet in the air, just past the breakers. Then the sea erupted into a furious geyser. After that, something magical hap-

pened. The plume transformed into an enormous hump-
back whale and her calf.

I watched spellbound as the two began an acrobatic display of splashing and flapping their tails. Then the mother
rolled her forty-ton carcass onto its side and jovially slapped
at the water. I was caught between laughter and amazement,
not wanting this moment to end. There was no question but
that something so incredible inspired thoughts of God.

I kept my eyes glued to the spot even after their antics
were over, hoping they would start again. My concentra-
tion was so focused that I jumped as a hand tapped my
shoulder, nearly scaring the life out of me.

Shit!

I whirled around, startled to find Sammy Kalahiki
standing there. I'd never even heard him approach. I
silently berated myself, knowing just how dangerous that
could be under the wrong circumstances.

He looked much the same as yesterday. Only his shirt
was different. Today's was bright blue with tiny white
flowers. However, it wasn't large enough to hide his bur-
geoning potbelly, or the love handles protruding around
his waist. Kalahiki was clearly a recipient of the "thrifty
gene" that afflicted so many native Hawaiians. On the upside, they retained calories to combat famine or food dep-
rivation. There must have been some Hawaiian in me. I
was constantly fighting the battle of the bulge myself.

The other thing I noticed was the smoldering anger in
his eyes. It made me all the more self-conscious over having been caught by surprise.

"I see you found the rock with no problem," Kalahiki
said, all the while staring at me.

"Yeah. After hiking in for a good forty-five minutes. So
now can you tell me what's so sensitive that we had to
meet all the way out here?" I queried gruffly.

Kalahiki blinked and his eyes came to rest on the boulder. I glanced at it, wondering what was so interesting about this particular rock.

"What do you know about sharks?" he finally asked.

Terrific. Had I been hauled all the way out here to be quizzed on zoology?

"Let's see. They've been around for four hundred million years, and they predate dinosaurs, making them one of the oldest species on the planet. They also have more than two hundred teeth, each as sharp as a finely honed blade, turning them into the perfect predator, at the top of their food chain," I rattled off like a verbal encyclopedia.

I figured that about covered the basics. What I didn't add was that shark pups can make their first "kill" while still in the womb, feeding on other embryos. Shark expert Peter Benchley had once described the species as the marine equivalent of Jack Palance: sleek, silent, and vicious. Since then I couldn't envision them without imagining the actor's trademark sneer plastered across their mouths.

"And how much do you know about the shark-fin trade?" Kalahiki continued, without missing a beat.

"Well, I'm not an expert on the subject," I admitted. "But I do know that shark finning's been banned in the States, even though it's legal in most of the rest of the world."

Kalahiki emitted a cynical snort. "A typical *haole* answer. Then you must also believe that weapons of mass destruction are still buried in Iraq, and that pigs have wings and can fly."

I could have gone into the office this morning in order to be insulted. As things stood, I was tempted to walk away and leave Kalahiki standing here alone. What stopped me was the fact I was still tired from my long hike in to meet him—that, coupled with my overwhelming sense of curiosity. Instead, I replayed what I knew about shark finning in my mind.

Sharks are one more species frequently caught in the

lines of tuna boats. The crew hauls the creatures on board, where their fins are quickly sliced off, the reason being that fins are the most lucrative part of the shark. After that, the fish is pitched back into the water. The rest of the carcass simply takes up too much room on the boat.

It made even more sense, once I'd learned just how much money fins could fetch. Dealers pay crew members roughly twenty-five to thirty dollars a pound for them, while shark meat itself brings in merely pennies. From there the price rapidly escalates. These same dealers then dry and resell the fins to a voracious Asian market for upwards of two hundred and sixty-five dollars a pound. That's when the job of processing begins.

The fins are repeatedly soaked, dried, and bleached with peroxide, after which they're simmered for hours. Only then are the small tendrils of cartilage extracted and rendered into much coveted stringy noodles. Their sole use is as the namesake ingredient in highly-prized shark-fin soup, a concoction that goes for one hundred dollars a bowl in high-end Hong Kong restaurants.

The fins are believed to contain both aphrodisiac and medicinal properties, elevating the soup to must-have status. It's now considered a mark of affluence and sophistication among an Asian middle class that continues to expand and grow ever more wealthy.

What had once been a culinary delicacy, eaten by a privileged few, has become standard fare among the majority. The soup is served not only on holidays, but also at banquets and business affairs, much the same as champagne and caviar. The increasing demand and high prices have whipped up an insatiable lust and fueled a feeding frenzy in which 100 million sharks are slaughtered each year. Another way of viewing it is, that's 10 million sharks killed for every person that sharks kill.

It struck me as darkly ironic that so many people were responsible for doing to sharks exactly what they, themselves, claimed to fear most—falling prey to bloodthirsty killers. It was enough to make one question who were really the aggressors and who were the victims in this world.

The craze for shark fins has steadily led to the sharks' downfall. Unlike other fish, sharks give birth to only a handful of pups at a time, each of which takes twenty-five years to mature. Meanwhile, they're being killed at a rate twice as great as they can possibly reproduce. The result is that nearly all shark species have declined by more than fifty percent in the past fifteen years. Still, what Kalahiki had said couldn't possibly be true.

"What are you talking about? I know for a fact that a law banning shark finning was passed in Hawaii only a few years ago," I insisted.

The bill clearly prohibits the landing of any shark fins without the accompanying carcass. And since most fishermen lack the storage space to transport large numbers of sharks, it was a clever way to stop finning.

"Then you're more naïve than I would have thought," Kalahiki scoffed. "Sure, the law got passed, and the public is happy. That's because they foolishly believe it's actually being enforced. But in reality, the bill's a complete joke. The trade is still going on, big-time. It's also the inhumane way in which finning is done that completely turns my stomach. Did you know that ninety percent of sharks are still alive when they're being finned?"

This was something I hadn't heard before.

"How is that possible?" I asked, unable to imagine it.

"Easy. A shark is lured in by the bait in longliner nets and becomes entangled. All those hooks instantly lodge themselves in its snout and eliminate any further attempt at escape. After that, the shark is hauled on deck."

"Wait a minute. A shark is far too dangerous to bring on board alive," I protested.

"That's right. Which is why crew members quickly move in and pin down its head with gaffes," Kalahiki explained. "Even then the shark continues to thrash about, probably because it's panicked at having been dragged out of the water, and is afraid that it's going to die. It generally takes about three to five minutes to cut off the fins using machetes and sharp knives. Once the deed is done, the mutilated bodies are dumped back overboard."

My own stomach turned at the thought.

Kalahiki raised a hand to his forehead, as though he were witnessing the event once again as he spoke. A star sapphire ring on his pinkie finger caught a ray of sun and glittered under its beam like the eye of an angry shark.

"The ocean is so clear that I've watched as terrified sharks spiral helplessly down to its floor, the water turning red from the blood pouring out of their veins," he continued. "It's not so much the finning itself that kills them. Rather it's the fact that they're unable to swim. They become like boats without rudders."

"What happens to them?" I asked, not really certain I wanted to know.

"They slowly starve to death, unless they get lucky. In which case, they're quickly ripped apart and devoured by their own brethren. It's not a pretty picture either way." A small shudder rippled through him. "But aside from that, the truly disgusting thing is the amount of waste involved. The fins comprise anywhere from one to five percent of their entire body. Think about it. It's kind of like what your people did to the buffalo when they slaughtered them, took their hides, and left the meat to rot."

He'd painted the picture vividly enough so that I found the scenario to be truly disturbing. However, there was still one basic problem.

"Horrible as that may be, it's important to remember

that finning itself wasn't banned. It was bringing the fins into Hawaii that was stopped," I reminded him.

Controversy had erupted when the bill first passed. Honolulu used to be the main port where domestic and foreign boats offloaded thousands of tons of fins each year. From here they were then dried, graded, and sent on to Asia. The local fishing industry lost mucho dollars when the ban took effect.

"And I'm telling you that's a bunch of bull. It's still going on like gangbusters in Honolulu," Sammy retorted caustically.

"If that's true, then why aren't you reporting this to the National Marine Fisheries Service?" I countered, beginning to have my doubts about the man.

The passage of the bill had not only been popular with the public, but had also garnered national press attention. It was crazy to think that anyone would get involved with something that had been so high profile.

"NMFS? I already have," Kalahiki responded with a grunt.

"All right, then. I'm sure they must be doing something about it. You know how these agencies work. They probably just aren't filling you in on the details." *This* was the big secret I'd been dragged all the way out here for? Great. It was yet another problem that NMFS would end up handling.

But Sammy looked at me grimly and shook his head. "That's where you're wrong. The truth is, I've been warned to keep my mouth shut."

I'd been told the same thing many times. However, it was always when I'd gone against my boss's wishes while in the midst of a case.

"And why would they do that?" I asked, wondering if he was an inveterate complainer.

"Because there's too much money at stake. Or is that so

difficult for you to comprehend?" he said bitterly. "It's gotten bad enough that I've even been threatened."

Sammy annoyed the hell out of me, yet his body language seemed to suggest he was telling the truth. His shoulders drooped and he looked nervously around, as if checking to make sure that we hadn't been followed. His facial bruises further intensified his glowering expression. I didn't know whether it was the situation, or Sammy's demeanor, but I was definitely beginning to feel on edge.

"Do you have any idea who's threatening you?" I questioned.

"It could be anyone," he responded with a tense shrug. "I've been receiving anonymous phone calls. Why else do you think I'm here? You're my last hope." He emphasized his desperation with a short, mirthless laugh.

I might have believed him more if he'd narrowed down the list. But "anyone" took in a whole lot of people. Surely the entire world wasn't against him.

"Sorry, Sammy. But I'm having a hard time buying this," I told him.

Kalahiki's stare was icy as a New York City sidewalk on a cold winter's day.

"Then you obviously don't know much about Hawaii. This place is corrupt to the bone. I'm talking every single agency, from the local police department on up."

I was beginning to think that Sammy was more than a little paranoid; he was pretty much whacked. But it was also evident that he was scared for his life.

"Oahu's like a fishbowl where everyone knows everyone else. The sleaziness, networking, and payoffs are rampant and in your face," he ranted. "Not only that, but the politics here are brutal. The intent is to keep the public fat and happy, while making sure they know as little as possible about what's really going on."

"Don't you think you're getting carried away with all this?" I suggested, trying to inject a note of reality.

"You're sadly mistaken if you don't believe that people are being bribed and paid off," he warned, a note of hysteria edging into his voice. "It's probably even going on within your own office."

I chose to brush off the comment. Norm Pryor might be a lot of things— such as a lazy, bureaucratic numbskull. But that didn't make him corrupt. Hell, I didn't think he even had the smarts for it.

"This is the federal government you're talking about," I pointedly reminded him.

"Yeah, you're absolutely right. And since when did the federal government become so squeaky clean that they're above deception?" Kalahiki's eyes blazed as he glared at me. "For chrissakes, why won't anybody listen?" he asked in frustration.

"Probably because what you're saying sounds crazy. Believe me, I know there are plenty of problems. But how can you accuse entire agencies of being corrupt?" I calmly questioned.

"Okay. So maybe it's not *entire* agencies," he admitted gruffly. "Just a few key players in Oahu. But that's more than enough."

"Those are serious charges," I responded.

Kalahiki picked up a stone and threw it into the sea, where it instantly disappeared.

"That's what I feel like, you know. A tiny worthless pebble. Look, I understand that if you want something done, you usually have to do it yourself. But I can't. Not with this. It's too big." Kalahiki's voice cracked, and his eyes welled up. "Why am I putting my own life at risk if someone like you doesn't even care? This is unbelievable. It's as if I'm one of those sharks that's gotten caught in a net that it can't get out of."

With that, Kalahiki turned and began to pound his fist on the coral rock.

"Okay, then. Convince me," I suggested. "Tell me why anyone in National Marine Fisheries would secretly decide to ignore the shark-finning ban."

Sammy rubbed his hands against his pants and took a deep breath.

"Think about it. What department does the National Marine Fisheries Service fall under?" he challenged.

"It's a division within the Department of Commerce," I automatically said, and then caught myself.

Damn! My mouth fell open as I began to realize what Kalahiki might be getting at.

"That's right," he verified with a tight smile. "And just how does the Department of Commerce make its money?"

"Through the exploitation of natural resources," I responded.

Which is exactly what the National Marine Fisheries Service is supposed to protect, I thought, filling in the blanks as a mental lightbulb went on.

"Exactly. Now you're beginning to get the picture," Sammy confirmed. "We're talking about one very schizoid agency. What do you think would happen to a senior-level manager who went to his boss and said, 'Excuse me, sir. But turtles, birds, and sharks are being caught in longliner nets. We've kept a lid on it so far, but we don't want to continue to hurt the poor things. Something will have to be done about it.'"

I laughed to myself, having a pretty good idea.

"He'd be out on his ass so fast that your head would spin," Sammy said, not waiting for a response. "No way is the Department of Commerce going to let anyone ruin a multi-million-dollar business. In other words, the commercial fishing industry."

Sammy was right about one thing. Industrial fishing

had been strip-mining the oceans for years, essentially wiping out ninety percent of large fish, and imperiling commercially valuable species. Even so, they continued to be protected, and suffered very little consequence.

"That does present one hell of a conflict of interest," I agreed.

"You damn well better believe it. So now tell me. How can National Marine Fisheries protect marine life *and* defend the fishing industry at the same time? I'll answer the question for you. They don't. Whatever information I give them goes right into a black hole."

"I think you're overstating it," I responded. "Certainly there are biologists within NMFS who care about the resource."

"Yeah. Except they're working for an agency that's skewed toward industry," Sammy countered. "They also get pressured by Hawaii's high-powered politicos."

If that were true, then it was the same old story. It all came down to a matter of job security. And it was well known what happened to whistleblowers.

"My bosses don't want to hear about any protected species interactions with longliners. Why?" Sammy held up a hand to stop me from interrupting. "Because the last thing they intend to do is cause the fishing industry any more harm. Longliners raked in well over a million dollars a year in Hawaii when shark finning was legal," Kalahiki revealed. "Why do you think that even NMFS fought against the ban?"

"But I'd always heard that fins were given to the crew as a bonus, and that their sale amounted to little more than beer money," I responded.

"Sure. That's exactly what the industry wanted the public to believe. But the truth is a far different story. As for those boat owners who *did* give the fins to their crew? It was only because they'd hired illegal Filipino workers who were being paid almost nothing. Shark fins were how their salaries were subsidized without money coming out of the owners' pockets," Sammy revealed. "However, that's just the tip of the iceberg, when it comes to what's really going on in the trade."

"Maybe so. But you just said it yourself. All of that took place before finning became illegal," I once again pointed out.

"Yeah, you're right about that," Sammy agreed. "Things have certainly changed. The trade has now gone underground and turned far deadlier."

"In what way?" I asked, my curiosity becoming even more aroused. Maybe there actually was something to what Sammy was saying.

Sammy bit off a hangnail and spit it out. "Okay, I'll give you an example. Do you remember hearing about a guy who was found off Pier 32 the other day?"

I nodded. How could I forget? It's what had prompted me to take an unplanned drive along the docks yesterday.

"Well, that was Charlie Hong, owner of Pacific Catch Products. Except the only product he ever dealt in was shark fins. And I can assure you that he didn't go for a swim in his business suit. The other thing I'm convinced of is that Charlie didn't commit suicide. He was a victim of the shark-fin wars."

"Do you want to explain what you mean by that?" I asked, having never heard the term before.

"Listen, shark fins are precious as gold. Charlie knew that better than most. After all, he'd been dealing in the stuff for years. In fact, the ban only made his business all the more lucrative."

What Kalahiki said made sense. It was a well-known fact that the price goes up when a resource becomes rare.

"The thing was that it also made him more greedy. Word has it that Hong tried to corner the market by undercutting another dealer. That bit of sticky business was resolved by giving Charlie the old heave-ho." Sammy gleefully swung his arms as though he were tossing a fish off a boat.

The shark-fin trade *had* to be worth big bucks, if people were willing to kill for it.

"But I thought he'd been eaten by a shark," I responded.

"Who? Charlie? Yeah, he was—once he'd been lying in the water for a couple of hours," Kalahiki said with a grin.

Funny what brought a smile to his face. This was the happiest I'd seen Sammy since we'd met. I filed away the information to be checked later on. Right now, I wanted to press Kalahiki on more personal matters.

"Tell me. Why was the crew so angry with you yesterday?" I questioned.

Sammy's eyes grew stormy as a pair of thunder clouds.

"I was an observer on their boat for a couple of weeks. Lots of things went on during that time. I was caught taking pictures they'd rather I hadn't. Some of the crew got pissed."

"Pictures of what?" I prodded.

"Oh, of dolphins and sea turtles that were snagged in their lines. Stuff like that," Kalahiki revealed, in a deliberately nonchalant voice.

The fact that he purposely kept his tone so blase sent up red flags. Something else was going on.

"Is that how you got those bruises?" I asked.

"Yeah, that was part of it," Sammy admitted, remaining maddeningly vague.

"Then maybe the crew members were also responsible for making those threatening phone calls," I proposed.

But Kalahiki promptly rebuffed my suggestion. "No. The calls began a few days before this last trip."

So much for trying to be helpful. I steered the topic back to the bomb that he'd just dropped.

"All right, then. What about the camera and film? Do

you happen to have those with you?" I asked, eager to see if any such photos really existed.

"No. They found the camera in my knapsack and threw it away," Sammy replied, dashing my hopes.

Damn! I needed some hard-core proof that Kalahiki's claims were actually true, and he wasn't just jerking me around. Otherwise, we were back to square one.

"Or at least they thought they did," he revealed, with a conspiratorial grin.

If the guy had been a Big Mac, I would have pounced on him.

"What do you mean?" I asked, verbally lunging.

"Here's the thing. Observers are only allowed to take one camera on board. And it has to have been issued by the National Marine Fisheries Service. It's always one of those cheap disposable jobbers. Well, that's easy enough to get around," he disclosed. "I just went out and bought myself an identical model. That way I not only have their piece of junk, but also my own personal click-and-shoot for catching those special Kodak moments. The camera they snatched from me was the authorized version that I use for NMFS's dog-and-pony show."

"So then, you *don't* hand all the photos over to your boss?"

Sammy looked at me as though I were exceptionally slow. "What, are you kidding? Of course not. I already told you. I learned long ago that any pictures I gave them would never see the light of day. They'd either be dumped in the round file, or buried where no one would ever find them."

My pulse picked up speed. If what Kalahiki said was true, then he definitely had proof.

"Instead, I've collected my own stash of highly sensitive material," he continued. "It catalogues everything that's been going on over the past few years. I've just been waiting for the right time to release it."

"And what makes you think this is it?" I asked, barely able to hear over the pounding of blood in my ears.

Kalahiki paused, and coolly observed me. His almond-shaped eyes crinkled in merriment, nearly disappearing beneath their lids, as a smile once again pulled at his lips.

"Maybe I'm hoping that a Fish and Wildlife agent has finally been stationed here with enough balls to look into what's really going on. 'Cause God knows, the special agents at NMFS are totally hog-tied. I guess I just didn't expect a woman to have bigger ones than a man."

I decided to take that as a compliment. After all, far worse things had been said about me. I also chose not to mention one little fact: that I was considered highly radioactive within my own agency. This case certainly wouldn't enhance my reputation. Far from it. Instead, it could spell big trouble all around. There's an unspoken rule within the federal government: You never go against a sister agency. Stepping into this would blow that maxim sky high. But it also wouldn't stop me.

"There's something else far more valuable on that roll of film than just a few dead animals, though," Sammy interjected, breaking into my thoughts.

"What's that?" I asked, eager for all the ammunition I could get.

"First, why don't you tell me exactly what you plan to do with the information that I've given you so far?" Kalahiki questioned me with the cunning of an attorney.

I wished he hadn't asked me that quite yet. Exciting as this was, I needed time to figure out what measures to take. Delving into another agency's business was foreign territory for me. Not only was it highly irregular, but it would require extreme caution. If Sammy was correct, the shark-finning law existed in name only, while in reality it was still going on. That could mean just one thing: NMFS officials were being paid to turn a blind eye, a practice that went directly against their mission.

I now realized something else as well, the implication of which hit me like a Mack truck. The Fish and Wildlife Service was involved with protecting both fish and marine mammals on the mainland, be it sturgeon, paddlefish, manatees, turtles, or walrus. However, that wasn't the case in Hawaii. Rather, I'd specifically been instructed that our policy was "hands off" as far as NMFS was concerned. It made me wonder if perhaps there was an ulterior motive at work.

What better way to protect the fishing industry than for National Marine Fisheries to claim absolute authority over those critters that impact fishermen and can cause problems? In that sense, NMFS were like bouncers at the door. They adamantly kept Fish and Wildlife agents from entering their realm. Fishermen couldn't be controlled if we didn't know how many albatross, turtles, whales, or dolphins were being killed. It was one more lesson on the workings of politics and endangered species. In this case, big business was being given free rein to continue on as usual.

Then there was that other little tidbit that Sammy had mentioned, the "shark-fin wars."

"I need a lot more information than you've provided so far, as well as evidence to back it up. But if what you're telling me is true, then I fully intend to do whatever's necessary to bring this matter to an end," I swore, meaning every bit of it.

Sammy nodded, taking me at my word. "Trust me, you don't know the half of it yet. What I'll tell you for now is that it leads directly to a high government official in Oahu, and all the way over to Hong Kong. You'll understand more once you've taken a look at my files."

"Something else," I said, not wanting to forget this last

request. "Who's the other shark-fin dealer that you were talking about? The one who you believe got rid of Charlie Hong?"

Kalahiki kicked at the ground with his sneaker.

"I'm not totally sure yet. But I'll try to get the information for you," he promised.

"Good. I'll need it if we're going to make this case fly," I replied, figuring that should add the necessary pressure.

Sammy bit his lower lip and seemed to think about it. "Okay. What say we meet at this same spot tomorrow around sunset? That way, you won't have to worry about your *haole* skin getting burned."

I looked at my arms. He was right. I was beginning to resemble a lobster.

"I'll bring some information along to back up what I've told you so far," Sammy added.

I wanted it all right now, but knew better than to push. Kalahiki would hand everything over soon enough.

"I can give you a ride back to Honolulu if you'd like," I offered.

I don't know why I assumed he lived there. Probably because that's where I'd first seen him.

"Thanks, but I came in my own vehicle. Besides, I'm staying with my mom over in Makaha on the West Coast right now," Sammy replied.

"In that case, I'll see you tomorrow at sunset," I said.

Kalahiki turned and walked in the opposite direction from which I'd come.

"Aloha till tomorrow then," he responded over his shoulder, and raised his hand in farewell.

His star sapphire lassoed a beam of light. The ring glowed so brightly that it nearly blinded me. I looked away for a minute. When I glanced back again, Sammy Kalahiki was gone.

Eight

I'd finished the last of my water before I'd made it halfway back to my Ford. Great. Now I'd not only be burned, but would also end up dehydrated. Visions of vultures flew through my mind when my cell phone rang.

Well, whadda ya know? Speaking of vermin, it was Rasta Boy on the line.

"Hey there, Special Agent Rachel Porter. Remember me?" he asked sarcastically. "It's Dwayne. The next megastar beachboy about to hit Waikiki. *Yeeeouch*!" he yelped. "I'm so red-hot that women are probably already lining up to get a taste of me."

Sometimes you had to wonder what God had in mind when he gave egos to men in the first place.

"What's up?" I asked, cutting to the chase.

"I'm sitting here in Waialua all by my lonely. So, are you anywhere in the area?"

I had to give him points for coming through. Dwayne must have already set up a meeting for me with his boss.

"Actually, I'm not far away," I replied.

That was true, as long as I made it back to my car alive.

He guzzled something and smacked his lips before responding.

"Goody. Then why don't you head on over to the Sugar Bar and come see me," Dwayne said, punctuating his suggestion with a burp.

Ooh, yeah. Females on Waikiki Beach were definitely in for a treat when it came to experiencing Dwayne's unique charms.

"I'll be there as soon as I can," I replied, and hung up.

I picked up the pace and arrived at my Ford without having become fodder for the local wildlife—although a few albatross did give me the eye. Opening the car door, I hit the portable cooler and quickly knocked back two cans of Coke. To hell with the calories. I figured I needed all the caffeine and sugar I could get. Then I planted my butt in the driver's seat and pointed the Explorer toward Waialua.

I once again passed the abandoned cane fields and sugar mill. Truth be told, Waialua had received something of a raw deal over the years in comparison to its neighbor. Haleiwa has always held the allure of being the "in" place for artists and surfers. That wrapped it in a sheen of gloss, while Waialua schlepped along as a working-class sugar town.

Now that those days were gone, the place had fallen into a scruffy state of disrepair. It's where sewage water was dumped, fields were sprayed, and birds were killed. Even the locals didn't seem to care. The proof was in the mounds of trash that littered the ground everywhere.

The Sugar Bar was set just off the main road. I turned in only to slam on my brakes, finding the right-of-way had already been claimed by a couple of roosters. They took their sweet time moving two feathered rear ends slowly across the street. I had no choice but to wait, while impatiently tapping my fingers against the steering wheel. Then I swung into a parking space, fairly certain that my winged friends would soon wind up as fricassee.

I got out of my Ford and headed toward a neoclassical

building. The words BANK OF HAWAII were inscribed above the front door. It would have been hard to believe this place was the Sugar Bar, but for a nearby sign that read NO LIFEGUARD ON DUTY. I knew it as a saloon that attracted mainly North Shore surfer trash. That and bikers, who tended to roll in every Sunday.

I walked inside and immediately spotted Rasta Boy. He sat fidgeting at the bar, maniacally spinning an empty beer bottle and cursing under his breath. He immediately perked up when he caught sight of me.

"Hey, Porter. It's about time you showed. Where in the hell have you been? Never mind. Now that you're here, you can buy me a beer," he said, with rapid-fire speed.

Lucky me. Not only did I get the pleasure of his company, but I was also supposed to pay for it.

I glanced around to discover that Dwayne was alone. The only other patrons were a half-dressed couple making out in the back of the room. If a meeting had been set up, it clearly wasn't taking place at the bar.

"So what's going on?" I asked, getting straight to the point. "Did you arrange a sit-down for me with your boss yet, or not?"

Dwayne snorted, rolled a pair of red-rimmed eyes, and wiped a layer of sweat from his brow. This was the first I'd seen him in the light of day, and he wasn't anything to write home about.

"Cool your jets," he replied. "I need another brewski first. Then we'll get down to business."

Running his tongue over his teeth, he picked a piece of food from between them.

I was left with the distinct impression that that amounted to their brushing and flossing for the day. If so, it hadn't helped. His teeth were ground down to little stubs, most of which were uneven. Equally unappealing was that they were the sickly color of puke—all except for his one gold tooth.

But Dwayne's lack of personal hygiene didn't end there. His body odor was even more noxious than I'd remembered. Forget about knocking out a courtroom. His perspiration was bad enough to make the dead roll over in their graves. It was then I also noticed that his pupils were dilated. That might explain it. He'd probably scored a recent hit of ice.

"What's the matter, Dwayne? Run out of your free stash of brew from the graveyard last night?" I asked, taking a step back for a breath of fresh air.

But Dwayne failed to appreciate my sense of humor.

"Very funny, bitch. Just buy me a damn beer already," he barked, and frantically began to pick at a scab on his arm.

You learn a lot by working in the animal world, like not to take any shit if you expect to be alpha dog. My hand flew out and wrapped itself around Dwayne's neck, firmly squeezing his windpipe.

"Uh, uh, uh. I thought we understood each other," I said, applying more pressure. "Didn't you agree to play nice?"

Dwayne thrashed about, looking wildly at me, his eyes beginning to bulge.

"What in hell are you talking about?" he croaked, starting to choke.

"You really don't know? Gee, that's too bad. Then let's try it again. You don't call me a bitch, and I don't act like one. Remember now?" I reminded him.

I heard a chuckle and looked over to see the bartender smirking, as if enjoying the show. Meanwhile, the couple still hadn't come up for air.

"What say we take this outside?" I suggested.

I didn't wait for Dwayne's answer, but led him through the front door, maintaining a tight grip on his neck.

"Are you playing games with me, Dwayne? Because I'm not in the mood and I don't have time to waste," I hissed in his ear.

"All right, already! I swear, no games," he said, his fingers prying my hand from his throat.

I released my hold.

"For chrissake, what's with you? I'm just a peace-loving surfer dude who grooves on the environment. You know, just like yourself, dudette," he said.

The next moment, he tried to punch me in the stomach.

I dodged the blow and, catching hold of his arm, jerked it behind his back. Then I threw him against the wall.

"Hey, I'm really a good guy. Hell, I even love Bob Marley. What do you have to push me around for?" Dwayne asked, screwing his face up into a tight ball.

For a moment, I actually wondered if he was about to cry.

"I mean it. You're hurting me," he protested.

"No kidding, 'dude.' That's the whole point," I replied.

"Okay. I give up. Uncle, already," he hoarsely surrendered, appearing to be truly upset.

"Are you absolutely sure? Because I have plenty more moves that I'd love to show you," I advised.

"Yeah, yeah. I'm positive. All right? I'll behave," Rasta Boy promised.

I let him go again, and Dwayne slowly rolled his neck, as if to make certain that it still worked.

"Jeez, what's your problem anyway, Porter? Have you ever considered Prozac? 'Cause you sure as hell could use some. You're just lucky that I didn't decide to hurt you back there," he said, gently stroking his throat. "Anyone ever tell you that you've got a real anger management issue?"

"Only those people that I've put in the hospital," I responded, figuring that ought to help keep him in check. "But thanks for the word of advice. What I really want is the name of the guy that you work for."

"Yeah, yeah. Like I don't know that," Dwayne said, fending me off as I took a step closer. "It's Stas Yakimov, okay. We're cool now, right?"

Not quite. The name wasn't exactly what I'd expected.

"Is he Russian?" I questioned.

"Russian, Chinese. It's all the same chop suey to me," Dwayne said with a shrug. "The only thing I know is that he was born here."

"Fine. Now I want you to call him," I ordered.

Dwayne looked at me, and flashed a dopey grin. "I can't. Don't have a cell phone. But I've got an idea. Why don't we use yours?"

The weasel was craftier than I'd imagined. Dwayne knew perfectly well that my number would turn up prominently displayed on Yakimov's phone register. The other option was that a message would appear saying that the number had been blocked. Either way, it could prove to be a tip-off that something was possibly wrong.

Rather than answer, I slipped my hand into each of his back pockets. Nothing there. Oh well, it was time to go Dumpster diving again. I quickly slid my hand down his front pockets.

"Damn, but you're determined to check out my package, aren't you?" Dwayne asked, wiggling around.

"It's what I live for," I replied, and pulled out his cell phone.

"Oops. I musta forgot it was in there," he said, grinning away like a baboon.

"I don't know why. It's the biggest thing that's in your pants," I parried. "Now make the call."

But Rasta Boy suddenly became indignant.

"Whoa! Not so fast," he objected. "What about our deal? You're supposed to set me up as a beachboy first. You do that, and then I'll come through."

"Sorry Dwayne, but it works the other way around," I

informed him. "Don't worry. I'll live up to my end of the bargain. Only it will be after this meeting takes place and I'm satisfied with the results."

"What are you talking about? You never said anything about 'results' before. What the hell's that supposed to mean?" Dwayne suspiciously countered.

"It means that you don't reveal my identity to your boss, or dream of selling me out. You play along, and I'll be happy to introduce you to Dolph once the case is over."

"Just great. And how long is *that* going to take?" Dwayne asked, pouting as he tugged on his ear. "Ouch!" A finger caught in his gold hoop earring and nearly pulled the lobe off.

"No more than a few weeks. Don't sweat it. You'll be on Waikiki Beach escorting wealthy women to all the hot spots in no time," I assured him.

I figured the first woman he approached would probably have him arrested and thrown in jail.

Dwayne remained silent while massaging his earlobe.

"Come on. You don't want to pass up the chance of a lifetime, do you?" I cajoled. "Just think. Beautiful women will be paying you to satisfy their every whim. It's either that, or I send your ass to prison for dealing in illegal reptiles," I reminded him.

"Oh, all right. Just give me the damn cell phone."

I handed it to him. "Okay. Now I want you to tell Yakimov that my name is Gloria Gaines and I own a pet store on Long Island. I'm just here on vacation for a few weeks," I instructed. "Got that?"

"Yeah, yeah. How did we meet? Oh, I know. I picked you up at the Sugar Bar and you took me back to your room for a good time." Dwayne chuckled. "Of course, you had to pay me for it, 'cause you're not my type."

I had a feeling that his "type" came in the form of meth heated in an ice pipe.

"If Yakimov asks, you'll say that we met near the Banzai Pipeline watching a surfing tournament," I corrected. "One more thing. You're also to tell him that you want a cut of any potential business that comes from this."

"You mean in addition to my being paid for catching the little squirts?" he asked, sounding surprised.

"Sure. For all he knows, I could start placing orders for lizards on a regular basis. That translates into big bucks. It will sound more convincing if you want a percentage. After all, you're the one that's bringing me in as a prospective client."

Dwayne regarded me with a hint of respect for the first time.

"Hey, that's pretty smart," he acknowledged.

"Can you remember all that?" I asked.

"Of course I can. Whadda ya think? I'm some sort of dummy?" he replied huffily.

I didn't respond but watched closely as he dialed, making a mental note of the phone number. His demeanor instantly changed as Yakimov answered the line.

"Hey, Stas! My main man. How's it hanging?" Dwayne asked, oozing his particular brand of charm.

He scratched his rear end and pulled at his crotch while listening to Yakimov's response.

"Yeah, yeah. Everything's cool here, dude. In fact, I may have something lined up for you. It's this older chick that I met on the beach."

What a schmuck, I thought, determined to make Dwayne pay for that remark.

"Yeah. She owns a pet store on Long Island and seemed to be real interested when I told her about the lizards."

The next moment, Rasta Boy's jaw dropped, and he began to pull on one of his braids.

"No, no. Calm down, man. It wasn't like that. I didn't bring it up," he quickly backpedaled. "She said she'd seen a few of them running around during this walking tour she took in the rain forest, and asked if I knew how to get some. All I said was that I might have a connection. I swear, Stas. That's it."

I learned, by listening to the conversation, that Yakimov was a lot smarter than Dwayne. My new informant began to nervously pick at his face.

"What? Does she have a business card?" Dwayne asked, obviously repeating Yakimov's question.

He looked at me and I nodded.

"Yeah, yeah. She does. Don't worry. Everything's legit."

I'd had a card made specifically for working under cover. Any incoming calls to the "shop" were picked up by an answering machine that reported that the store was closed while I was away on vacation.

"Anyway, I was thinking that I should probably get a piece of the action if she starts placing orders with you. Whadda ya say?" he queried tentatively.

I was equally curious to hear Yakimov's response.

It must have been good, because Dwayne broke into a high-pitched giggle and roundly slapped his thigh.

"No, man. She already tried to hop on me and I turned her down. Yeah, she caught a look at my package in my swim trunks yesterday and got all turned on. But like I told her, she's not my type. Anyway, I don't want to be paid off in trade, just cold, hard cash."

Right about now, I could have killed the guy. I was going to hurt Dwayne big time for that miserable lie.

"Uh-huh. Okay, Stas. No problem. That sounds fair to me."

I pinched his arm and silently mouthed, *I want to see him today*.

Rasta Boy nodded and pushed me away.

"So listen. Any chance she can stop by your place sometime this afternoon?" Dwayne asked, still scratching at his face.

He opened a pimple that began to bleed.

"Cool, dude. I'll tell her. Yeah, yeah. Don't worry. I'll let her know about that, too. Catch you later," he said and hung up.

Then Rasta Boy turned and grinned at me. "So did I do good, or what?"

"Yeah, except for the fact that you made me sound like an over-the-hill sex maniac," I snapped. "What the hell's with you, anyway?"

"Aw, don't get so bent out of shape. It was just guy talk," Dwayne retorted, continuing to dig at the open wound.

"So what did he offer to pay you?" I asked, my curiosity overcoming my bruised ego.

"Actually, it's a pretty good deal," Dwayne revealed, looking mighty pleased with himself. "Stas is gonna give me ten bucks extra for every order you place. That money'll sure come in handy until this beachboy gig comes through."

I didn't respond, but looked at him in amazement. The only explanation was that crystal meth was eating away at his brain.

He caught my expression and immediately turned hostile.

"What's your problem?" he asked darkly.

"No problem," I answered.

There seemed little point in reminding him that I wasn't really going into the pet trade, but just running a sting operation.

"Good. Then how about a few bucks so I can buy myself a beer?"

I peeled off a ten and held out the bill.

Dwayne grabbed it and began to walk inside.

"Aren't you forgetting something?" I questioned.

"Please and thank you, ma'am," he called over his shoulder.

"No. I'm talking about Yakimov's address," I responded, chalking the 'ma'am' up as another black mark on his record.

"Oh yeah. I guess you need that, don't you?" Dwayne said with a snort.

I copied down his garbled directions, fervently hoping they were correct. Then I headed to my Ford, as Dwayne took a seat at the bar. But I hadn't seen the last of him yet. Rasta Boy stepped outside as I turned on the engine.

"Oh, by the way. Yakimov said that you should meet him in his backyard. Be sure and say hello to all the little animals for me," he added with a broad grin.

"You're sounding pretty chipper," I warily responded. "What's up?"

Dwayne shook his braids and laughed at me. "I already told you. I'm a peace-loving dude who believes in letting bygones be bygones. You should try it sometime, Porter. You'll live longer."

I pulled away and he raised his beer bottle in farewell. The image stayed with me long after the Sugar Bar disappeared from sight. Something about it didn't feel quite right. All I knew for certain was that Dwayne had been far too happy.

 *Nine*

There was no getting around the fact that I had to report in to work. The other sure bet was that I had no intention of heading there now. Not when I had an appointment with Stas Yakimov looming so soon in my future.

Instead, I punched the office number into my cell phone, hoping that Pryor wouldn't be there.

"U.S. Fish and Wildlife office," Jaba the Hut answered the line.

Damn, damn, damn.

"This is Rachel," I responded, having little choice but to stick my neck in the noose.

"And just where the hell are you?" he snapped irritably. "I don't know how things worked at your last posting, but this isn't some social club where you can waltz in and out as you please."

The two options were either to lie or to tell him the truth. I made the only sensible decision.

"I know, Norm. And I'm really sorry, but this couldn't be helped. I got a call from one of the state conservation officers first thing this morning. Some birds were shot in Kualoa Park last night, and he asked for my assistance. I'm still here investigating what took place."

Pryor sighed so deeply that I could almost smell the sweet scent of cherry Danish wafting through the phone.

"Don't these guys know that sort of thing is really *their* job?" he complained.

There are times when a girl's got to do what a girl's got to do. This was definitely one of them.

"You know that state officers don't get anywhere near enough the training they need. Besides, I think it's important to help them out whenever we can," I responded, ever the little diplomat.

"I suppose you're right," Pryor agreed. "God knows, it's best to keep good relations with the state. But just remember that you've got a time sheet to fill out, and I want every minute of your workday accounted for."

I knew that only too well. I also had the sneaking suspicion that Pryor didn't really care if it was one hundred percent accurate. Not as long as it looked good to his superiors back in D.C. That brought me around to thoughts of Sammy Kalahiki and our meeting this morning.

"Something's been bothering me that I'd like to ask you about," I heard myself say.

I was nearly as surprised by the statement as Pryor seemed to be.

"What is it?" he asked, sounding startled.

What the hell. I might as well jump in and find out if he had any knowledge of what was really going on.

"Can you tell me why Fish and Wildlife has jurisdiction over protected species like walrus in Alaska, and manatees on the mainland, but it's hands off as far as marine mammals here in Hawaii?"

I heard Pryor's chair squeak, and knew he was squirming around in his seat. Maybe he'd wondered the very same thing. Whatever the reason, it took him forever to answer the question.

"It's because that's the way National Marine Fisheries likes it," he finally responded.

That was it? I felt like a three-year-old who'd asked why the sky was blue and just been told, *Because that's what God decided.*

"But you see, that's what I don't understand. How can NMFS be so powerful when it comes to this state?" I continued to stubbornly press.

I didn't have to be standing beside him to feel the tension begin to build.

"You're sticking your nose into matters that clearly don't involve you," Pryor retorted, his voice sounding strained.

That's where he was wrong. As far as I was concerned, every species with a heartbeat fell under my jurisdiction. And I had no intention of forsaking a single one of them.

"I'm not trying to annoy you, Norm. Really, I'm just curious," I softly replied, falling back on a tried-and-true method: my feminine wiles.

Why stop there? I decided to go for broke and blatantly stroke his ego. "Besides, you're so well connected with the higher echelons in both agencies that I felt certain you would know the reason. But if you don't, it's all right. I understand," I conceded, allowing the slightest hint of disappointment to creep into my voice.

"It's not that I don't know *why* the policy was put in place. It's just complicated, is all," Pryor genially responded in kind. "You see, there are a number of issues that go into it."

"I'd love if you'd explain them to me," I coaxed, doing my best to keep up the sugary-sweet front.

But my cover must have slipped a bit, because Pryor started to withdraw.

"What do you want to know for?" he suspiciously countered.

We'd plainly danced around the issue long enough. It was time to lay down my cards.

"I've been hearing rumors that shark finning is still going on, and that Honolulu dealers are involved in a major way."

"That's totally ludicrous. There's a law banning that sort of thing," Pryor replied with a cynical grunt. But his tone held a slight edge.

"I know. That's what makes these rumors so disturbing," I agreed, secretly hoping he'd prove me wrong.

"And just who is it that you've been hearing them from?" Pryor questioned, turning the tables on me.

I hesitated, having learned not to trust anyone—not until I knew which side they were on.

"I can't help you unless you're willing to confide in me, Porter," he tried to coerce. "For God's sake. I'm not the enemy here. We're with the same agency, remember?"

Pryor was right. He sounded so reasonable that I nearly told him the name of my source. It was pure gut instinct that kept me from blurting it out.

"It's just gossip that's been floating around," I asserted.

I knew I'd made the correct decision upon hearing Pryor's response.

"That's right, Porter. Idle gossip is all it is and nothing more," he concurred, neatly clipping each syllable. "I'm going to give you the benefit of the doubt, and clue you in on something that you might not yet realize. It's always best to keep your nose out of another agency's business, no matter how tempting it is to get involved."

I didn't need to be told. I already knew what happened to those who opposed a sister agency. They were labeled troublemakers and promptly ostracized for having dared cross the line.

"Hawaii is a small pond where people play for big

stakes, and gossip can be a very effective tool. Come to think of it, I've already heard a rumor or two about you. Nothing you need to worry about, of course. But then again, one never knows," Pryor lightly warned. "Just remember, the nail that sticks up is the one that gets hammered down."

I didn't know whether I'd just been threatened or given sage advice. What I did know was that if rumors were going around, it was best to stop them now. They could effectively destroy an agent's career.

"What have you heard?" I asked, curious as to what was being said about me.

"Just idle gossip. Probably the same sort of thing you're encountering with those malicious rumors about shark finning," Pryor insinuated, making his point.

I had no idea if what he said was true. But the fact that I was beginning to worry was proof enough of the power that rumors could hold. His unspoken threat danced in the air between us.

"I plan to head to the airport and check in with Customs once I'm through here," I said, ending the conversation and, at the same time, providing my excuse for this afternoon.

"Good idea," Pryor agreed, his voice turning smarmy with newfound confidence. "Do us both a favor and just stick to your job."

That's exactly what I am doing, I thought.

"So I probably won't be in the office until tomorrow morning," I informed him.

"No problem," he replied, as if granting me absolution. "As I said from the start, this posting can either be very easy or extremely difficult. It's all up to you. The smart thing to do is to stay below the radar and keep a low profile."

Now where had I heard those sentiments before? Oh yeah. From just about every Fish and Wildlife resident agent in charge that I'd worked for. What did these guys do? Take an oath to keep a tight grip on their agents and never ruffle any feathers?

The thing that continually astonished me was why they'd joined the Service in the first place. It certainly wasn't because they were conservationists at heart, or gave a damn about saving species. All I could figure was that it was for the paycheck and prestige.

Hanging up, I took his advice, rolled it in a tight wad, and slam-dunked it into a mental trash basket. I had every intention of playing by my own set of rules. And as of now, that included an appointment with Stas Yakimov.

Turning south, I drove past miles of military land. A quarter of Oahu's territory is in the armed services grip, with more than a hundred military installations on the island. Defense is such big business that it ranks just below tourism, pouring three billion dollars into the local economy each year.

The dark side is that the government illegally took possession of all of this without giving the Hawaiians any compensation. What private land remains lies in the hands of fewer than fifty individuals and corporations. As a result, large numbers of natives live in poverty, many of them homeless. They're still waiting for land promised to them since 1920 under government programs. More than five thousand Oahuans remain on the list today, while others have died having never been resettled.

I approached Schofield Barracks, the largest U.S. base in the world. Across the street were a variety of fast food shops, tattoo parlors, and a bar famous for its Jell-O shots. A sign announced that the bands Pimbot, Slug, and Primal Tribe, with their trippy vibes, would be performing live over the weekend. It was the perfect idyllic retreat for those hankering to indulge in a slice of headbanger heaven.

Hopping onto the H-2 Freeway, I experienced a little headbanging of my own, by joining in an endless line of traffic. This afternoon, paradise consisted of brake lights for as far as the eye could see. There was little choice but to take a deep breath and try to relax. I improvised on that by unleashing a stream of new curse words with each exhalation.

The blue waters of Pearl Harbor and the U.S.S. Arizona Memorial came into view. The stark white shroud sits atop the sunken hulk of a battleship bombed by Japanese torpedo planes more than sixty years ago. Entombed inside are the remains of more than a thousand sailors. The ship's ruptured fuel tank still bleeds oil, as if crying tears for its crew, producing a kaleidoscopic slick that floats on top of the water's surface like a burial garment.

Legend has it that locals were upset when the U.S. Navy dug Pearl Harbor's dry dock in the same area where the shark goddess, Kaahupahau, supposedly lived. There must have been truth to their concerns, for the entire structure collapsed after only four years. Prophetically, a giant shark skeleton was found among the rubble.

I left the military base behind and began my ascent up the West Coast, where few tourists stray, frightened away by its reputation of being unreceptive to outsiders. This is the last stronghold of Hawaiian culture, where the old customs and traditions still prevail. It's also one of the poorest and most drug-riddled corners of the island.

The West Coast differs from the rest of Oahu in other ways as well. The vegetation is much more sparse, the landscape embedded with rocky crags and cactus-studded hills. I passed through one small town after another, each consisting of little more than a small grocery store and a couple of drive-in restaurants. My sole companions on the road were locals driving their pickup trucks, with pit bulls riding shotgun in the rear.

I continued with Dwayne's directions, hoping I was on the right track. But after a while, I started to wonder if Stas Yakimov really existed. Perhaps this was just some clever ruse to lead me astray.

I was whiling away the time imagining the horrors I'd inflict on Rasta Boy for having tricked me, when a street sign flew by bearing a name that sounded vaguely familiar. Checking my directions, I saw that this was the street where Stas Yakimov lived. I performed a tire-squealing one-eighty and quickly turned onto it.

I wandered through an area where Hawaiian and Samoan farmers tended dusty fields behind sunblasted homesteads. Their hoes dug at dry, baked soil, the particles of which hung like a dingy red curtain in the air. Pigs and chickens paid little heed to the sound of my Ford, but pecked and scratched around junked cars that sat like pop art sculptures in the front yards.

A wave of relief rushed over me as I spotted Stas Yakimov's house. I had to hand it to Dwayne. So far, he'd proven to be a stand-up guy.

I parked behind a dark blue van, got out and faced a typical standard tract house. Only this one had a chain-link fence encompassing its property. Discolored bedsheets covered the windows, looking like a poor man's version of a patchwork quilt, and the yard was a barren field of bare dirt. The house itself was painted a moldy yellow with cinder blocks lining the contours of the roof as if to hold it on.

Dwayne had said that I was to meet Yakimov in the backyard. That was fine with me. Just like one of the three little pigs, I worried that if someone huffed and puffed hard enough, this house might fall down. Besides, I was curious to see the rest of the property.

I pushed the front gate open and walked through, picking my way past sheets of plywood that had been thrown on the ground. It was obvious that Yakimov didn't put a lot of time into lawn care. In that sense, he was a man after my own heart. I'd always figured, why pluck weeds when they were only going to grow back again, anyway?

It was then that I heard a strange sound. What could only be described as chorus of grunts and trills was coming from somewhere close by. The noise grew in volume as I tiptoed up to the corner of the house and peeked around.

Holy leaping lizards! The backyard was filled with at least fifty cages, each of which contained different varieties of iguanas, chameleons, and geckos. All were ready and waiting to be packed up and shipped out.

There were green anoles, whose heads bounced up and down like little bobble-head dolls while they did what appeared to be pushups. They emphasized the movement by fanning a flap of skin beneath their throats like a banner. Next to them was a cage with Jackson chameleons, their stubby bodies queued up as if they were a factory line of miniature triceratops. Each bore three sharp little horns on its head. They sat and stared at their neighbors, a group of Indonesian tokay geckos that touted light gray bodies flecked with bright orange and red spots. The geckos noisily barked as if to say, *We're the bad boys on the block*. On that account, however, they were definitely wrong. I'd already spotted a cage filled with Australian bearded dragon lizards. The ominous-looking creatures lived up to their name, with large triangular heads and spines that ran along the sides of their bodies.

But even these were dwarfed by a crate packed with bright green South American iguanas, each of which measured over five feet in length. They barely acknowledged the other reptiles, knowing that when it came to size they were clearly the winners.

I gazed about in wonder, feeling as if I'd stumbled upon Ground Zero for invasive species. Everywhere I looked, there was something new to see. Other cages held poison-dart frogs, silvery brown skinks, bird-eating Cuban knight anoles, ball python snakes, and blue and red Madagascar geckos. Last, but not least, I caught sight of twenty-five veiled chameleons. They were easily identified by the three-inch shield resembling a shark fin on top of their heads.

My own head was spinning, barely able to process it all, when an angry explosion of barking erupted behind me. I whirled around, my heart racing wildly. What I saw was a vision that had sprung to life from one of my worst nightmares. Five pit bulls, with lips pulled back and teeth bared, were flying through the air, their sights dead set on their target. These were no docile versions of Spam, but five hounds from hell, with only one thing on their mind: to attack and kill.

I grabbed a piece of plywood and held it in front of me like a shield, all the while knowing they'd slice through it as easily as a pack of karate champs. But there was nothing else with which to defend myself. Fear's a strange thing. My heart beat so loudly that I could no longer hear the roar of their howls, and I had to tell myself to continue to breathe. As for my sight, it had narrowed to such a fine point that I was unable to see beyond a speeding blur of fur and teeth.

I said a quick prayer and braced myself for the worst when a voice, so low and rough it must have slithered up from the bowels of the earth, screamed out one single word.

"SPARTACUS!"

The dogs screeched to a halt, as if having hit an electrified fence. Even so, two of the beasts were unable to stop, their bodies sailing through the air. They slammed into the board with such force that I was knocked off my feet. I held the plywood tightly against my face, fearing that I was about to be mauled. Opting for a face-lift was one thing. Undergoing reconstructive surgery was quite another. But all I heard was a chuckle, its resonance falling somewhere between a diesel engine and the rumble of an earthquake.

"It's all right. You can get up now. Don't be afraid. The dogs won't hurt you," instructed the voice that had issued the command.

Easy for him to say.

I lowered my wooden shield and caught sight of a guy who could have been part reptile and part human striding toward me. Oh yeah. And there were five vicious pit bulls cheerfully wagging their tails. This was what the legendary Charles Atlas might have resembled, had he been blown up into a giant Thanksgiving Day parade balloon. Stas Yakimov was a body builder who had clearly lost all control.

Yakimov's arms stuck out from his sides, rather than placidly lying against his body. His muscles were so pumped that the veins popped up like lines on a 3-D relief map. As for his thighs, they rubbed together with the perseverance of a camper with two sticks determined to start a fire. The sound they produced was a *swish, swish, swish*, generated by a pair of nylon blue gym pants that fluttered against his Paul Bunyon–sized legs.

But what really caught my eye was that Stas had breasts nearly the size of mine. Even more demoralizing was that the he didn't need a bra. An "Italian Stallion" T-shirt allowed me a glimpse of his rock hard pecs. Unbelievable. They never once jiggled as he walked. Had he been a girl, I'd have been totally envious. As things stood, I was pretty miffed.

An enormous neck held up a head that looked way too small for his body. It featured a face smothered with acne and a tongue that darted in and out of his mouth. But the real showstopper was the creation erected with his bleached blond hair. It had been gelled into a stiff fin that rose straight up in the air, mimicking the raised spine of a pissed-off komodo dragon. There seemed no question but that Yakimov was either working out twenty-four hours a day, or this guy was one hell of a serious steroid freak.

"You must be Gloria Gaines," he said, holding out a hand. "I'm Stas Yakimov."

I grabbed onto a paw the size of a baseball mitt and was almost lifted off my feet. The five pit bulls promptly began to snarl. Yakimov kicked at the hounds, who scurried away with their tails tucked tightly between their legs.

"Sorry about that," he apologized. "I told Dwayne to make sure you came to the front door. Otherwise, the dogs are bound to think you're a trespasser and are trained to attack."

Why, that lying little bastard, I thought, making sure to keep a smile plastered on my face. No wonder Rasta Boy had looked so happy as I drove away from The Sugar Bar. He'd planned to get rid of me.

"He probably just forgot," I said, and pretended to brush it off.

But Yakimov had a lethal security system. It explained how he was able to keep all these reptiles outside without being robbed.

"Dwayne tells me that you have a pet store on the mainland," Yakimov said, checking out my physique.

It was at times like this that I wished I were more pumped up. I was daydreaming about what body parts I'd improve when Stas reached out toward me. I nearly jumped, wondering what he was up to. His hand encircled my bicep, and gave the muscle a squeeze.

"You must work out," he declared. "You have well-toned arms."

"Why, thank you," I responded, and began to blush.

I couldn't have been more flattered if I were a school-girl. What I didn't tell him was that it came from wrestling lowlifes like Rasta Boy.

"So, where did you say your pet store was again?" he asked, getting down to business.

"East Meadow, Long Island," I replied, figuring it was a safe bet that he'd never been there.

"East Meadow? Sounds like a nice quiet place," Yakimov responded, slipping into salesman mode.

Just as I'd thought. He clearly didn't know the area.

"I don't usually work with small individual stores," he continued. "I generally prefer to deal with only the larger chains."

"Really? Why is that?" I asked.

"Because they don't give me any trouble. You know what I mean? They order in bulk, pay on time, and that's that. No fuss, no muss, no pain in the ass," he explained.

Stas was decked out in a variety of gold baubles, making me wonder if he and Dwayne patronized the same jeweler. A necklace the size of a snow-tire chain hung from his neck. It matched the heavy link bracelet on his arm, and the solid gold *S* weighing down his ring finger.

"Then your business must be very lucrative," I responded, blatantly gawking at his jewelry.

Stas followed my gaze and laughed. "You bet it is. I made close to four hundred thousand dollars last year."

Yikes!

"You grossed all that just from selling reptiles?" I asked, in amazement.

No wonder invasive species were booming in Hawaii, with that kind of money to be made.

"Who said anything about gross? I'm talking net,"

Yakimov bragged, lightly fingering his massive gold necklace. "And yeah, it's mainly from selling reptiles, along with one other sideline that I've got going."

"And what might that be?" I casually inquired.

"Nothing you'd be interested in" he said matter-of-factly.

That's what *he* thought. In any case, the invasive species trade was more lucrative than I could ever have imagined. I was equally struck by the fact that Yakimov felt safe enough to speak about it so openly. He'd obviously never been hassled by state or federal authorities, regardless of what the law might be.

"Well, you have quite an impressive array of lizards and my clientele goes nuts for this stuff. So why don't we talk prices and see if we can't do some business? My store might not be large, but I move an amazing amount of inventory. Plus, if things work out, I have friends in other states that might also be interested," I added, hoping to sweeten the pot.

"All right, then. Let's get down to it," Stas agreed, rubbing his ring as if for good luck.

We walked by cage after cage, as Yakimov rattled off prices.

"These rosy boas generally go for forty-five dollars, while the panther chameleons are one-hundred twenty bucks apiece. Those Jacksons over there? They sell for fifty-five smackers. As for the bearded dragons, they usually run forty for males and sixty for females."

I quickly realized why Yakimov was doing so well. His prices were better than any I'd heard on the mainland.

"Of course, that's if you're buying in bulk," he clarified. "You know, like a Pets Galore or Leapin' Lizards chain. But you seem like a nice woman, so I'll give you a special introductory deal. After that, we'll see what happens based on how much you order and if you bring in other clients. Who knows? Maybe I can even come up with some better prices."

Stas was definitely savvy when it came to doing business.

"Do you mind if I jot those numbers down?" I asked, trying to keep them straight without wanting to make him suspicious.

"Of course. Go ahead. Be my guest," he magnanimously said. "Now see these beauties over here?"

We stopped in front of a crate of veiled chameleons. They stared at me reproachfully, as if aware of my secret.

"These are my pride and joy. They're a hot, hot item on today's reptile market. In fact, I can barely keep up with the demand for them."

Yakimov ran a hand lightly over his spiky blond hair. The chameleons seemed to nod their own fins in agreement.

"Do you have any idea how hard it is to get them out of Saudi Arabia and Yemen these days? I'll tell you. It's damn near impossible. Let me fill you in on something else. You have these babies in your store window and they'll be snapped up faster than you can say Al Qaeda. In fact, I'm going to make you a terrific offer. Order ten or more, and I'll let you have them for the same price I give Pets Galore. One hundred twenty-five bucks a piece. Be sure to write that down," Stas instructed, stabbing a sausage-sized finger at my pad.

What a guy, what a guy, I thought, and quickly made a note of it.

"I'm going to give you another hot tip," Yakimov said. His tongue nearly darted in my ear as he pulled me close, as if to tell me a secret. "Advertise them as 'bin Laden's beasts,' and I guarantee you can jack the price up to three hundred and fifty smackers each. All the local yahoos will be buying them faster than if they were hotcakes. Pretty smart idea, huh?" he said with a laugh.

His muscles had a life of their own, as they jumped and jerked and vibrated. The guy would have made a hell of a Chippendale dancer with this kind of muscle control. As it was, I half expected him to turn into the Hulk and rip off his clothes.

I pulled away, pretending to take a closer look at the chameleons.

"That's terrific, Stas. They're definitely on my 'to buy' list. In fact, I'm thinking of ordering two dozen," I replied, figuring that ought to make him happy.

I was right. Stas wrapped his arms around me, nearly breaking my bones.

"See how well we're getting along already?" he cheerfully said, his fingers prancing up and down my spine.

It actually felt pretty good, and was one way of getting a free massage. However, Yakimov seemed to be getting the wrong idea about us. I placed my hands against his chest and pushed him away.

"What's the matter? Is something wrong?" Stas asked, scrunching his face until his acne turned into one giant pimple.

"I have to admit, I am a little worried about something," I said, pretending to pout the slightest bit.

"Don't be silly. You're in Hawaii and you've just met *me*. What could possibly be better?" Stas modestly countered. "Unless you're concerned that I'll sell to competitors in your area. In which case, you'll have to make it worth my while."

I didn't even want to ask what he meant by that.

"My concern is if you'll be able to meet my demand," I retorted, giving his chain a yank.

"Oh you are, are you? Why? Are you all that insatiable?" Yakimov asked coyly. "Because I have something that will take care of that."

Oy veh. Now I got it. He was out to prove himself more of a sex toy than Rasta Boy.

"Very funny, Stas," I responded, and shot him a withering look. "I'm talking about the reptiles. You have such a large and unusual assortment that I'm worried what will happen if *your* suppliers dry up."

"That's something you don't have to fret your pretty little head about," Stas said with a wink.

"And why is that?" I questioned, ignoring his sexist comment.

"Because I'm growing them right here on Oahu," Yakimov revealed, proudly puffing out his already enormous chest.

"That's amazing," I responded, feigning astonishment. "How did you ever manage to do that?"

Yakimov's cockscomb stood up a bit straighter, as if pleased that I was impressed. "I'm a friendly guy. I go and talk to people at bars in Waikiki. You never know who you might meet. It turned out, one of my "new friends" was a reptile wholesaler who was vacationing in Honolulu. We had a couple of drinks and soon he started to tell me his life story."

It seemed that Yakimov and I used some of the same techniques. Stas placed his hands on his hips, so that the veins in his arms popped out and stood at attention.

"It didn't take long for him to complain about having to place five-dollar-a-minute phone calls to Madagascar to try and track down lizards," Stas continued. "Not only that, but he was handing out hundred-dollar bribes just to get the damn things shipped over to him. Except that half the time, people would take his money and never send the critters. He said he'd gotten tired of it and asked if I'd like to take a shot at raising them here in Hawaii. I thought, why the hell not? So, he smuggled a few over. The next thing you know, I've got myself a booming business," Yakimov crowed. "Best of all, there's not much overhead since everything is ranched in the wild."

Now all I needed were the names of those people that Yakimov dealt with on a regular basis. I figured that should be easy enough to learn in another visit or two.

"You mean, I could send a couple of water monitors over here, and you'd actually start a colony of them for me?" I questioned, hoping to gather more information.

"Absolutely. Except you'd have to come up with something better than that. I've already got plenty of those," he revealed with a shrewd smile. "In fact, they're just about ready to be caught and shipped to the mainland."

"You've got to be kidding," I replied in disbelief.

Water monitors grew to be seven feet in length, and were highly aggressive. Someone was in for a hell of a shock the next time they jumped in their local water hole to go for a swim.

"Why don't you think of a reptile that's a little more original? Perhaps along the lines of what I have back here," Yakimov suggested.

He led the way to a bunker built out of cinder blocks. Sitting in front was a crate that had been raised off the ground.

"I bet you have no idea what those things are inside," he challenged.

My breath caught in my throat at the sight of six long, graceful critters with whiplike tails and small, pointed heads. Light forest green in color, each had black stripes running down its back, and sharp claws attached to big strong feet. I instantly knew that I was looking at one of the rarest lizards on the planet.

"Oh my God. Those are green tree monitors from New Guinea," I responded in a hoarse whisper, unable to imagine how he'd gotten hold of them.

"How did you know that?" Yakimov sharply questioned and stared at me. "The only people who usually recognize those are experts in the field."

Damn! I should have known better than to appear quite so knowledgeable. I quickly scrambled to cover my tracks.

"I own a pet store. Remember? Besides, I've always loved chameleons. I had every lizard memorized by the time I was eleven years old," I brazenly lied. "Not only that, but I recently read an article that green tree monitors are being captive bred at the Bronx Zoo."

That seemed to temporarily appease him. Yakimov's complexion returned to normal, and he unclenched his fists.

"Oh yeah. I think I read about that too," Stas said with a slight nod, as if recalling the information.

I leaned in for a closer view and let loose a low whistle. My heart jumped as it was answered by a hissing and spitting that hadn't come from the three-foot lizards standing in front of me. Rather, the sound emanated from somewhere inside the cinderblock prison. I gazed up to meet a pair of feline eyes that angrily glared out through a small window.

"Holy shit!" I exclaimed in surprise and leaped back. "What in the hell have you got in there?"

"Well, well. Look who's asking. If it isn't the big animal expert," Yakimov gloated in unconcealed delight. "I guess you aren't as smart as you think. What you just saw is my cougar, Rocky."

I flashed back to the streak of brown that had run across the road the other night. Could Stas be crazy enough to attempt to breed mountain lions in the rain forests of Oahu?

"You aren't ranching those things, are you?" I asked, almost afraid to know the answer.

If so, he'd never be able to catch them again.

"Not yet. I'm still waiting for his girlfriend to arrive. She'd better come soon, though. 'Cause Rocky's getting impatient for female companionship, if you know what I mean," Stas imparted with a laugh.

He kicked at something, and I saw that it was a piece of cougar scat.

I pointed to it and asked, "You don't let Rocky outside by any chance, do you?"

Hopefully, he had more sense than to play at being Siegfried and Roy.

"No, no. Rocky goes into a large crate whenever I clean his shed. I'm not about to let him escape like the last one did. That cost me way too much time and money."

Whadda ya know? So I hadn't been crazy, after all. There *was* a cougar running around loose in the mountains. I could already see the headline that would one day be splashed across the *Star Advertiser* and the *Honolulu Bulletin*.

MAN-EATING MOUNTAIN LION GOBBLES YET ANOTHER HUMAN

That should do wonders for Hawaii's tourist industry.

"Why don't we go inside and finish our business? That way we can relax and you can give me your order," Yakimov suggested.

My, my. But wasn't Stas eager to seal the deal? It was fine with me. I'd get a chance to snoop around inside his house.

I peered through the bunker window once more. Rocky anxiously paced back and forth, as if he were a condemned prisoner. I'd certainly hate to be his girlfriend when she finally arrived.

We approached the house, where a large mobile hung outside the back door. It looked like something that Fred Flintstone might have owned, touting real bones in place of chimes or cute little figures of angels. A whisper of a breeze made them clatter together like skeletons engaged in a macabre dance. The sound reverberated in the air, ominous as a death rattle.

Yakimov played with them as we stood near the door.

"You like this thing? I made it myself," he announced.

"It's very interesting. What sort of bones did you use?" I asked, curious as to the type of animal he'd killed.

"These are from my old pit bulls," Yakimov divulged with a peculiar grin. "This way, the dogs are always with me. I like to think of myself as a sentimental guy."

Funny. I was beginning to think of him as a muscle-bound, lizard-breeding, environmentally polluting pervert.

I scurried past the mobile and followed Stas into what appeared to be the kitchen. The interior of the house perfectly mirrored its shabby exterior. The only thing that could have helped the place would have been a wrecking ball. Paint was peeling off the walls, and pots and pans were scattered about.

But it was the mind-boggling noise inside that made it seem as if every critter he'd ever sold had come back to haunt him. The ruckus was nearly deafening. It sounded as if something large were pinned behind the walls and desperately clawing to get out. It reminded me of hundreds of feet shuffling against gravel.

"Sorry about the racket. A delivery of crickets came today," Stas shouted, and pointed to dozens of boxes piled high on the kitchen floor. "I like to feed them to the lizards right before they're packed up for shipment."

So that was it. The sound came not from one creature, but thousands of crickets crammed inside boxes. Terrific. Yakimov was importing alien insects to *feed* his invasive species, in a never-ending cycle that spelled disaster for Hawaii.

We picked our way through the mess and headed into the living room, where I viewed its unique decor. The place had a definite S&M feel about it. Probably because the furniture looked as though it had been beaten with chains and smothered in dog hair. All this was set against walls that were painted Day-Glo red.

But the true piece de resistance was the life-size pit bull that stood stuffed and mounted on a glass coffee table covered in dust. The pooch wore a tight spike collar, with teeth bared, as if ready to attack on command. Stas walked over and affectionately petted the thing before leaning down to give it a kiss.

"This is Sparky, the love of my life. I think my wife knew it as well, which was why she didn't like him. The bitch finally gave me an ultimatum. Only one of them could stay. The other had to go. So guess which one ended up getting the boot?"

I looked at Sparky and hated to imagine what must have happened to Yakimov's wife. Stas seemed to confirm my suspicions as our eyes met. Suddenly, something didn't feel quite right. Perhaps it hadn't been such a wise idea to come into the house, after all. A subtle change appeared to be taking place within Yakimov. It was definitely time to wrap things up and vamoose.

A flurry of dog hair rose in the air as Stas sank into the couch. The fur fell like a gentle mist as he stretched out his arms, as if unfolding a pair of wings. Then he pointed for me to sit in the chair opposite him.

"Okay. Now you're going to give me a great big order, right?" Yakimov asked with a smile. But his voice held a thinly disguised threat.

I hoped to pry a few contacts from him before bolting for the door. Taking a deep breath, I launched into my spiel.

"Of course. But first I'd like the names of some wholesalers that you deal with on the mainland. I want to check and make certain that everything's on the up and up," I said, congratulating myself for being oh-so clever. "After all, I plan to order quite a bit of inventory from you. That translates into a large chunk of cash. I'm sure you understand."

Then again, maybe not. For the strangest thing started to happen. Stas's eyes bulged as if they were about to pop out of their sockets, and his grin grew so wide that I thought his face would explode. All the while he sweated profusely, as if a faucet had been turned on over his head. However, that wasn't the end. The muscles in his arms sprang to life, expanding and contracting, until his veins joined in the dance, in what must have been some sort of horrible steroid reaction.

"What's going on? Now you don't trust me? This is complete bullshit! Why did you come here in the first place if you were just going to waste my time?"

Yakimov's mood turned on a dime, as he suddenly rose from the couch and came toward me.

Oh shit. There was no question but that I didn't stand a chance if it came to fighting the guy.

"Be sensible, Stas. Why don't we talk this over? I'm sure we can work things out," I tried to reason.

But Yakimov kept moving forward like a bulldozer intent on mowing me down.

Quickly looking around, I picked up the only thing that might possibly fend him off—his former true love, Sparky.

"Don't hurt the dog!" Stas wailed in a high-pitched howl as I raised the stuffed mutt high above me.

"I won't," I tried to reassure him. "Just as long as you calm down."

But I kept a tight grip on the pooch, ready to use it as a club if necessary. Yakimov must have realized I meant business, because he started to back away.

"Okay, Gloria. You've made your point. Tell you what.

I'll give you two references. After that, you've got five days to place an order before the prices go up."

Who knows? Maybe this was the way business was normally conducted in Hawaii. All that mattered was that the tactic had worked. And, at this point, I was willing to settle for whatever I could get.

"You've got a deal," I agreed. "Do I have your word that we have a truce?"

The man looked at Sparky, and I could have sworn that his lips began to tremble.

"Yes, I won't touch you. Just put down the dog."

I had no choice but to believe him, having locked my gun in the glove compartment of my vehicle. I'd wrongly figured that a pet-store owner from Long Island would have little reason to pack heat while vacationing in Hawaii. But then I hadn't known that I'd be dealing with a nut case like Stas Yakimov.

Stas wiped a layer of sweat from his brow as I placed Sparky back down on the table.

"I have those contacts in the other room. I'll get them for you," he offered.

Right. Like I trusted the man out of my sight.

"I'll come with you," I countered, stating it more as a fact than a suggestion.

Yakimov's kamikaze dogs broke into a round of maniacal barking before either of us could make a move.

Stas rushed to the front window, where he pushed aside the ragged curtain and peered outside.

"Damn. My other appointment is already here."

It seemed that Yakimov was a busy man. I glanced over his shoulder and spied a black Lincoln Continental that sat parked near my vehicle. A check of the license plate revealed it was a rental. Obviously, Stas wasn't the only one making money off the Hawaiian reptile trade.

"Call off your dogs, or I swear to God I'll shoot the damn things!" shouted a voice that sounded vaguely familiar.

"I've got to do what he says," Stas muttered, clearly beginning to panic. "You don't know this guy. He's totally crazy."

I figured it must be true if he could make even someone like Yakimov nervous.

"All right, go ahead," I agreed.

But Stas wasn't waiting for my permission.

"Spartacus! Spartacus!" he'd already begun to yell, while running outside to herd the dogs into their pen.

With any luck, this just might work in my favor. It was possible that I was about to meet one of Yakimov's major wholesale connections.

My palms grew damp, and my pulse sped up. The reaction wasn't one of fear but of excitement at the prospect of snagging yet another fish on my line. However, my hopes were dashed as Yakimov quickly hurried inside.

"You're going to have to leave now. We'll finish our business later."

"Like hell we will," I protested, as Yakimov began to brusquely steer me toward the front door.

I tried to put on the brakes—until I caught sight of his visitor.

A pair of pointy alligator shoes emerged from inside the car, followed by white polyester pants and a garish Hawaiian shirt. The cheesy attire covered a six-foot-five, three-hundred-pound frame. The only way to describe the outlandish sight was *Blue Hawaii* meets *Saturday Night Fever*.

But the situation grew even more bizarre as the man's face came into view. He had the pompadour hairdo of a fifties rock star and the nose of a punch-drunk fighter, crookedly embedded in a mound of puffy flesh. Forget

Saturday Night Fever. This was definitely a scene straight
out of *The Sopranos.*

If Yakimov hadn't been holding me tight, I might have
fallen flat on the ground. But I also knew it was necessary
that I keep my wits about me. The man walking toward
the house was none other than Vinnie Bertucci—former
bodyguard of a perp I'd busted in New Orleans for smuggling drugs inside wildlife shipments. Bertucci had moved
to New York since then, where he now worked for a
prominent Sicilian crime family.

I no longer argued with Yakimov, but hastily strode out
the door. My eyes remained glued to Bertucci, who lowered
his sunglasses and stared in surprise. Vinnie was about to
speak, when he realized that I was silently mouthing the
word *NO.* Instead, he slowed down as I approached.

"My name is Gloria Gaines," I whispered while passing by.

Then I continued on to my Ford as the two men went
inside and shut the door.

The smart thing would have been to immediately split.
But there was something that I wanted to do first. I
waited until I was certain that the two men were occu-
pied. Then, unlocking the glove compartment, I grabbed
my gun along with a baggie, and snuck into Yakimov's
backyard.

The dogs remained locked in their pen, where they continued to bark. I figured the noise wasn't a problem, since
Yakimov wouldn't be suspicious of trespassers. It gave me
the chance to scurry over to Rocky's shed, find the piece
of scat, and scoop it up into my bag. Then hastening back
to the Explorer, I turned on the engine and left.

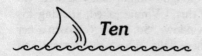

Ten

I got as far as the main road before pulling over to park. Only then did I allow the torrent of thoughts, percolating inside my head, to break loose. What in hell was Vinnie Bertucci doing at Stas Yakimov's? Had he finally broken his word and gotten involved in the illegal wildlife trade? I couldn't imagine any other reason for his visit. If so, the delicate friendship we'd developed over the years was about to come to an end.

My stomach twisted at the thought. Vinnie had helped me out of a couple tight spots. In return, I'd agreed to overlook his mob "activities" as long as they didn't impact wildlife. Not only had that pleased Vinnie, but also the FBI, which had his New York crime family dead in their sights. They didn't want me getting involved with any individuals in whom they might have an interest. Perhaps they had good reason to worry. I'd intruded on their territory in the past when it had served my purpose.

My heart hadn't stopped pounding since his Lincoln Continental appeared in front of Yakimov's house. Now it was hammering for a different reason. I was trying to figure out how to bring down Vinnie Bertucci.

An hour crawled by before Bertucci's black Continental

glided into view. The Lincoln pulled up beside me and the window lowered as if of its own accord.

"Hey there, Gloria. I thought I might find you here. We gotta stop meeting like this," Vinnie joked, sticking his beefy head out the car window. "So, I hear you own a pet store in East Meadow these days. What's the matter? You don't make enough dough to open a shop in a fancy place like Great Neck?"

Bertucci's laugh was rough as a chunk of Parmesan cheese being shredded on a grater.

"What say you lead the way back to Waikiki and civilization, and we get the hell out of this place. I'm staying at the Royal Hawaiian. We can ditch the cars there," Vinnie instructed.

Of course. Only the best hotel in Waikiki would do.

I guided the way back through a torturous line of traffic, glancing into my rearview mirror every so often to see how Vinnie was doing. He handled the rush-hour melee pretty much as I'd expected. Bertucci kept his middle finger raised in the air, with his other hand planted smack on the horn. Naturally, all the other cars assumed his efforts were directed solely at me.

We finally escaped the highway and crossed the canal into tourist heaven.

"Now this is more like it," Vinnie said when we arrived at his picture-perfect pink hotel.

He stretched his limbs and rubbed his stomach, which growled as rabidly as one of Yakimov's curs.

"What I need is a thick, rare steak and a coupla shots of scotch," Bertucci announced, and gave me the once-over. "From the look of things, you could use a good meal yourself. Whadda ya livin' on these days? Bananas and coconuts? I swear to God, it looks like you're fadin' away. But you're still as gorgeous as ever."

I nearly kissed the guy, tempted to overlook any differences there might be between us. That was the nicest compliment I'd been paid in years.

"Just don't take me to any of those native places where they try to foist that Spam or poi crap on you," he warned.

Instead I took him for a stroll along the strip, where we passed kitschy souvenirs made in Taiwan, an assortment of hot-looking hookers, and pain-in-the-ass street performers. It seemed to take all of Vinnie's willpower not to run off with one and whack the other. But what really caught Bertucci's eye was a two-story cylindrical fish tank that comprised the front window of a chi chi clothing store.

"See? Now this is the way to get people interested in wildlife," Vinnie informed me, his complexion glowing bright cobalt blue in the tank's reflection. "You gotta capture animals and put 'em where they can be seen as people walk by. You should learn a thing or two from this."

"I'll keep that in mind," I retorted, not bothering to tell him that such places already existed. They were known as zoos and marine aquariums.

Down the street were Gucci, Prada, and Hermes boutiques, where every customer inside seemed to be Japanese and spoke little English.

"For chrissakes. What's going on? Hasn't anybody ever told these people that *they're* the ones that lost the war?" Bertucci grumbled irritably.

What Vinnie didn't comprehend was that Waikiki is as much a Japanese resort as it is an American one, a town where numerous businesses are Japanese owned and run.

So much for sightseeing. It was time to stop and eat. I settled on a restaurant that any carnivore would have loved—a place that specialized in Kobe beef.

"How's business going these days?" I asked, making small talk as Vinnie dug into his salad with gusto.

"Which one are you talking about?" he responded, through a mouthful of lettuce.

I picked a shred of romaine off my arm and placed it in my napkin.

"I don't know. How many have you got now?" I queried.

"What, are you kiddin' me? I'm a regular fuckin' Trump," Vinnie retorted, shooting a shard of carrot my way.

The guy could be lethal, even while eating.

"Not only do I look after the family's holdings, but I also got my own business interests, if you know what I mean."

I'd learned that firsthand while working a case in Montana. Vinnie and I had both been after one Benny Gugliani, a former wiseguy who was placed under the federal witness-protection program. By the time the dust cleared, Vinnie had taken control of Gugliani's booming business in survivalist gear.

"Such as your business venture in Montana?" I inquired.

Vinnie broke into a high-pitched rat-a-tat-tat giggle, as if still tickled by the memory. "Yeah. That was a good one, huh? We had fun together on that thing. In fact, remember that Indian friend of yours?"

Vinnie caught me off guard and I nodded, unable to speak over the lump that formed in my throat. I'd been thinking of Matthew Running all too much lately.

"Well, we still send each other postcards every once in a while," Vinnie continued. "Come to think of it, I got one not too long ago. It said he might be coming to New Yawk. Ain't that a kick in the rear?"

"Unbelievable," I agreed.

What was going on? Was everyone in touch with Matthew Running except me? I quickly changed the subject, not wanting to dwell on something that might have been.

"Speaking of surprises, what brings you to Hawaii? In particular, to see Stas Yakimov? Don't tell me that you've gotten involved in the reptile trade?" I questioned him, figuring we might as well get right down to business.

Vinnie threw his fork on the table and actually stopped eating.

"No way. Now you're insulting me. Haven't I always told you that I'd never harm a living, breathing thing?"

Vinnie looked at me with a pair of sad eyes and, for a moment, I was ready to apologize.

"That is as long as it has four legs or more," he added with a chuckle. "Besides I don't wanna have to take on someone like you, unless it's absolutely necessary."

Evidently we were both thinking along the same lines.

"Then what brings you here?" I once again asked.

Vinnie pushed aside his decimated salad and leaned in closer.

"Okay. This is just between you and me, right? A coupla of friends shooting the breeze."

A spider vein on his nose twitched, and I nodded in agreement.

"You know my policy," I reminded him.

"Yeah, yeah. Don't worry. No little four-legged creatures are involved in this deal. Although a few males in the animal kingdom probably wish they could be," Vinnie said, with a twitter. "My business associates . . ."

"You mean the Travatellis?" I interrupted.

Vinnie skewered me with a look. "Hey, you know better. No names in public, okay?"

"Sorry about that," I responded, having been put in my place.

Vinnie raised a chastising eyebrow and then continued.

"My business associates are big into the black-market trade for Viagra these days. Of course, I don't need that kind of thing myself," he quickly added. "But there's a helluva market out there for guys that could use a helpful boost—or those hoping to land a four-hour erection. Our friends at Lehman Brothers figure that demand is soon gonna triple to six billion dollars a year. And that's just the tip of the iceberg, so to speak."

"Yeah, but where do you come in? After all, the drug is already legal," I reasoned.

"Sure. But you still gotta have a prescription for it," Bertucci explained.

Vinnie grew silent as a waiter placed a large slab of beef in front of him. He sliced the meat with expert precision and stuck a chunk of it into his mouth.

"Hey, this is terrific. What did you say this stuff was called?" he asked between bites.

"Kobe beef," I replied, tasting my own well-done steak.

"See? That just shows you how screwed up the legal system in this country is," Vinnie complained, with a shake of his head. "First O. J. walks, and now Kobe Bryant gets a cut of beef named after him."

I decided it was probably best to leave it at that, and not mention where the meat really came from, based on Vinnie's reaction to all the Japanese tourists in Waikiki.

"Anyway, we're tapping into those countries where Viagra hasn't been approved yet," he said, continuing to eat as he spoke. "This thing is huge—no pun intended. And I'm not talking about that twenty-five- or thirty-milligram crap. We're dealing in one-hundred-milligram pills only. That way, you get more bang for your buck. My associates are pipelining these goodies around the world for twenty-five smackers a pop, and people still can't get enough of 'em."

That was interesting to know. In a strange sense, maybe Vinnie and Viagra would actually help with my work. The drug might take some pressure off those creatures whose bones and body parts were believed to be magical aphrodisiacs. Those species ran the gamut from snakes to turtles, whales, monkeys, and bears, along with tiger bone, rhino horn, and seal penises. I was all for Viagra, if it cut down on the slaughter of innocent creatures.

As much as I enjoyed the idea, it still didn't explain what Vinnie was doing here, and why he'd paid a visit to Stas Yakimov. It was as if he had read my mind when he spoke up.

"Stas has been doing some work for us. The only problem is that a large chunk of change keeps disappearing from this end. I'm here to straighten out any financial problems. I guess you could say I've become a regular CPA enforcer."

Vinnie daintily picked a piece of meat from between his teeth with his little finger.

"I don't get it. Is Yakimov selling the stuff or stealing it for himself?" I questioned.

"I'm figuring little of both. He's got a problem, in case you haven't noticed. It probably comes from shooting up too much juice."

I looked at Vinnie, not quite certain what he meant.

"You know. I'm talking gym candy, Arnolds. That kind of stuff," Bertucci rattled off.

He waited for me to react and then impatiently shook his head, frustrated that I still wasn't getting it.

"For chrissakes, Yakimov's a steroid freak."

"I'm perfectly aware of that," I responded.

"Well, you know what that does to a guy's erector set, don't you?" he asked.

"Not really," I admitted.

"Then let me fill you in," Vinnie cheerfully offered. "To put it in plain English, Stas can't get Jimmy and the boys to stand up. My guess is that's why he's been helping himself to a good deal of the stash. Of course, he'd never admit it. Instead, he's blaming late payments on some big fish that's supposedly been hooked on the island. So, it's my job to check it out."

Vinnie burped and ordered two pieces of macadamia nut fudge cake, along with a couple of cappuccinos.

"You mean, you flew all the way over here just because you got stiffed on a few pills?" I joked, and enthusiastically dug into the thick gooey mound of calories placed before me. Even better, I didn't feel the least bit guilty as I polished off every single last crumb. How could I, when Vinnie had said that I was fading away?

"A few pills?" Vinnie snorted. "Try ten thousand of 'em. Figure it out. That's ten thousand erections for a quarter million bucks. Now *that's* what I call cold, hard cash."

Bertucci gave his stomach a satisfied rub, and then wrinkled his nose at me.

"Hold still a minute," he ordered, and dunked a napkin into his water glass.

The next thing I knew, Vinnie was dabbing a smudge of dirt off my face.

"How'd you get so filthy, anyway?" he asked, taking a closer look at my clothes.

"It's a long story." I sighed, feeling as though I were being cleaned by a mother cat. "I caught this guy snagging illegal reptiles up in the mountains, and twisted him to learn who he was working for. That's how I got to Yakimov. I had him introduce me to Stas as a buyer. Except the kid proved to be smarter than I thought. It turns out that he set me up," I revealed.

"How do you figure that?" Vinnie asked, and took a sip of his cappuccino. He quickly pushed the cup away. "This place should be closed down for mutilating good Italian coffee."

However, he seemed to reconsider a moment later. I watched as Vinnie pulled the cup back and dumped three heaping teaspoons of sugar into it.

"Okay, now go ahead. Finish what you were saying," he instructed, and tasted the brew once more.

"This kid told me to meet Stas in his backyard. Only Yakimov had specifically warned him that I was to come to the front door, knowing that his dogs would be loose. Naturally, the pit bulls thought I was a trespasser and began to attack as soon as I set foot on the property. I would have been a goner if Stas hadn't been there to call them off. That was probably the kid's plan all along," I theorized. "My concern is that he'll rat me out when he learns that I'm still alive."

"So, where does this kid live, anyway?" Vinnie casually asked, beginning to clean his nails with a file.

I instantly regretted having told him the story.

"Uh-uh. Thanks for your concern, but I'll handle this on my own," I warned.

"Don't be such a hard-ass, Porter. I'll just pay the guy a visit and we'll have a friendly little chat," Bertucci replied.

Tempting as that might be, I couldn't possibly allow it.

"I'm serious, Vinnie. I know you mean well, but stay out of this," I firmly advised.

Vinnie shrugged and put away his nail file. "Whatever you say. It's your neck. Besides, I've got my own problems to handle."

We walked back to the Royal Hawaiian, where I picked up my Ford.

"I plan to be around a few more days. What say we get

together one night and take in Don Ho's show? I love that
Tiny Bubbles crap," Vinnie said with a straight face.

"Sure. That would be fine," I replied, gambling that
he'd probably never call.

Then I got in my vehicle and Vinnie closed the door.

"Take care of yourself, Porter. I'd hate to see you end
up as dog chow."

I drove off thinking about Vinnie, how to get even with
Rasta Boy, and the black-market trade in Viagra.

I heard the sound of talking and laughter as I walked
through the door. For once, Spam didn't come running to
the kitchen to greet me. Neither did Tag-along sashay in
to rub against my legs and beg for food. Things were bad
when even the damn cat couldn't be bothered.

I headed into the living room, where Kevin and Santou
were drinking a few beers and reminiscing about old
times together. Funny how my radar instantly flew into
action, hoping to pick up any juicy bits of gossip.

Half the time, I wondered if it would have been any easier if Kevin were a woman. At least then I'd have known
what I was up against and how best to deal with it. As
things were, I simply felt left out. What can I say? It sucked
having to compete with a man for Santou's attention.

"Hey, chere. You didn't come home for dinner tonight,"
Jake said with a smile.

I took that as a good sign. It could have been worse. He
might not even have noticed that I hadn't been here. As
for Kevin, he was back to being his old self again.

"You look a little worse for wear. Hot date tonight?" he
asked with a smirk, bringing the bottle of beer to his lips.

"Yeah. As a matter of fact, I got together with your old
girlfriend and she filled me in on all the dirt," I countered,
slipping back into our familiar roles. "Actually, I bumped
into Vinnie Bertucci. Remember him?"

Both men instantly perked up.

"You're kidding. Bertucci's on Oahu?" Santou asked, with more interest than he'd shown in a while. "That can only mean one thing: trouble. Any idea what he's up to?"

I hesitated, not all that eager to share information with them.

"Not really. Maybe he's just here on vacation," I replied.

"Sure. I hear the guy's really big into whacking fish." Kevin sneered. "Only instead of using a rod and reel, he's partial to a nine-millimeter Uzi. If Vinnie the Vault is in town, then you can bet something's going down."

"Vinnie the Vault?" I dubiously inquired, never having heard the nickname before.

"Yeah, it's because of his size," Kevin retorted.

"I hope you don't plan on spending any time with the guy," Santou added. "Bertucci's moved up the ladder since his days in New Orleans and, trust me, it's not the kind of company you want to keep."

"I don't see why there should be a problem," I responded. "It's not as if he's involved in the wildlife trade. Vinnie even said he'd never harm a living, breathing thing, as long as it wasn't a human being."

Santou looked at me in amusement, "Now that's an interesting comment. And just what category do you suppose you fall under, chere?"

I opened my mouth to speak, but nothing came out. Damn it. I hate when I don't have a good comeback.

"Jake's right," Kevin said, unexpectedly turning serious. "The guy's bad news. Nothing but trouble follows wherever he goes."

Or maybe he follows trouble, I thought. In which case, we have the trait in common.

I decided to play it smart, and not argue the matter any further.

"Why don't I let you two finish your beers? I'm beat. I'm going to call it a night and head into bed," I said.

Jake gave me a kiss. "I'll join you in a little while, chere."

Spam didn't follow, but remained where he was, with his chin solidly planted on Santou's foot.

I'd apparently been telling the truth. No sooner did I hit the pillow than I instantly fell asleep. Neither Spam nor Santou roused me as they entered the room.

I continued to sleep the sleep of the dead, until a strange chirping worked its way into my head. I awoke in the dark, unable to determine what the odd noise was, or where it was coming from. I strained to listen as the sound morphed into what seemed to be the smacking of lips, along with the rapid pitter-patter of tiny feet. Quickly looking around, I spied a bizarre sight silhouetted in a shaft of moonlight. There on the wall were a small gecko and a cockroach, of nearly equal size, engaged in a deadly stand-off.

I stared, transfixed, as the two now entered into battle. The cockroach lunged, as if hoping to fake out its attacker, and then began to swiftly scuttle away. But the lizard held the definite advantage. Its long tongue lashed out with the speed of a whip, its sticky tip latching onto its prey. The bug's horror was so palpable that it conjoined with the pounding of my blood upon slowly being reeled back into the lizard's waiting jaws. With the bug firmly in grip, the gecko then turned its graceful neck and proceeded to bash the roach, over and over, against the wall.

The cockroach flailed its legs in a desperate attempt to escape. Its wings scraped against the cracked paint with the herky-jerky movement of defective window wipers, fluttering frantically until they were torn. Though the bug did all it could to cling to life, it finally gave up, unable to fight anymore. The last of its energy ebbed, along with the thrum of my blood. The struggle ended, and to the victor went the spoils.

Then the lizard turned its head and held me captive with its eerie eyes while clutching the corpse in its mouth. My stomach tightened in a virulent knot as the lizard now began to devour its prey, with its pupils still glued to mine.

Rolling over, I pressed myself against Santou, no longer able to watch. It wasn't the life and death battle that bothered me. But rather the uneasy premonition that I was also about to fall victim to the ruthless law of the jungle. I somehow knew I'd already been strapped into a roller coaster ride from which there was no breaking loose.

The noxious *crunch, crunch, crunch* of the bug's shell being consumed echoed in the room as I slowly fell back into a restless sleep.

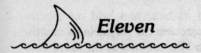

Eleven

The lizard was gone by the time I awoke the next morning. All that remained were a few tiny legs to confirm what had taken place the night before. A chill sped through me, even though the air was already heating up. Grabbing my clothes, I started for the bathroom, only to feel Santou reach out and grab me. The next thing I knew, I'd been pulled back into bed.

"How about a proper hello? You were already fast asleep when I came into the room last night," he said, wrapping his arms around me.

"It's not my fault that you prefer Kevin's company to mine," I lightly retorted, letting my feelings show.

Santou propped up his head and looked at me. "You don't seriously believe that, do you, chere?" he asked, with a note of concern in his voice.

Even now, Santou had the salty aroma of the ocean, and the sharp, clean smell of the beach, about him. I took a deep whiff and reveled in the scent while running my fingers along his bare skin, its hue as golden brown as finely burnished leather.

"Maybe I just don't like having to share you," I whispered in his ear.

But I knew it was far more than that. I worried that Kevin might be closer to Jake than I would ever be. It was something that bothered me as much as any physical betrayal.

Maybe Santou wondered the same thing as he rolled me onto my back and pinned my hands near my head. I didn't fight, but steeled myself to hear whatever he had to say.

"Let's get one thing straight, chere. You'll always be the most important person in my life, no matter what. But Kevin and I have a history together. That doesn't take anything away from you and me. In fact, I want to make sure that we both stay around for a good, long time. So much that I'll make you a deal. I won't surf the big waves until I get more experience. However, you have to promise me something in kind."

"What's that?" I asked, already dreading his request.

"You keep me in the loop concerning whatever it is that you're doing. I don't like to think of you being on your own out there, high and dry. I know you're not crazy about Kevin. But believe me, both of us can help you more than you realize. Take advantage of what we're offering here. It'll make me feel better, and will give you an edge that others working alone in the field don't have."

I could feel my resistance begin to crumble as easily as a castle made of sand.

"Do I have your word on that?" he asked, slowly lowering his body against mine.

"You've got my word," I promised, and closed my eyes, seduced by Santou, the smell of the ocean, and the sound of the tide.

Sometimes, while stuck in my seventh-floor office, it was hard to believe that I was actually in Hawaii. I could have been anywhere, doing the same mind-numbing paperwork, the same tedious dumb-ass reports. Even the low hum of the planes ferrying tourists back and forth added to the growing sense of monotony.

I'd heard the problem described as the downward spiral of tropical entropy. The work speed is barely moving, and all plans tend to fall apart. Most blithely let it flow over them like a tidal wash. Blame for it is placed on the constant state of humidity that eats away and causes everything to rot. Maybe so. But from what I could tell, most federal agents stationed here were routinely deballed and broken by their superiors until they reported in to work each day as zombies. That wasn't true in my case. It came from feeling that time was speeding by without me.

Revving my engine this morning was the knowledge that I'd soon be meeting with Sammy Kalahiki. I was anxious to see what sort of hard-core evidence he'd produce. Kalahiki had done a superb job of snagging me on his hook. Now all he had to do was come up with the goods tonight in order to reel me in.

Truth be told, anticipation had gotten the better of me hours ago. I could already tell that his story had all the earmarks of a big case. Some people are good at reading tarot cards, others at unmasking stock-market fraud, while there are those who excel at diagnosing disease. As for me, simply point toward corruption and let me go. Unfortunately, I had Norm Pryor trying to hang on to my reins.

He walked in that morning dressed in his usual attire: white leather mocs and a pair of camo pants that could have doubled as pajama bottoms. Today's shirt was decorated with palm trees, surfboards, and antique "woody" station wagons. Pryor glanced in as he strolled past my office, reminding me of the gecko on my wall last night.

"Good morning, Porter. Glad to see that you made it in to work today."

Good morning, teacher, I silently responded, waiting

until he'd settled at his desk and begun to open the bag that held his breakfast pastry.

Then I got up, walked into his office, and plunked my own bag of goodies in front of him.

"Here. I thought you might enjoy this with your coffee," I offered.

"What is it?" he asked suspiciously, pursing his lips into a perfectly round O. "Don't tell me it's another one of those damn lizards."

"No lizards in there," I promised. "Remember the deal we made?"

Pryor's expression remained as blank as an unpainted canvas.

"Deal? What sort of deal?" he questioned, his apprehension beginning to grow.

"You said if I could prove that a cougar was running around in the mountains, you'd gladly eat its scat."

Pryor glared at me, his lips compressing into a thin, straight line.

"Well, I hope you're hungry, because here's your proof," I responded, barely able to keep the grin off my face.

Pryor cautiously opened the bag and peered inside.

"Shit!" he exclaimed, and pushed the sack aside.

"Exactly," I confirmed.

"And what makes you so certain that it comes from a mountain lion?" he scornfully questioned, as if hoping to trump bureaucratic muscle over science.

"Because I saw the cat for myself," I replied. "Those lizards that I brought you the other day? I tracked down the person responsible for breeding them. There's a guy on Oahu that's in cahoots with pet store chains on the mainland. Stas Yakimov is being sent a wide variety of reptiles. In return, he's establishing colonies in the wild and then pipelining them back to those stores to be sold. That's where I got the scat from. I paid Yakimov a visit. He also has plans to start breeding mountain lions for profit."

"In other words, this thing's living in a cage at his house. That's not exactly the same as a cat running wild in the mountains," Pryor said, looking relieved.

"Sorry, but you're wrong about that. Yes, this one's in a pen. But his first cougar got loose. That's the one that people are seeing. We've got to bust this guy. Only I don't want to do it immediately. Instead, I'd like to work him undercover for a while. That way, I can discover which wholesalers are sneaking reptiles in to be illegally bred. I'm also hoping to get evidence on all the pet stores that are involved," I revealed, figuring my plan amounted to a major coup.

I had expected Pryor to be ecstatic. It could very well mean a gold star from D.C. for him, too. Which was why I was surprised by his reaction.

"Whoa! Hold on there a minute." Pryor balked. "You're not going to do a damn thing until I've had time to think this thing through."

"Why? What's the problem?" I asked, my insides beginning to do flip-flops.

"This could prove to be a real Pandora's box," he replied, nervously licking his lips and tapping his fingers together. "After all, how much do we really want to hurt pet stores on the mainland? Especially in this economy? And then of course, there's this fellow, Yakimov, that you keep talking about. I need to find out exactly who he is, and his connections. For all we know, he has the tacit approval of the state."

"What are you talking about?" I nearly howled. "This is a state law that's being broken."

"Listen, Porter. There's something that you still don't seem to understand. Everything in Hawaii runs according to who you know. That being the case, there's not a hell of a lot of reason to enforce things," he snapped. "Which means that I'm not about to jump into this without first studying the problem. We don't need to go and embarrass ourselves."

"And just how would we do that? By carrying out our job?" I retorted angrily.

"No. By stepping into a matter that we shouldn't," Pryor countered.

There was no question that it was business as usual with Pryor in charge. The big boys in D.C. had again seen fit to tie me to a boss who believed if you ignore a problem long enough, it would just go away. Putting the two of us together was as good as placing TNT and nitroglycerin in the same room. All they had to do was chuck in a rabid mongoose with a lit match.

I turned, ready to storm out of his office, unable to believe I'd been stupid enough to reveal anything about Yakimov in the first place. However, Pryor's voice stopped me in my tracks.

"By the way, Porter. I hear that you're trying to stick your nose into that other bit of business we discussed."

A chill wrapped itself around me, tight as a wetsuit. How could Pryor possibly have known? Secrecy was the entire reason that Kalahiki had decided to meet me at Ka'ena Point.

I turned back to face him, wondering if this might be about something else.

"What business is that?" I asked, working hard to keep my tone neutral.

"Those shark finning rumors that you told me about." Pryor's normally bland gaze now sharpened into steely determination, driving the point home that the matter was serious. "I'm going to tell you one more time, and I expect you to listen. We don't need that kind of trouble."

"Why should there be any trouble?" I questioned, equally determined to dive headlong into whatever was going on.

"You know damn well why. I've already told you that sharks aren't under our jurisdiction," he barked in frustration.

Enough of this crap. It was time to discover where Pryor's loyalty really lay.

"But what if it turns out that NMFS actually knows shark finning is still going on and yet refuses to do anything about it? Who's responsible for what happens to sharks then?" I queried, refusing to hold my tongue.

Only good sense kept me from revealing the equally tantalizing rumor that finning led all the way up to a powerful government official.

Pryor's eyes narrowed to two sharp pincers, and his hands scuttled across his desk, his limp thumb dragging behind like a useless claw.

"And why would you think that?" he asked.

His voice no longer held its usual bluster, but had become soft and low, reminding me of a snake that was about to attack.

"It just strikes me as odd that an agency responsible for the well-being of the fishing industry should also be solely in charge of marine species whose numbers keep dwindling. Doesn't that bother you, as well?" I challenged.

If Pryor had rattles attached to his rear, I would have heard them shaking by now.

"Be careful what you accuse NMFS of. That kind of slur can bury someone," he warned. "Your transfer to Hawaii is a double-edged sword. This is the land of starting over again. But fuck up, and your career can very well die here. It's your choice. Just remember that you can't sneeze on this island without me knowing about it."

Pryor's threat made me absolutely furious, but I wisely kept my mouth shut. Arguing any further would lead nowhere. It was little wonder so few people realized that Fish and Wildlife agents had been stationed in Hawaii before me. Those agents had played by Pryor's rules and never made a ripple. Their reward was to be promoted up. As for Pryor, he'd never voluntarily leave this job. And the man wouldn't be fired unless caught selling crack cocaine in the governor's mansion, or was found to be sleeping with one of bin Laden's wives.

Know thine enemy, was the phrase that flit through my mind, as I slipped back into my office.

As of now, I'd identified Norm Pryor as my number-one nemesis.

I passed the time typing out reports and listening to the overhead drone of planes. But my thoughts were on other matters.

How had Pryor managed to learn that I'd gone against his advice and plunged feetfirst into investigating the shark-finning trade? Had he been tipped off, or just made an educated guess? And, if so, had I been tricked into foolishly revealing my hand? Thoughts such as this kept tumbling around in my brain, driving me crazy.

Fortunately, Pryor remained in his room all day and stayed far away from me. Not that it really mattered. All I wanted to do was ask Kalahiki who else knew about our meeting. But the sun wouldn't be setting for hours.

By the time 4:30 rolled around, I was nearly climbing the walls and had begun to identify with my poster of the shell-shocked duck probably a little more than was healthy.

True to form, Pryor walked out the door at 4:34. I waited five minutes more and then quickly followed.

Rush hour traffic seemed benign compared to the proverbial prison I'd been stuck in all day. For once, I didn't even curse at the other cars around me. Instead, I spent the time daydreaming about the possible results that could come from breaking out of my cage.

What if I were able to bring down Yakimov and make a dent in the invasion of alien species? What if I were allowed to shut down the shark-finning trade? What if I were given leeway to actually make a difference when it came to the decimation of Hawaii? What if, what if, what if? Who'd ever have guessed those two little words would so completely rule my life?

There had been plenty of time when I'd left the office, but it was quickly eaten away. I dismissed the burger and fries that were beckoning to me, and headed straight for Ka'ena Point.

Soon I was shaking, rattling, and rolling across ground that was as pockmarked and potholed as any New York City street. I once again went as far a I could along the rugged jeep trail before finally abandoning my vehicle. This time I opted to take two bottles of water, instead of just one, as I struck out on my own.

Even at this time of day, Ka'ena Point was hot as hell. But then, I suppose it only made sense considering that *ka'ena* was Hawaiian for "the heat."

The sun hung low, a molten ball of flame, as though suspended from the heavens by a string. I glanced to my left where Jesus rays hovered above the Waianae range, their halo of light transforming the verdant pali into a strand of ghostly mountains. The sight was so intensely beautiful that I had to force myself to look away, fearing it might prove to be taboo and I'd be turned into a pillar of salt.

Instead, my gaze fell upon hundreds of pale orange il-ima blossoms that covered the ground. They could have been mistaken for crepe-paper leis, so tightly were they threaded together. I sidestepped them and hurried on, passing a few roving albatross along the way. The birds flew out to sea and then swooped back over the dunes, as if in search of one last snack before settling down for the night.

The large coral rock eventually came into view. It must have been gathering the sun's rays all day, for it practically pulsated and glowed in the last of the light. It was almost as if the rock contained magnetic powers, so strongly was I drawn to it. I didn't question the sensation, but pulled myself onto the boulder, hoping to catch a glimpse of Sammy in the distance. However, he was nowhere in sight.

I worried at first that Kalahiki might have changed his mind. For all I knew, he'd received another threatening phone call and been frightened away. Perhaps he was try-ing to contact me even now. Then again, he'd also been late for our first meeting. I probably should have realized that the guy operated on a different clock—one that kept Hawaiian time.

It was something I'd been warned about by other main-landers who resided here. There's simply no structure to things. Maybe it has to do with the fact that the tempera-ture is always the same, as if regulated on a hidden ther-mostat. It probably helped explain the origins of a favorite Hawaiian expression: "whateveh." You set your watch back five hours and two hundred years. Then you're pretty much running on the same type of schedule.

With that in mind, I turned my attention to the sunset and the Waianae coastline.

The winter waves were notorious for being larger here than anywhere else on the island. I relaxed and watched the display as they angled in from both sides of the point.

They swept across a chain of rocks, gathering strength along the way. It was as if a giant hand had slapped the water hard, so that the waves kicked up plumes of mist. They hung in the air before slowly dispersing, their long wisps the phantom tails of mythological creatures galloping out across the sea.

I leaned back and basked in the last bit of light as the water turned liquid gold, stretching against a cloudless horizon. But what literally took my breath away was a flash of green so bright that I wondered if there'd been an explosion. It lasted just a brief moment before the seething sun puddled and oozed into the ocean. However, I was greedy for more and not yet ready to let it escape. I quickly scrambled to my feet and stood on top of the rock, determined to follow its course. It didn't matter that it was already too late. I stubbornly refused to give up.

I continued to scan the water with my binoculars, hoping to catch a glimpse of a whale, a monk seal, or a spinner dolphin, anything that would fuel my interest as I waited for Kalahiki to arrive. My wish seemed to be granted as I caught sight of something fluttering in among the rocks. I leaned forward as far as I could without falling off. But I still wasn't able to see directly below into the water. I solved that problem by jumping from my perch and standing along the cliff's edge to get a better view.

All I could see at first were the waves relentlessly pounding layers of hardened lava. I continued to stare at the landscape of rocks, adjusting my gaze until I finally found what I'd been searching for.

That was when a creature, cold and clammy, slithered beneath my skin and wouldn't go away.

Pinned under a jagged boulder was a shape that slowly mutated into an arm. Its hand moved back and forth in the current's frothy spittle, as if frantically waving to say,

"Help me. I'm here." A dying ray of light skipped from finger to finger, as if in a child's game of hopscotch, its dwindling beam caressing the waterlogged flesh.

It was then I spied a glint reflecting off one of the digits. I crept to the tip of the cliff and adjusted my binoculars, hoping to get a closer look. A smooth blue stone burned with a life all its own, encompassing a six-pointed star beneath the surface.

Superstition has it that the gem brings peace, happiness, and purity of soul to those who wear it. But as with most fairy tales, that simply wasn't true. Rather, the bearer's life had been filled with mistrust, broken promises, and disillusionment. The fire within the star sapphire ring slowly began to diminish until it finally disappeared.

Paradise had once again proven to be elusive for those living within its purlieu. And along with that came the realization as to why my contact was so late. Sammy Kalahiki had been there all along. He lay floating below, dead in the restless water.

Twelve

I pulled out my cell phone and called the police.

"Ka'ena Point? Terrific. The guy couldn't have picked an easier spot?" grumbled the voice on the other end.

"Yeah, it was pretty inconsiderate. But then he probably wasn't thinking about your convenience at the time," I snapped.

My bitchy remark was met by a moment of stony silence.

"Stay where you are and don't leave the scene," the desk duty officer instructed icily.

"Don't worry. I know the drill. By the way, how soon do you think someone will arrive? I'm an agent with the U.S. Fish and Wildlife Service," I informed him.

Maybe that wasn't such a smart move on my part.

"Why? What's the problem? Are all the animals out rioting tonight and you've gotta rush back to work?" he sarcastically responded. "Cool your heels. We'll get there when we get there."

He hadn't been kidding. I stood at the edge of the cliff and waited for what seemed like hours. If nothing else, it gave me plenty of time to think.

The hand continued to wave, though not so urgently

now. It was almost as if Sammy knew he had been found. Still, what was he trying to tell me?

I turned my head, not wanting to stare at the disjointed arm. However, Kalahiki refused to let me look away for too long. Having no choice, I tried as best I could to disassociate myself from the limb. An arm is an arm is an arm. This one just happened to belong to my latest informant.

I wondered when Kalahiki had arrived. Sammy must have been anxious about our meeting tonight. Otherwise, why would he have shown up so much earlier than expected? There was that, along with Pryor's blatant warning. Combine the two and I was left with a feeling of unease.

Kalahiki had grown up in these parts and probably knew every rock and stone. Had he become so cocksure as to have misread his surroundings and accidentally plummeted to his death? Every instinct within me refused to believe so.

Besides, this place was like an echo chamber, with nothing but albatross around. I'd certainly have heard a scream or the clatter of rocks during my walk to the point. On the other hand, if a fight had ensued, I would have heard that also. My skin was cold to the touch, even though the evening air was humid and warm.

I needed to kill time until the police arrived. Especially if I hoped to keep my sanity. With that in mind, I decided to do what I love best: snoop about while carrying out my own mini-investigation. Flicking on my flashlight, I proceeded to carefully search the area. No litterbugs here. In fact, there wasn't a damn thing on the ground that could have been deemed the least bit suspicious.

Having no luck, I stood on the brink of the cliff and felt the pull of the rocks below. Had Sammy become so despondent about events that, rather than resist the tug, he'd finally given in to temptation? Once again, gut instinct told me no.

"Rachel!"

I whirled around, expecting to find the police behind me, but no one was there. My flesh turned to chicken skin and my body became icy cold.

"Rachel!" the call again pierced the night.

I could scarcely breathe, having realized that the cry wasn't coming from behind, but was carried on the waves like a ghostly song. My God! Could it be that Sammy was still alive? My heart raced double time as I dashed to the edge and flashed my light on the rocks below.

"Sammy? Are you there?" I called out.

But there wasn't a sound. Rather, the disembodied hand giddily mocked me by waving hello. I hastily retreated to my perch of stone as the night ominously closed in around me.

Every shadow, every rustle came to life, magnified a hundredfold. My nerves nearly reached their breaking point as fear planted itself deep, spreading its tentacles throughout my entire being. That was when a noise sprang to life and echoed in the night, turning the darkness into a living, breathing creature.

I jumped as a stone unexpectedly fell into what sounded like a bottomless well. That was followed by the clatter of another stone, and then another. Something was scrambling up the rocks, as if pulling itself from the bowels of a watery death. The clawing echoed in my head until my stomach was reeling.

"Sammy, is that you?" I weakly called.

But the only response was fractured, disjointed breathing.

The flashlight shook between my trembling hands, not

knowing what it would find: the mutilated figure of a man or an angry wraith in the night.

I remained where I was as if paralyzed, until the murmur of distant voices broke the spell.

"Over here!" I screamed out, not knowing if they were friend or foe, or really caring. All that mattered was that they were flesh-and-blood human beings.

I stared into the darkness, finally spotting a procession of lights like a dislocated band of fireflies. There were four in all, each of which continued to grow in size. I urgently blinked my flashlight to the beat of the song playing inside my head, the Rolling Stones' diabolic tune "Sympathy for the Devil."

A cluster of bodies emerged from the night, their movements as tenuous as that of a spider picking its way across rough terrain without any sight. The forms gradually crystallized into a responding officer with three morgue technicians bringing up the rear. It immediately became clear that the trio in back had been hired for their muscle rather than brains. I could already hear them snickering about what kind of moron would come all the way out to Ka'ena Point just to fall off a cliff. As for the officer, he looked more annoyed than anything else. No matter. I was relieved to no longer be alone.

"Officer Eddie Fong," he said upon finally reaching me.

The man was slightly built, with sparse dark hair and a pair of sleep-deprived eyes. Deep lines tugged at the corners of his mouth like a couple of tiny anchors.

"I'm Special Agent Rachel Porter. The body's down there," I informed him, pointing toward the spot. "I found Sammy Kalahiki right around sunset."

"Hey, Officer Fong. You wanna go down first and check out the scene before we haul him up?" one of the technicians asked.

"What for? I can already see everything I need to right here. Besides, why would I want to get my uniform wet?" Fong dryly retorted and then began to move his flashlight around.

Its beam came to rest near where Sammy had apparently gone over.

"So this is where you think the accident happened, huh?" Fong asked, in a tone of nonchalance verging on boredom.

"I believe so. If it really was an accident," I replied, always curious as to how someone else carried out an investigation.

"What are you saying? That it might have been suicide?" he promptly followed up.

"No. Not at all," I answered, feeling sure of my response.

"Okay then. You said you weren't in the area at the time. Is that correct?" Fong inquired, proceeding on with the interview.

"Yes. I didn't get here until afterward. I spotted the body while waiting for him to arrive," I clarified.

"Then how can you be certain that this is the location where he fell?" Fong quickly countered.

"Call it an educated guess. Take a look for yourself. Kalahiki's body is lodged directly below here, under a rock," I calmly responded.

He walked to the edge and flashed his light in the water, where Sammy waved to him in hello. Fong looked at me in surprise.

"Interesting story, except for one problem. All I can see is a hand. Which leads to the next question. What makes you so certain that this is your friend?"

"Take a closer look and you'll spot a star sapphire ring on one of the fingers. It belonged to Sammy," I explained.

"What was the relationship between you two, anyway?

Was he just an acquaintance, or perhaps something more?" Fong asked, now turning to look directly at me.

What did he think? This was the result of some sort of lovers' quarrel?

"We were friends," I lied.

"It seems like rather a strange place to meet a friend at night. Wouldn't you agree? What did you come here for, anyway?"

"Sammy said it was a great spot to watch the sunset. I decided to take him up on the offer," I replied, purposely choosing to remain vague.

I was grateful that Fong was at least asking the right questions. Now all he needed to do was dismiss me as his prime suspect. Apparently, Fong came to the same conclusion.

"Sorry about your friend. But you'd be amazed how often this sort of thing happens around here.' "

"What's that?" I inquired, wondering what he was getting at.

"People lose their footing and fall off cliffs on this island all the time."

Two of the technicians began to climb down, and we shined our lights on the rocks to help guide their way.

"Damn, but this guy's pinned under here pretty good," one of the men called to us, as they tried to pull him out.

Their struggle continued until the flow of the tide finally helped to dislodge him. Once that was done, a body bag and stretcher were lowered, and Sammy was packed and strapped onto it. Then Fong helped the third technician lift the parcel back up the cliff.

We waited until all were again on firm ground before zipping open the body bag.

Sammy stared up at us, as though wondering why he was on his back and we were all standing around gaping at him. I'd seen that same expression on others whose lives had been cut short. The disbelief that this couldn't be all there was to existence. But there was something else in his eyes, as well: a silent demand for retribution.

"Take a look at this," Fong said, and aimed his flashlight on Kalahiki's torso. "Pretty nasty, huh?"

A series of ugly red gashes had been torn across his body, ripping through muscle, flesh, and bone. I tried hard not to gag at the sight of Sammy's intestines hanging half out.

"Those slashes could have been made by only one thing: a shark. That should answer any question as to how your friend died. That is, if the fall didn't kill him first," Fong theorized.

The same lacerations covered Sammy's chest and throat, making him look more like the victim of a slasher than any meals-on-wheels for a shark. That was the other thing. He'd clearly bled out.

Kalahiki's complexion was chalky, as if a vampire had fed on him. Though I couldn't quite put my finger on it, I knew that something was wrong.

I took a deep breath, and waited to hear what else Fong had to say.

"Okay, boys. That's it. Let's get him out of here," he ordered.

Sammy's eyes were the last thing I saw as the bag was closed up. They bore into mine, as if determined to extract a promise.

"I'm sure you'll learn more during the autopsy. In any case, I'd like to be kept in the loop as the investigation progresses," I said, having regained my composure.

Fong regarded me strangely, his expression oscillating between irritation and amusement.

"And what makes you think there's going to be an investigation? This was clearly an accident," he responded.

"Wait a minute. You don't know that for certain," I disputed. "There are still too many unanswered questions."

"Such as?" Fong challenged.

"Such as things which simply don't add up," I obstinately replied, unable to conjure any specifics—except for one. "A shark wouldn't have attacked Kalahiki like that and then just left him. Not without at least eating part of the body."

"Maybe your friend didn't taste so good," Fong retorted, abruptly dismissing my concern. "Anyway, that's not my area of expertise. All I can tell you is what I found, which is nothing. There's no other explanation but for the fact that he stood too close to the edge, stepped on a loose stone, slipped and lost his balance. As I said before, this kind of thing happens all the time. You want to go interview a bunch of sharks, be my guest. That's your business. But as far as I'm concerned, this case is closed."

Fong said nothing more, but turned and walked off. The two technicians tottered behind like crabs, balancing Sammy's body between them, while the third man directed his light on the path. I reluctantly followed. Though I didn't agree with Fong's conclusion, neither did I want to be left in the dark.

We silently parted ways upon reaching our vehicles, and I guided the Explorer toward home. The moon hid behind clouds, as though it were also protesting Fong's decision.

Sammy was supposed to have brought evidence with him tonight. I now wondered if he had and, if so, what could have happened to it? There'd been no sign of papers in among the rocks—unless the sea had chosen to wipe away all clues of their existence. Not only that, but I couldn't erase the image of Sammy's shredded flesh from my mind. It had hung from his bones like tattered rags.

Fong was right. Sammy did appear to have been killed by a shark attack. Yet there was something about it that simply didn't make sense.

The sound of the waves helped lull my nerves as my tires raced down the road. I parked in the driveway and followed my nose along the beach to where Kevin and Jake were cooking dinner.

"How did I know you'd arrive home in time to eat?" Santou asked with a grin.

I think it's the one talent I have left," I glumly responded.

Kevin threw me a beer and popped open a can for himself.

"Tough day, huh? Well, we're nothing but a couple of beach bums with plenty of time on our hands. So, why don't you tell us about it?" he suggested, stretching his legs and wiggling his toes in the sand.

His one-eighty-degree change in demeanor took me by surprise. I was about to ask if he'd spent his day undergoing a lobotomy, when Santou caught my eye and slyly smiled.

At the same time, Spam crawled on his belly through the sand, until he was close enough to lay his head in my lap. Lifting a paw, he demanded that I scratch him behind the ears. I idly did so.

What the hell. The worst Kevin could do was to try and knock me down a couple of pegs. And in my mood, I'd simply beat the crap out of him. When considered in that light, it was a win-win situation.

"There's another case I'm working on at the moment. One I haven't told you about, that involves shark finning," I revealed.

"Shark finning, huh? Didn't I read something about that just a few years ago?" Kevin retorted. "I seem to remember the governor signed a bill declaring it to be illegal. That's right, and the local fishermen were pretty pissed."

"Yes, it's both a state and federal law," I said, impressed that he actually recalled the occasion. "In any case, it's still going on gangbusters in Oahu. Or at least, that's what I've been told."

"Then you don't know for certain?" Jake inquired.

"Let's just say I'm met with plenty of resistance whenever I ask any questions. Even more upsetting is that my informant died tonight."

"Accident or murder?" Kevin asked, cutting straight to the point.

"Who knows? It looks like he fell off a cliff and was attacked by a shark, but I'm not buying it. This was a native guy who knew the island inside and out," I replied. "Kalahiki was also an observer with the National Marine Fisheries Service. He'd recently accused the agency of turning a blind eye to shark finning, at best, and possibly giving it their tacit approval, at worst. Whichever it is, Kalahiki was supposed to bring along evidence. However, by the time I got to our meeting place, he was already dead."

"Don't tell me. And the evidence was gone," Kevin surmised with a chuckle.

"Not only that, but the responding officer on the scene called his death an accident, and refused to consider anything else," I revealed.

"Of course. Why should he make problems for himself, when it can be bagged, tagged, and cleaned up so easily?" Santou concluded.

Then he stared at me, his eyes narrowing in suspicion. "This doesn't have anything to do with Vinnie Bertucci, does it?"

"No," I said, with a shake of my head. "You know how the Statue of Liberty's inscription reads, 'Give me your tired, your poor, your huddled masses yearning to be free'? Well Vinnie's motto is Give me your men with limp dicks. He's busy selling black-market Viagra to all the needy Joes of the world."

Santou burst into laughter. "Oh, that's perfect. Now

the mob's dealing in Mr. Blues? The pharmaceutical industry should love that. They'll have to create another pill just to counteract all the out-of-control erections."

"Not so fast," Kevin bantered. "That's not necessarily a bad thing."

"Getting back to the topic at hand, did your boss know that you planned to investigate shark finning? It's a pretty sensitive matter if it involves another agency," Jake commented.

"That's the thing. I mentioned it to him. But sharks fall solely under NMFS's jurisdiction, not Fish and Wildlife's. Pryor said I was to stay the hell out of it," I conceded.

"Yeah. But you went ahead anyway, didn't you? Because you're that kind of gal. A fucking *haole*, right?" Kevin responded, with a cynical snort.

Now *this* was the Kevin that I'd come to know: a sarcastic jerk without an ounce of humanity in him.

"Don't you realize that island life is all about getting by? You don't do anything to rock the boat," he continued, seeming to go out of his way to egg me on.

I looked out at the water and swore I could see Sammy's hand still waving, imploring me not to give up.

"I'm an investigator. That's what I do. I investigate," I retorted between clenched teeth. "As far as I'm concerned, there's no such thing as 'my jurisdiction.' If something is illegal, I enforce the law. The rest is a pile of crap."

Kevin stared at me and then slowly nodded, as if in agreement.

"Congratulations, Jake. I didn't realize you had such a hard-ass fighter on your hands. Maybe she really can get something done."

Santou grinned at him in return. "That's what I've been telling you all along. The woman's a wolverine."

Kevin crossed his legs in half lotus position, and leaned in toward me.

"Then it's high time that you learn a few cold hard facts about Hawaii. This place works differently from just about anywhere else."

"So I gathered," I morosely responded, having begun to wonder if I'd already come to a dead end.

"Everything in Hawaii is based on politics and who you know. It's incestuous as hell. Oh, yeah. And there's one other thing that makes this tropical carousel spin round and round," he added.

"What's that?" I asked, forced to admit that Kevin knew more about the island than I did.

"Money, money, money talks," he said, rubbing his fingers together. "Everything runs on a cash economy here— be it drugs, meth, shark fins, or anything else illegal. This place is *Apocalypse Now* without the war."

A shiver raced through me as I flashed back to the note left by the prior Fish and Wildlife agent on my computer. The phrasing was exactly the same. Could it be *that* was what he had meant?

"Hawaii is where deals are cut. The hula shows, the sun and the fun? They're just a thin layer of icing for tourists on top of a very dark cake. This is by far the most corrupt place in the U.S. And I'm not only referring to what goes on inside most agencies. I'm talking about high-level corruption. You can easily lose your soul in this place," Kevin acknowledged, with a note of regret in his voice.

For a moment, I wondered if he was talking about himself.

"The question you need to ask is who's running the shark-fin trade in Hawaii." he pressed. "Is it just a bunch of local fishermen hacking off fins to make a few extra bucks? Or is it something bigger and more insidious? And if so, what?"

He'd given me plenty to think about as I gazed at the stars, my mental postcard of paradise becoming increasingly frayed.

"After hearing all this, are you still certain you want to take shark finning on?" Jake questioned, his hand coming to rest on my back.

"I don't see that I have any choice," I responded, knowing if I didn't rock the boat, there was little hope that anyone else would give a damn.

"You really care that much about this stuff, huh?" Kevin asked.

He pulled a pack of Marlboros from his shirt pocket and lit up a cigarette. The tip glowed, bright as a burst of blood in the night. I looked at him in surprise, having never seen Kevin smoke before.

"Yeah, I know. It's a lousy habit that I gave up years ago. Still, we all need our little vices every now and then. Don't we?"

His eyes met mine, and I realized he knew more about me than I would have liked.

"But you haven't yet answered my question," Kevin reminded me, as if it were a challenge.

"I'm sure that you gave a hundred and ten percent to your job." *Whatever that might have been,* I thought. "Why should I be expected to do any less?"

Kevin took a deep tug and blew a lazy ring of smoke into the air. It performed a seductive hula before languorously drifting up to join the clouds.

"Okay then. I have friends here that owe me a favor or two. Let me make a few calls and see what I can find out for you."

Santou looked at me as if to say, *See? I told you that Kevin is a good guy.*

But I knew he was doing this for Jake. That was all right. At this point, I was willing to take help where I could get it. There seemed little question but that I was about to jump head-long into a battle that would pit a couple of federal Goliaths against one very determined Fish and Wildlife agent.

Thirteen

I should have realized that my day was off to a bad start when I ordered a latte at Starbucks and left with a cup of cold tea. My morning immediately went downhill from there. I walked into the office, earlier than usual, only to find Norm Pryor already waiting for me. My first step inside promptly set off an explosion of fireworks.

"What in the hell do you think you're doing?" Pryor demanded, his face turning an impressive shade of purple.

"Showing up for work?" I brazenly responded, determined to ride out the storm.

With any luck, Pryor would decide to back off. I must have been living in a dream world.

"You know damn well what I'm talking about. You arranged to meet Sammy Kalahiki last night, didn't you? I want to know exactly why you were planning to see him," he yelled.

Word clearly traveled fast via the coconut wireless. I watched as Jaba the Hut transformed into the Raging Bull before my eyes.

"We realized that we enjoy taking nature walks together," I retorted dryly, partially to see if Pryor would get any angrier.

My wish was instantly granted.

"Bullshit! Don't hand me that line of crap," he erupted, his face mutating to bright red. "Sammy Kalahiki was an observer with the National Marine Fisheries Service, and a disgruntled one at that. Now I know why you've been harping away about shark finning these past few days. The guy was nothing but a troublemaker. In fact, he'd been fired just yesterday. Did you also happen to know that? It's probably why he jumped off that damn cliff last night. He was embarrassed that he'd lied about things and made such an ass of himself."

This was the first I'd heard that Sammy had been let go. I wondered if it was true. If so, it shined an even darker light on last night's events. It also threw a layer of guilt on me. Perhaps I'd pushed too hard for evidence. What if Sammy had tried to get more and been caught? The truth of the matter would be hard to uncover. A document could easily be created claiming that he'd been fired.

"I warned you before. This time I'm ordering you to stay the hell out of National Marine Fisheries' business," Pryor fumed.

The man was so worked up that he was nearly apoplectic.

"I don't get it. Why should everyone be so upset that I'm asking a few simple questions about shark finning?" I inquired.

Pryor looked at me though if I were the village idiot.

"For chrissakes. What rock have you been living under? Don't you know that Senator Shirley Chang takes a personal interest in anything to do with Hawaii's commercial fishing industry? If you don't back off now, both our heads will roll."

I was well aware that Chang, as a member of the Senate Appropriations Committee, had funneled mucho government funds to both the Hawaiian Fishing Council and the longline fishing industry. Her picture was constantly in the newspaper, where she was lauded for all her good work.

Chang had managed to secure $250,000 from the 2004 budget alone to fund the Council's "coral reef ecosystem" fishing plan. That was in addition to the $8,000,000 she'd already finagled for longliners under a little something called "economic disaster relief."

To my mind, "relief" was a questionable term, considering that it helped to further devastate a number of already endangered marine species. The fishing industry returned the favor by helping to finance Chang's campaigns and supplying all the necessary labor votes.

It didn't take much digging to discover that Chang was also responsible for a good deal of money acquired by the National Marine Fisheries Service. Word had it a close look would reveal that a number of Chang's friends generally wound up as beneficiaries of NMFS grants and contracts. She clearly knew how to work the system by rewarding her chums and punishing her enemies.

Interesting that Pryor should mention her. It led me to further question why Senator Chang, the National Marine Fisheries Service, and Pryor should be so concerned about my poking around if nothing was wrong.

"Are you saying that one senator is powerful enough to dictate policy to Fish and Wildlife?" I needled.

Pryor massaged his temples, as if to calm himself down, before forced to give yet another explanation.

"Listen, Porter. There's more that goes into the fishing industry than you obviously realize. So let me give you a quick reality lesson. A number of those boats out there— just where do you think they come from?"

I looked at him blankly.

"They're built and purchased from shipyards in Biloxi, Mississippi. Except most of them probably aren't fully paid off yet. Now you put those boats out of commission, and what do you suppose is going to happen to that state's economy? If you don't already know, I suggest that you call their senators and congressmen and find out," he snarled. "For the last time, people at National Marine Fisheries have assured me that no illegal shark finning is going on. And you know what? We're going to take them at their word, and that's the end of it."

I spent the rest of the morning commiserating with the sitting-duck poster in my office. If I listened closely enough, I could almost hear the bullets whizzing past my own head.

This must have been exactly how Sammy had felt, I mused. Funny thing. I was beginning to believe him even more now that he was dead.

A tremor shot through me. Is that what it would take before someone believed me, as well?

The hours crept by as I tried to do paperwork. However, my attention kept wandering to the window. I watched the planes fly in and out of Honolulu, attempting to guess how many boxes filled with illegal reptiles were probably on them. But nothing could completely take my mind off Sammy.

By mid-afternoon, I'd decided enough was enough. The least I could do was to track down his mother and pay my respects. Sammy had said that she lived somewhere near Makaha. I dragged out the phone book and looked up her address. Then, grabbing my bag, I shut the door to my office and left, without so much as a good-bye to Norm Pryor. As far as I was concerned, he could go screw himself.

I flew by the docks with their boats bobbing up and down. Most likely, they carried bags filled with illegal shark fins. I didn't stop at the airport or slow down as I approached Pearl Harbor, which was crying its daily allotment of tears. Instead, I continued on Route 90 until it merged into Farrington Highway. Then I headed up the coast road, past the posh condos, toward what many locals consider to be the real Hawaii.

One little town dissolved into another, until even these began to disappear. Soon my Ford traveled between wild ocean and scrub-covered mountains as civilization receded into the distance. The land became increasingly isolated and rural, its beauty marred by just one thing: all the homeless that were camped along the beaches. Although I'd heard about it, the sight had still taken me by surprise. Hundreds of people were living like squatters in paradise.

Their population appeared to be a mixed bag of druggies, nonconformists, criminals, and those who were just plain down on their luck. Many had the same story to tell: they'd lost their jobs, landlords had raised their rents, and they couldn't afford to live anywhere else. Seventeen hundred people camped on the west side of the island—three hundred of which were children—having fallen on hard times. Some resided in tents made of bright yellow and blue tarps, while others lived in ramshackle wooden huts. A bumper sticker on one of the cars seemed to sum it up: DUE TO RECENT CUTBACKS, THE LIGHT AT THE END OF THE TUNNEL HAS BEEN TURNED OFF.

Equally heartbreaking was that most were native Hawaiians. But then their community was a troubled one. Comprising less than twenty percent of the state, they have the highest rate of unemployment, welfare dependence, and drug abuse. Factor in that Hawaiians also have the lowest life expectancy, and are the worst educated group in the nation, and it was yet one more reason why they consider their homeland to be paradise lost.

I pulled off the road and stopped at what appeared to be a neighborhood store, no longer certain of where I was going. I walked inside to spy an array of fried foods that must have been sitting on the counter for too long. It's always a bad sign when not even the flies will land on them. Leaning against the register was a handwritten sign that read CASH ONLY. Two elderly women turned in unison to stare, as though I'd just landed in the parking lot on a ship from outer space.

"Hello. I'm wondering if you can tell me how to get to Ellen Kalahiki's house?" I politely inquired.

Neither spoke for a moment. Then the woman closest to the door broke the silence.

"She must mean Auntie Ellen, one of the local *kupunas*," she said, as if interpreting for me.

I'd heard the word before, but wasn't quite sure what it meant.

"A *kupuna*? I'm sorry, what's that?" I questioned.

"It's an elder who's considered to be a source of traditional knowledge and wisdom. They're called Auntie or Uncle, as a term of respect," she explained, peering curiously at me over the rim of her glasses.

The store owner then began to clear her throat, as if determining whether I was worthy of such information. When she finally spoke, her voice came out in a wheeze.

"If you want to find Auntie Ellen, you still have a ways to go. Look for a skid mark on the mountains, and make a right turn there. Then continue on that gravel road. You'll eventually reach her house," she instructed, beginning to gasp for breath.

"Thanks," I replied and turned to leave.

"Wait!" the first woman called after me. "You don't plan to go empty-handed, do you?"

"Why? Should I buy something?" I asked, wondering if I'd been expected to purchase the information.

"Of course," she answered, and tugged on her flowered

blouse as though adjusting an arrangement. "No one ever pays a visit without taking a *pu'olo*."

"A *pu'olo*?" I repeated, having no idea what she was talking about.

"A gift," she responded with a sigh, as if speaking to a dim-witted child.

Of course. To show up without one would have been thoughtless and a sign of disrespect. I glanced around the store, wondering what might be appropriate. The store owner seemed to sense I needed help, and graciously came to my aid.

"Here. Take a can of Spam. She can always use that," the old woman advised, her words carried on top of a whistle.

I would have considered the suggestion crazy, had I heard it anywhere else. But here in Hawaii, Spam made perfect sense. Residents consume 7 million cans of the gelatinous pink pork brick each year, making it more than a staple food; it's become part of the island culture. After all, what's not to like? It's cheap and it never spoils.

There's Spam fried rice, Spam sushi, and Spam McGriddles, which is served every morning at McDonald's for breakfast. Should there be even the slightest hint of a hurricane, people immediately rush to stock up on it. And woe to the grocery store that runs out of the canned luncheon meat. That's been known to cause riots.

"What the heck. Give me three cans," I replied, opting to go for broke.

My decision made the two women smile.

I took the supply of Spam and continued my drive up the coast.

White sand beaches stretched on my left, seeming to claim the land for their own. To my right, the ground was strewn with large black boulders, as if a game of checkers were being played by giants. I kept looking for some kind of skid mark, all the while wondering if the old woman had actually known what she was talking about.

I finally spotted a deep vertical groove that slashed its way through the mountain like a scorch from a lightning bolt. Sure enough, a gravel road appeared on my right and I took it. My Ford bounced along a path that eroded into a potholed track, as I headed for a vista dotted with green, scalloped cliffs.

Yap! Yap! Yap!

A little red puff ball shrilly barked and, jumping in front of my vehicle, forced me to slam on the brakes. Having put me in my place, the Pomeranian then turned on its scrawny legs and bounced along the trail, as if springs were attached to each of its paws.

I crawled along behind the brazen sucker until a house came into view. Then I zipped around the walking, barking mound of fur, proving not only who was boss, but that size really does count.

Auntie Ellen's cottage stood on stilts, like an old plantation house. The frame was painted sea-foam green, offset by tidy white wooden shutters. Flowers and vegetables were neatly planted in prim little rows inside a fenced-in garden. But that wasn't the only thing that was sprouting in her yard. A collection of shiny silver CDs hung from wooden poles, modern-day versions of scarecrows, their purpose to frighten the birds away.

I gathered up the cans of Spam and walked up the steps, only to feel myself hesitate. Though I wanted to pay my respects, I was equally tempted to turn and run. I've always hated death and anything to do with it. It was one of the reasons I worked so hard to try and keep critters alive. Taking a deep breath, I screwed up my courage, climbed the last step, and tapped on the front door.

My knock was answered by a hefty Hawaiian woman dressed in a shocking pink muumuu. A red hibiscus fluttered like a tropical bird in her hair. The flower matched a pair of red-rimmed eyes, marred by hours of endless crying. It looked as if all the world's sorrow had gathered together and welled up inside her. That same sadness flowed into me, as I felt myself begin to choke up.

"I'm so sorry about Sammy," was all I could manage to say.

She gazed blankly, as though uncertain that someone was really standing there.

"Who are you?" she softly questioned.

"I'm Rachel Porter, the woman that found your son."

A strand of wavy white hair fell out of its bun, and her stubby fingers dutifully brushed it from her face.

"Then you're partially responsible for my Sammy boy's death. You're the one that he went to see," she quietly stated.

Her voice was as flat as the sea just before it's whipped up by a storm. I could only imagine the pain she must have been feeling.

A sharp prick nipped at my skin, as if to let me know. The Pomeranian had obviously made it home. I knew, because the canine was biting my leg with its sharp little teeth. Auntie Ellen bent down and scooped up the dog in her arms. The pooch nestled against her neck and licked her face.

"Sammy had called and asked for my help. That's why I went to meet him," I tried to explain, not knowing what else to say.

"I'm aware of that. I warned him there would be trouble if he dealt with outsiders. But he insisted on trying to live with his feet in both worlds. That was a mistake. You see for yourself what happened," Auntie Ellen replied, refusing to release my eyes from her gaze.

"Once again, I'm terribly sorry. It was a horrible accident," I mumbled, wishing I was anywhere else but there.

That seemed to bring some life into her.

"What accident are you talking about?" Auntie Ellen sharply retorted, her eyes flashing in rage.

The anger in her voice grabbed me around the neck and gave me a hard shake.

"The fact that Sammy fell off the cliff and was killed by a shark," I responded, beginning to feel somewhat off-kilter.

I hadn't come all the way out here expecting to be attacked.

"That's pure rubbish. No such thing ever happened," she brusquely snapped.

At first, I was taken aback. Then I finally admitted what had been eating away at me all along. I didn't really believe that Sammy's death was an accident, either.

"What makes you say that?" I asked, wondering why she felt the same way.

Auntie Ellen scrutinized me so closely, it was as if she could see beneath my skin. What in the hell did the woman possess? Some sort of X-ray vision?

"If you know anything about Hawaiian culture, it should be that sharks are sacred to us as a people. They're the greatest *aumakua*, or guardian spirit, that we have. In Western terms, it's akin to a guardian angel watching over you."

I tried to shake off the feeling that she could read my every thought.

"But why sharks? What makes them so special?" I pressed, curious as to why Hawaiians viewed them so differently from the rest of the world.

Auntie Ellen nodded, as if she understood why I would ask such a question.

"It's because sharks display many of the same attributes as humans. They're fierce and stealthy, graceful and magnificent, just as in the best and worst of man."

In a sense, that made me all the more wary. Humans and sharks are both perfect predators, each lethal in their own way.

"It's also believed that sharks embody the spirits of our departed ancestors, which is why it's their job to protect each family," she continued. "The Kalahikis have a very powerful *aumakua*. That's another reason why no shark would ever harm us."

If true, it was one hell of a family god to have looking out for you.

"Then how do you explain the bite marks that were found on Sammy's body?" I questioned.

A dark cloud came over her face, and I immediately regretted having asked.

"I don't know," she softly replied. "But that's why Sammy boy chose to meet you at Ka'ena Point. It's the legendary home of the Sharkman. That's the place where he felt most safe."

I had heard tales of the Sharkman, a creature that was human on land. However, the space on his back turned into the mouth of a shark upon entering the ocean. It was a story that I didn't find terribly comforting.

"There is one thing I am curious about, though," Auntie Ellen wistfully remarked.

"What's that?" I asked, anxious to help in any way that I could.

"Will you tell me exactly where the two of you were supposed to meet at Ka'ena Point?" she questioned.

"Sammy was very specific about the spot," I replied. "It was the same place that we'd met the day before. A huge coral rock along the north side of the point."

Auntie Ellen sharply exhaled, as though the wind had

been knocked out of her, and her complexion turned visibly pale.

Then it's almost as if he knew," she responded in a whisper, causing chills to run down my spine. "That coral rock is the leaping-off point."

"Leaping-off point for what?" I asked, the words sticking to the back of my throat.

"For Hawaiians when we die. It's believed that the soul leaves the body and travels along the ridges to the west side of the island. Once there, it goes to that large coral rock that you found. The spirit stands on top and then jumps off into the afterworld. Only your soul can sometimes end up there before you die."

"How does that happen?" I questioned, caught up in her tale.

"Your spirit can wander away if you fall into a deep sleep or lose consciousness. Then it's up to your *aumakua* to guide you back home. Otherwise, the soul will have no choice but to leap into the abyss of endless night," she explained.

I tried not to let her see how much the legend affected me. I also knew that it was time to reveal the reason for my visit.

"I assume Sammy must have told you why he asked for my help," I began.

Auntie Ellen wordlessly nodded, but offered nothing else.

I took a deep breath and plunged in.

"He was supposed to bring evidence to our meeting that night. Sammy said it would support his claims that sharks were being illegally slaughtered for their fins. The problem is that I never found anything. Do you suppose that he might have left those papers here?" I fished.

But Auntie Ellen didn't so much as blink.

"Maybe he took evidence with him and maybe he

didn't. But he left something of far more value at Ka'ena Point. Sammy boy gave his life for what he believed in. What are you willing to give?" she responded, with a question of her own.

There were those eyes again, looking straight through me. I had no choice but to answer truthfully.

"Whatever is necessary."

Auntie Ellen's lips twitched, and I knew she believed me. It opened the door for another important question.

"Sammy told me that he'd received threatening phone calls. Do you know anything about them?"

"No," she said, with a shake of her head. "But then he wouldn't have wanted to worry me. What I do know is that he came home very late two nights ago. He must have been somewhere unusual, because his clothes smelled bad and were dirty."

That would have been the evening before his death. Our first meeting had taken place earlier that day. It was also when I had pressed him to get more evidence.

"Have you washed them yet?" I asked, trying not to seem too eager.

"Why? Do you want to see them?" she asked, with a puzzled expression.

"Yes, as long as they're still dirty."

I remained standing outside the door as Auntie Ellen went to fetch them. She came back with a pair of jeans in her hands. Even from this distance they retained a strange odor. Whatever it was, the pants reeked to high hell. She held them toward me, and I realized that I still had three cans of Spam in my hands.

"Here. These are for you," I said, and awkwardly exchanged them for the jeans.

"Thank you," Auntie Ellen murmured, seeming to be pleased.

I took a whiff of the pants. A pungent aroma that was

oddly familiar raced up my nose. Either a cat had peed on his leg, or Sammy had been hanging around a New York City subway station in his off hours. His jeans held the distinctive stench of urine.

My hands proceeded to travel down along the pants and discovered the fabric was sticky and stiff. Something clicked, and I realized what I'd been smelling all along. The odor was that of ammonia. Even so, it didn't help to explain the glutinous substance on the legs. Not only that, but I now saw that the bottom of his jeans were stained. I licked my fingers, rubbed them against the denim and examined my hand. A dull red matter came off, staining my fingertips. It was the same color as that of dried blood.

I looked up to find Auntie Ellen intently staring at me.

"Do you mind if I take these?" I asked, planning to turn them over to a lab.

She hesitated briefly, as if trying to make a decision.

"Did you really intend to help my Sammy boy?" she asked once again.

"Yes," I responded. "I believed what he told me to be true."

"And what about now? Do you still plan to help?" Auntie Ellen questioned.

"I will if I can," I replied. "Only it will be more difficult now. Sammy took whatever information he had with him when he died."

Auntie Ellen cocked her head for a moment, as if listening to something.

"Wait here," she instructed and disappeared. When she returned, there was a hat box in her hands.

"My son is dead. Nothing can ever change that. But maybe Sammy boy will rest better if I give you this," she said and handed the box to me.

My fingers trembled as I anxiously took it from her. I

didn't bother to ask what was inside. I'd find out soon enough.

"I'll do whatever I can," I promised, and turned to leave.

"Do you know what *aloha* means?" she asked, firmly stopping me.

I turned back to face her, hoping I'd done nothing to insult the woman.

"Hello and good-bye?" I responded, feeling slightly awkward.

"Yes, that's what all *haoles* tend to believe. But the word has a much deeper significance. *Alo* is space, and *ha* means breath. So when you say *aloha*, what's really being said is, 'Come share my space; come share my breath.' We've been a generous people, but outsiders have bought and sold *aloha* until there's no more left. Our people have been decimated by your diseases, missionaries have destroyed our culture, and our kingdom has been overthrown by American business interests. We've been betrayed and our trust has been continually broken over the years. You find out who killed my Sammy boy and then you'll have helped to repay some of the *aloha* that's owed us. That's when you come back to see me again," she said.

I stood in silence, unable to speak. What was there to say? Every word that Auntie Ellen had said was true. I felt like one more barbarian at Hawaii's gate. I simply nodded and began to walk away, afraid of adding on yet another empty promise.

"Tread lightly wherever you go, and leave no permanent footsteps," her voice snuck up behind me.

My heart ached, and I spun back to tell her so, intending to vow never to harm the land, only to find that no one was there. At the same time, the air grew so thick and still that chicken skin broke out on my arms. It was almost as if a ghost had spoken those words to me.

I made my way to the Ford, climbing inside as the island held its breath, the mountains looming like foreboding sentinels behind me. Then I drove down the gravel road, knowing full well what I'd have to do if I ever hoped to be viewed as anything other than one more invader.

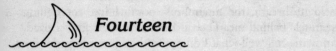 *Fourteen*

It was as if the box were a magnet and my fingers were made of steel. They kept gravitating toward the carton, itching to pull off the damn lid. Finally, the temptation grew to be too much, and I stopped at a roadside dive. What the heck. I figured I might as well grab something to eat while I was at it.

The choice of menu was simple. All that was offered was the usual down-and-dirty fare: the infamous Hawaiian plate lunch. It consisted of two scoops of sticky rice, one lump of macaroni salad—extra heavy on the mayo, please—and a thick slice of Spam. Yum, yum. If the food is full of heart-clogging starches, fats, and gravies, then you'd better believe that you're eating local.

Having placed my order, I next turned my attention to the hat box. It was almost as if an electrical current shot through my fingers as I removed the lid.

Lying on top were copies of letters that Sammy had written his bosses at the National Marine Fisheries Service. I carefully read through each one. Together they amounted to no more than a bunch of nitpicking complaints.

The food and hygiene on the boats wasn't up to snuff. The sleeping quarters weren't comfortable. The crews were unfriendly and hostile. Even the office work required between fishing trips was ridiculous and mundane.

My heart sank as I sifted through each sheet. I was beginning to worry that Norm Pryor might have been right, after all. Perhaps Sammy *had* been no more than a disgruntled employee. It certainly was beginning to look that way.

The waiter returned and set the lumps of rice, macaroni, and cold Spam before me. My stomach joined my heart, slowly sinking in a leaden swan dive. I pushed the plate aside and continued to dig through the box, determined to quench my curiosity. What I found next was nothing less than the beginnings of a scandalous paper trail.

There could be little doubt that the Service had wanted to fire Kalahiki. But Sammy had cleverly fought back by maintaining his own logbook of dirty laundry.

He'd somehow obtained evidence revealing government kickbacks and illegal inter-office deals. Pay-offs were routinely made to keep observers from going out on certain fishing boats. In addition, "pass-through" money was consistently siphoned from grants, so that only some of the funds were ever used for their actual purpose. While this was dynamite information to have, it did little to help my own particular concerns.

I took a bite of the macaroni lump. The gooey salad turned to glue in my mouth, and I quickly washed it down with a can of lukewarm Coke. The waiter kept glaring at me, and I wondered which he found to be more rude—the fact that I wasn't eating my food, or that I wasn't sharing the contents of the box with him. He'd have to deal with whatever it was, as I once again focused on my scavenger hunt.

Oy veh. There seemed to be nothing but endless lists of Sammy's constant gripes and complaints. This was shaping up to be one hell of a frustrating exercise in futility. That is, until my fingers touched what felt like a satiny smooth surface. My heart beat a little faster, hoping that I'd finally struck proverbial gold.

Eureka! I pulled out a photograph, and quietly thanked Auntie Ellen for having given me something other than a box full of junk. However, one quick glance at the photo instantly dashed any such hopes. All that could be seen was the silhouette of a longline fishing boat. At least, that's what I assumed the image to be. It was difficult to tell, since the boat looked like nothing more than a large grainy black dot bobbing on the horizon.

So much for Sammy's photographic skills. I imagined him standing on deck for up to twelve hours a day. He'd probably spent his time idly snapping away, hoping to relieve the boredom while spending grueling weeks on board as an observer. The guy should have learned how to better use a camera, if this was an example of his work. I tossed it on the table, and idly continued to poke through the papers.

My mind started to wander as I removed a few more photographs and quickly flipped through them. Yeah, yeah, yeah. They were all of the same damn boat, only taken from a closer distance this time. Great. I'd apparently put myself on the line, only to end up looking like a fool.

But wait. It was then that something strange caught my eye. My fingers froze as I focused more closely on the longliner's mast. Was I imagining things? Or could it be that what I saw was real?

I'd learned early on to carry a small magnifying glass in my bag, never knowing when it would prove to be useful. I pulled it out now and began to study the photograph.

Holy shit! I suddenly realized why the boat looked so

dark. Hundreds of shark fins flew from the pole in place of sails. The membranes fluttered up and down the length of its mast like a cotillion of flags. I'd heard stories of how fins were hung from hooks this way—the reason being that it kept them from rotting, while allowing the fins to partially dry.

In the past, a boat like this would have carried giant bales of fins on board. The trawler would then have either brought them into Honolulu or, if they weren't yet ready to return, offloaded the bales onto another ship that was headed toward shore.

I quickly flipped the snapshots over and checked the date stamped on back. January 24. They'd been processed by a photo lab only a few weeks ago. It appeared to be hard-core proof that illegal finning was still going on. If so, there was no question but that the fins were being offloaded, dried, and graded right here in Hawaii.

I was determined to find the name of the boat. However, the camera angle blocked it from view. All I could spy was what appeared to be the first letter of a word. I was fairly certain that what I saw was an *M*. No matter. My spirits soared as I now began to furiously dig deeper.

My persistence paid off as I next stumbled upon a bunch of handwritten papers stapled together. They seemed to be some kind of report. Each sheet was divided into five columns listing the species of shark, the date caught, the number of fins, their weight, and the amount that had been paid for them.

I was amazed to see that blue shark, white tips, thresher, Mako, and scalloped hammerheads were still being hunted. But it was the total amount of fins harvested that really blew me away. Eleven tons had been purchased in one sale alone.

I now knew that Sammy had been right all along. While

it was possible that some fins had slipped into Oahu unnoticed, no way could eleven tons have been discreetly offloaded. Not on the Honolulu docks, without at least a few state and federal agents knowing about it. Just the thought of what was going on set my teeth on edge.

"Is everything all right?" the waiter asked, sidling over to me.

He looked at the barely touched plate and must have wondered if my *haole* stomach had contracted food poisoning.

"Everything's fine. Just the check, please," I said, carefully covering the information with my hands.

He tried to eyeball it, but without any luck. Then he shot me a glance, as if wondering what I was up to. I could have told him the truth: that I didn't have the foggiest notion, but was flying by the seat of my pants.

I waited until he walked away, and then studied the report once again.

Where had Sammy possibly gotten hold of such detailed information? The papers appeared to be the bookkeeping records of either a commercial marine dealer or a broker. Except neither would have willingly handed over such incriminating evidence.

I glanced at the date on the pages. February 13. Two days ago. That was the same night that Sammy arrived home late.

It now began to make sense as to why Kalahiki had taken precautions not to be seen with me. He'd been safeguarding my life as well as his own. That led me to wonder what else he had known. The question haunted me as I once again remembered Auntie Ellen's words.

No way was his death an accident.

I believed she was right. Something else bothered me, as well. I felt certain Sammy had brought evidence with him the night we were to meet. Possibly information that was even more compelling than the papers inside this box. So what in the hell had happened to it?

I wasn't quite through yet, having come upon a clear plastic bag tucked away near the bottom. I pulled it out and immediately recognized the scent. It bore the same slight aroma as that which had been on Sammy's jeans. But it was the bag's contents that made my heart begin to pound.

Inside were long white tendrils, nearly as thin as strands of fine hair. Reaching in, I twined my fingers around them. The fibers were a clump of processed shark fins that had been repeatedly soaked, dried, and bleached with peroxide, until they'd reached this final state.

So this was what all the fuss was about: a product that amounted to threads of treated cartilage. I could only wonder how many dead sharks I held in the palm of my hand. Was it possible that Sammy Kalahiki had been killed just because of this? I stared at the lifeless bundle of strings, and my stomach churned a little more. The lengths to which man's greed would go never ceased to amaze me.

There was one last sheet of paper, and I felt a twinge of melancholy while extracting it, not yet ready for the journey to end. I'd come to know Sammy better in these past few minutes than might have otherwise been possible. It was as if he were speaking to me through the box, offering what clues he could. The rest would now be up to my own initiative.

I felt the weight of this responsibility more than ever before—partially because of Auntie Ellen's request, possibly because federal agents could be involved, definitely because I feared that I might not live up to what was expected of me.

I unfolded the final piece of paper, curious to see what it revealed. The contents caught me by surprise, and I very nearly laughed out loud. It held the crude drawing of a shark with razor-sharp teeth. How strangely ironic. But there was something else, as well. Three names were written beneath the cartoon sketch.

Leung. Ting. Yakimov.

A jolt of recognition shot through me. Could it be that Stas Yakimov was somehow involved in the shark-fin trade? And if so, did that mean Vinnie Bertucci was entangled, as well?

I stared at the other two names. As for Leung and Ting, they could be anyone. Especially in a state whose population is mainly Asian.

I put everything back inside the box and closed it up. Perhaps it was time to pay an unannounced visit to Stas Yakimov. It would be easy enough, since I'd pass by his place on my way home.

I paid the bill and left a good tip, considering I'd been sitting there for so long. Then I took my box of goodies and split, driving back down along the coast.

My Ford once again passed through the same small dingy towns. There were rumors that cockfights went on in this area at night. An investigation into that would have to wait for another time. I turned onto Yakimov's street and parked in front of his house.

I got out and walked up to the gate. Even though his dark blue van sat in the driveway, it appeared as if no one were home. The place was unusually quiet.

"Stas, are you here?" I called out, anxious to see if either he or his pack of crazed dogs responded.

But all remained oddly silent.

I opened the gate and entered the grounds, tiptoeing past the mounds of strewn plywood. Then I headed around and peeked into the backyard, feeling amazingly brave. Why not? After all, I now knew the magic word with which to control his dogs. All I had to do was say *Spartacus*.

I took a deep breath, prepared to yell out the command, only to find that the dogs were all locked in their pens. They broke into an unearthly howl upon catching sight of me.

Aaaoooooowww!

It wasn't the ferocious barking that I'd formerly heard, but rather a mournful dirge. A flurry of eight-legged, creepy crawling shivers scurried up my spine, the sound penetrating deep inside me.

I didn't tarry, but hurried toward Yakimov's handmade mobile of pit-bull bones. It still struck me as a gruesome memorial to have constructed from the remains of his pets. How had he managed to lose so many of them, anyway? A little voice whispered that they hadn't all died from natural causes.

I arrived at his back door, and proceeded to knock on it.

There was no answer. However, the door stood slightly ajar. I pushed it open and stepped inside.

"Hello? Stas? Anybody home?"

Every nerve ending in my body warned I should go no farther. Instead, I stood in the kitchen and intently listened as the door creaked closed behind me. There was almost no other sound. Even the crickets in their boxes were oddly muted. Or perhaps it was due to the roar of blood that was pumping in my ears.

My feet felt like two leaden weights as I slowly began to move forward, my body heavy as stone. By the time I reached the living room, I no longer needed my senses to know that something was terribly wrong.

Stas's beloved pit bull, Sparky, had been knocked off the glass table and thrown on the floor. The taxidermied pooch lay covered in blood that matched the red of the walls. Its carcass was surrounded by papers and books that were scattered about.

I didn't have to think twice, but automatically pulled out my gun. Then I followed the fresh, wet trail of blood down the hall.

Red splatters leading to the bedroom door told of a struggle. All I could wonder was, Who had Yakimov killed? Rasta Boy? Vinnie? Or a dissatisfied customer? It wasn't hard to imagine him snapping. Stas was downing steroids, Viagra, and who knew what the hell else? I just hoped that he wasn't in the throws of 'roid rage, or I'd never stand a chance against him.

The macaroni salad I'd eaten at lunch now rose into my throat as I tried to sidestep all the blood. But I could almost feel it seeping through my shoes and into my skin. It thrummed through every vein and capillary, until the victim and I became one.

The hairs on the nape of my neck began to bristle and I whirled around, certain someone must be behind me. But it was only Sparky's lifeless cadaver listlessly gazing from the floor. I turned my attention back to the bedroom, using my toe to push open the door.

The first thing I saw was a bureau, its drawers jerked open and their contents torn apart. Then I heard the most ghastly sound—a gurgling, as if someone were submerged and blowing bubbles underwater. Each one *pop, pop, popped* as they rose and hit the surface, exploding in the air like miniature bombs.

The strange noise came from somewhere on the other side of the disheveled king-sized bed in the middle of the room. I moved closer, my pulse beating wildly.

Lord, protect me from all things both lethal and demonic, I quietly prayed.

The sound came from where Stas Yakimov lay sprawled

in a pool of blood, with his chest slashed open and his throat cut.

"Oh my God," was all I could utter, too stunned to say anything else.

Yakimov looked as though he'd been sliced, diced, and carved alive. Then I realized that Stas was staring at me with glassy eyes, his lips moving as though he were trying to speak. I slipped the gun into the back of my pants and knelt down beside him.

A bout of light-headedness caught me in its grip me as the warmth of his blood oozed through my jeans. It was followed by a wave of nausea, so that I broke into a cold sweat.

Get a grip, Porter! I reprimanded myself.

But the viscous fluid continued to leak through my clothes, where it stuck to my soul like adhesive. The sickly sweet scent filled the room, as well as my nose, making me feel woozy.

"You'll be all right, Stas," I lied, trying to convince both of us.

But that only seemed to agitate him even more. Red-tinged globules rose in his throat, as if they were tiny cartoon captions, each of which bore some kind of message. All the while, he continued to frantically gurgle. The sound was that of a drowning man. He'd be lucky if he lasted another two minutes.

"Who did this to you?" I asked. "Is there any way you can let me know?"

He responded by latching on to my wrist with a strength that surprised me. The bubbles came faster and more furious as he continued to try to speak, his eyes drilling into mine, as if desperate to tell me something.

"Save your energy, Stas," I pleaded, aware that it was a lost cause.

He refused to let go. Rather than attempt to speak, his eyes now rolled up to the ceiling. Then Yakimov squeezed my wrist, as if demanding I follow his gaze. I did so and saw that a mirror hung over the bed. We were framed within the looking glass as if playing out a death tableau. But something else had begun to appear in its reflection, as well.

It slithered across the mirrored surface, as if sliding onto a movie screen. I watched in stunned silence as a figure dressed in black now silently approached from behind. The man's face was covered by a mask, revealing only a pair of cold, calculating eyes—ones that were fixed on me.

I quickly reached back to get my pistol, my fingers tightly wrapping around its butt. I started to pull it from my pants when something sharp slashed at my arm. The pain seared through my skin and stole my breath away, as though I'd been branded with a white-hot iron.

I jerked away, horrified, as the .38 flew from my grip and slid under the bed, in a perverse game of hide-and-seek. Then glancing back around I saw the man about to attack again. I could almost feel him smiling behind his mask.

I wasted no time, but again rolled out of the way as fast as I could. The black clad figure followed, dogged as the Grim Reaper, determined not to let me escape. Stumbling to my feet, I raced across the room. I almost made it to the door, when I tripped on something on the floor, and fell down hard on my hands and knees.

I turned to get up, only to see my archangel of death hovering over me. However, rather than a sickle, he held an unusual type of weapon in his hand—one that appeared to be oval and was attached to his wrist with a loop. In addition, some sort of studs were embedded all around the periphery.

He raised it high above his head, preparing to come down for the kill. I steadied myself, having little choice but to fight to the bitter end—though without a weapon of my own, the game was virtually over. I took a deep breath, not wanting to think about what would happen next.

I was just about to lash out with my legs, when a deep voice came booming from the living room and raced down the hallway.

"What in the hell's going on in this damn place?"

A second intruder now succeeded in startling both of us. My assailant's attention was drawn to the doorway, and I took advantage of the moment to try and kick him in the knees. But he was prepared for such a move, and quickly jumped out of the way.

"You got lucky this time," he hissed, while running for the open bedroom window. "Wise up and take this as a warning to stay out of business that doesn't concern you."

He slipped through the portal as I dashed to the bed and, reaching beneath it, managed to grab hold of my gun. At the same time, Vinnie Bertucci lumbered into the room brandishing an Uzi while taking in the scene.

"Quick! He escaped through there," I yelled, and pointed to the open window.

Bertucci hurried toward it and, sticking his head outside, tried to search the grounds.

"I don't see nothin'. The guy must already be gone," he responded.

By the time Vinnie turned back around, my gun was pointed at him.

He stared at me as his face began to glower.

"What the hell kinda game are you playing, New Yawk?" he ominously questioned.

Funny he should ask. As far as I was concerned, his timing seemed a bit too convenient. Besides, I no longer knew exactly who to trust, or what was going on.

"I'd like a few questions answered," I told him.

Unbelievable. The guy didn't flinch, but had the balls to respond by aiming his own gun at me.

"Okay now. You got a choice. You can either put that thing down, or we can play shootout at the OK corral. Only our gunfight's gonna take place in some shit hole in Hawaii."

I had to admit, the man had a way with words. I looked at Vinnie and knew that I couldn't shoot him, but was unsure of what to do next.

"I don't know what your problem is, Porter, but you're treading on dangerous ground. Besides, you're in no shape to take me on," he warned.

He was right about that. I was suddenly aware that I wasn't feeling too good. The realization opened the door for a flood of pain to kick in. I looked down and saw that my arm was bleeding. At the same time, I remembered Santou's words of warning not to trust Vinnie.

"Don't make me do something stupid that I'll regret. You're gonna have to trust me for now," Bertucci advised, as if he could read my mind. "The way I see it, you've run out of options."

I looked at him standing there. His massive frame was covered in a pink Hawaiian shirt with hula girls playing ukuleles, and I almost wanted to laugh. Then again, I was beginning to feel a little light-headed. I lowered my gun, knowing that Vinnie was right. If I tried to fight him, I'd lose.

"That's better," he responded, and padded toward me.

Vinnie removed the gun from my hand, and then grabbed one of Stas's shirts off the floor. He couldn't have been more gentle as he bound it around my wound.

"What the hell's the matter with you, anyway?" he gruffly questioned.

"I don't know. I'm sorry. I walked in here and found Stas. Then I was attacked," I explained.

"Yeah. A thing like that happens, I guess you can get a little crazy," Vinnie grudgingly conceded.

He then moved over to Yakimov.

"Holy crap. Whoever did this, sure as hell filleted the guy," he said, almost in admiration.

"Is he still alive?" I questioned, no longer hearing the popping of bubbles.

"Hell, no. Would you wanna be in his condition?" Bertucci responded, with a small laugh.

I looked at the man and a shiver kicked through me. "Do you have any idea who did it?"

Vinnie looked at me closely and his eyes narrowed. "Now, why would you think I'd know something like that?"

"No reason," I said, but my mind was going a mile a minute. Somehow I didn't buy the fact that their only connection had been Viagra.

Vinnie walked over, and I involuntarily flinched. Fortunately, he didn't seem to notice.

"That cut isn't deep, but it sure looks nasty," he said, loosening the shirt to examine my wound. "Come on. We gotta get you to a doctor, pronto. I know of someone where there'll be no questions asked."

"And why would I care if there were?" I countered.

Vinnie shrugged. "Maybe you don't. In which case, I'll drop you off at a hospital, if you want. You can phone the cops from there. Or you can stay here by yourself, call in the troops, and deal with them right now. The choice is yours."

I knew that getting involved with the police would only

place me in even deeper trouble. According to my boss, I wasn't supposed to be here at all. Should he find out, I'd never get to the bottom of what was really going on. Rather, it would be swiftly covered up, especially if Yakimov had been embroiled in the shark-fin trade.

Funny, how a single incident can lead to a critical decision in one's life. I could either play this by the book, or try to hide the fact that I'd ever been here.

Vinnie had already removed his shoes and was using paper towels to wipe away his bloody footprints. He must have gone into the kitchen at some point, because he was disposing of them in a black plastic bag.

"Would you mind getting rid of mine also?" I requested.

Vinnie gazed at me and slowly began to smile.

"Well, well. I guess you made your decision, then. You wouldn't happen to have another pair of pants with you, by any chance?" he questioned.

I looked at my bloody jeans.

"Yeah. In my Ford," I replied.

I'd gotten used to carrying around a change of clothing, never knowing when I might need it.

"And what about shoes and a shirt?" he inquired, as if going through a mental check list.

"Uh-huh. Those too," I replied.

"Okay then. Let me finish up here and we'll get 'em on our way out."

I took off my shoes, grabbed some paper towels, and began to try and help.

"Slow down there, New Yawk. I don't need you bleeding all over this nice, new clean floor. Why don't you just watch and wait," he suggested.

I hated standing around feeling helpless. But he was right. I didn't want my arm to start bleeding any worse.

Vinnie did such a bang-up job, he could have been in the cleaning business.

"Okay, the coast is clear," he said, having quickly peeked outside before we left the house.

I walked barefoot to the Ford and grabbed my satchel of clothing.

"Do you think you can drive a little ways?" Vinnie asked. "We can't leave either of our vehicles here. There's a store close by. We'll ditch your Explorer there for a while."

"No problem," I said, though I was feeling a bit faint.

"Oh yeah. And change your pants and shoes before you get in the car. You can throw them in here," he instructed, handing me a black plastic bag.

I headed into the backyard once more, and did as I'd been told. The dogs watched me strip like a bunch of four-legged voyeurs. Had I known there'd be an audience, I might have been tempted to wear nicer panties. Then I followed Vinnie down the street to a local mom-and-pop grocery store.

"Wait in the Lincoln. I'll take care of this," Vinnie said, and disappeared inside the shop.

I opened the Lincoln Continental's passenger door. A plastic drop cloth had been carefully laid over the seat. Vinnie must have had it tucked away in the trunk of his car. I didn't even want to contemplate the reason he was carrying it around with him.

"Okay, your Ford will be fine here," he said, slipping in beside me. "Now let's go take care of that cut. Here's the address. Just get me there."

The information was written on a piece of flowery notepaper. I pulled out a local map, which guided us into the down-and-dirty outskirts of Honolulu. We ended up at a dilapidated house just off an H1 Freeway ramp. It was indistinguishable from the other dwellings on the block, all of which had a bunch of roosters and hens clucking in their front yards.

"You stay here while I check this guy out," Vinnie directed.

Bertucci would have made one hell of a micro-manager.

I watched as he knocked on the front door. A man answered, listened to Vinnie speak, and then nodded. Little Italy turned and waved for me to come in.

I got out of the car and walked through the yard, making my way past a cluster of chickens that pecked at my shoes. Then I was whisked inside and led into a back room. Funny, but it didn't look anything like a doctor's office. The mint green walls were peeling, the room held two metal chairs, an examining table, and a desk with a bunch of crap on it.

A man dressed in an Aloha shirt, polyester pants, and flip-flops approached. He was small, bald, and had a head that was shaped like a cue ball. All it needed was a number printed on the side. He removed my makeshift bandage and began to cluck as though he were one of the chickens.

"Is it bad?" I asked, not liking the sound of that at all. "And I'm terribly sorry, but I didn't catch your name."

I figured knowing that he was a real doctor might help to make me feel better.

"Doc will do," he replied, not bothering with further formalities.

Ooh, yeah. That was a lot more reassuring.

"I can tell you this much. You're a very fortunate girl," Doc confided. "I've never seen a cut quite like it. There could have been real damage had it gone any deeper. Whoever did this used a very unusual knife. I'd love to know what it was. Anyway, I'll get my equipment and be right with you."

I waited until he'd left the room.

"Are you sure this guy knows what he's doing?" I asked Vinnie.

"Yeah, yeah. Don't worry. He's a real pro," Little Italy insisted.

But I had the feeling that he was trying to sound convincing.

Doc No-name came back with a medical bag that contained lots of goodies. I winced as he began to clean my wound.

"You wanna hold my hand?" Vinnie offered. "I don't mind if you squeeze it."

I took him up on his offer as Doc No-name threaded a needle. I clutched his paw tightly as the good doctor began to stitch up my arm.

"Hey! Not so hard," Vinnie protested as I firmly gripped his hand.

What a wuss.

One tetanus shot later, I was nearly as good as new. At least that's what Doc No-name told me.

"Here. And take these," he said, handing me a bottle of amoxicillin.

How convenient. I didn't even need a prescription.

Vinnie paid him for his trouble and we got back into the Lincoln and hit the road.

"You know, I wasn't jerking you around before. I really don't know who iced Yakimov," Little Italy disclosed. "Anyway, you never told me what *you* were doing there today."

"Same old, same old," I coolly lied. "I was just following up on those chameleon sales. How about you? Why did *you* stop by?

"Same old, same old," Vinnie responded, in blatant imitation. "I'm trying to track down the damn money that Yakimov owes my boss. I gotta find it soon, or there'll be hell to pay."

"What about that big fish you mentioned the other day?

You know, the one that Stas supposedly had on his hook? Any idea who it might be?" I questioned, trying to be of help.

"That's what I went there to find out," Vinnie acknowledged.

We remained silent for a moment and then looked at each other, knowing what had to be done. Vinnie didn't stop to get my vehicle but continued on, aware there were more pressing matters to be dealt with first.

Perhaps the intruder hadn't intended to simply kill Stas, but had also been searching for something. If so, it was vital that we find it before he had a chance to return—or the police got involved. We headed straight for Yakimov's house.

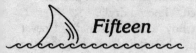

Fifteen

All was quiet, as before. The only difference was knowing that Yakimov lay on the floor like a gutted fish.

"Why don't we divvy this up? That way, if there's something to be found, we might come across it faster," Little Italy suggested.

I agreed, being that it made perfect sense.

"I thought I'd start in there," Vinnie said, with a nod toward Yakimov's office. "How about you take the bedroom?"

"Wait a minute. Why don't *you* take the bedroom?" I protested. The only thing I didn't add was *I got here first*.

"For chrissakes, do we really have to argue about this?" he asked, beginning to look embarrassed.

I stared at him without saying a word.

"Okay, here's the God's honest truth. I'm not all that crazy about dead bodies. They kinda give me the heebie jeebies," Vinnie admitted.

I understood that. On the other hand, there was a lot that could be learned from them. It's where most deep, dark things tend to be hidden.

"Yeah, okay. But we share whatever information we find. Agreed?" I proposed.

"Absolutely. You got my word on it," Vinnie confirmed.

I reached into my purse, as Vinnie stuck a hand in his pocket, and we each pulled out a pair of latex gloves.

"I see you came prepared," I noted dryly.

"Yeah. I'm a goddamn Boy Scout. Personally, I never leave home without them," he replied, slipping on the gloves with the ease of a surgeon.

Vinnie headed for the office, and I walked into the bedroom. I tried not to look at Yakimov, but it was nearly impossible. A lot of good all of his muscles and steroids had done him. However, truly unnerving was that he seemed to stare at me where ever I moved.

I turned my back to Yakimov and began to rummage through the open drawers of his bureau, though most of its contents were already on the floor.

I may be a slob, but there are certain things that bother me. I can't stand sleeping in an unmade bed, I always close closet doors—you never know where the boogie man might lurk—and partially open drawers drive me crazy.

I began to close each drawer now. However, there was one that was stuck. Something was jammed tight against its runner. The only solution was to reach in and remove whatever it might be.

I pulled out the drawer, knelt down and took a look inside the bureau. There it was: A large manila envelope had fallen behind and become lodged against the back wall. I reached in and removed an envelope that was partially torn and crumpled.

Its contents were a thick stack of papers that appeared to be legal documents of some sort. I realized they were articles of ownership for a number of different restaurants both in Hong Kong and in mainland China. All were listed under the umbrella of Magic Dragon Chinese Restaurants Incorporated.

A quick look through the pages revealed that each

restaurant listed the same exact group of officers. They included a G. C. Leung and S. M. Ting. Something struck me as peculiar, and I realized what it was. Leung and Ting were two of the names that had appeared on Sammy's doodle of a shark.

I didn't care how many Leungs and Tings there might be in Oahu. This was definitely too unusual to be a mere coincidence. I rolled up the papers and stuffed them in my bag.

There was one last item left inside the envelope. It was a business card for a company called Magic Dragon Medicinals. The tagline read, DISTRIBUTOR OF HEALTH AND VITALITY PRODUCTS.

I interpreted that to mean, "We sell shark fin, rhino horn, bear gallbladder, and lots of other animal parts to keep you potent and feeling young."

It wouldn't have surprised me to learn that they were also selling black-market Viagra. Come to think of it, Vinnie Bertucci could very well be in cahoots with them.

Magic Dragon Medicinals and Magic Dragon Chinese Restaurants were clearly interconnected in some way. Both companies had the same name, were based in Hong Kong, and had been of interest to Stas Yakimov.

"How's it goin' in there?" Vinnie called to me from the other room.

I slipped the card into my pocket and walked out to meet him.

"Pretty much as I expected," I replied, wondering if Vinnie had found anything of interest. There was nothing in sight. If so, he'd decided to keep it well hidden.

"What does that mean? Did you come up with anything or not?" he asked impatiently, dismembering a fingernail with his front teeth.

I noticed that he didn't spit it on the floor, but slid the sliver of nail into his pocket.

"Not really. How about you?" I responded, feeling the slightest twinge of guilt.

"Nope. Not a thing."

Call me crazy, but Vinnie reminded me of the cat that ate the canary. All that was missing were the feathers sticking out of his mouth. Little Italy narrowed his eyes, and seemed to regard me with the same sense of suspicion.

"Okay then. In that case, we should probably get out of here," he advised.

We left as we came, removing all signs of our presence. Climbing into his Lincoln, we headed back down the street to fetch my vehicle.

We both remained silent, as if afraid that the least hint of sound would put a tear in our resistance. But the urge to speak continued to build inside me. I felt as if I were smuggling nuclear secrets out of the country, the papers nearly burning a hole in my bag. It was Vinnie that finally broke the deadlock.

"Okay. Enough with the bullshit, already. Who do you think you're kiddin' here? We both know that we each found something. So what say we lay our cards on the table and reveal exactly what it is?" he proposed.

Damn, but he was good at this. Vinnie pulled a white envelope from beneath his shirt that was boldly marked CONFIDENTIAL.

"You show me yours, and then you get this," Bertucci bartered.

My fingers itched to snatch the envelope from him. Maybe it contained something. Then again, maybe it didn't. There was only one way I'd ever find out. Besides, I've always been the kind of gal who rarely bets when the stakes are low, but gambles the house and goes for broke. I figured it was worth a shot.

"Here. You might be interested in this," I said, removing the Magic Dragon Medicinal card from my pocket.

Vinnie seized it from my fingers.

"Distributors for health and vitality products, huh?" he grunted. Whadda ya think? Maybe they're selling erector pills to help guys launch their own personal-sized rockets?"

"Yeah, it could be that they're offering bootlegged Viagra," I responded.

"Yakimov might of had some kind of secret deal going on with these bums. For all I know, he coulda been supplying them with pills from our stash and pocketing the profits. That would explain where the money went."

"Anything's possible," I agreed.

Vinnie snorted in disgust. "Terrific. A helluva lotta good this does me. The damn place is in friggin' Hong Kong. What am I supposed to do? Catch a plane over there? I gotta find the guy that's here on *this* end."

I was well aware that Vinnie bordered on being computer illiterate.

"Tell you what. I'll check this company on the Internet and see what I can find out," I offered. "Now it's your turn. Let's see what you've got."

"I don't know if these will be of any help with your lizards, but it must have been important to Yakimov."

I tried to take the envelope from him, but Vinnie held it just out of reach.

"Of course, if it has anything to do with Viagra, you gotta tell me about that also," he insisted.

"I wouldn't dream of withholding information from you," I assured him.

Vinnie handed me the envelope, and I plucked out two business cards. One was for Tat Hing Products, and the other for Africa Hydraulics. Both of these companies also were based in Hong Kong. The second card produced the same sensation I'd experienced earlier—the strong feeling that I'd seen this name somewhere before. Then a sickening feeling set in as things began to click together.

A former boss, Charlie Hickok, used to brag about taking part in major sting operations during the "good old days" of Fish and Wildlife. Naturally, there'd always been those Moby Dicks that had gotten away. Africa Hydraulics had been one of them.

They were a front company that smuggled and laundered vast quantities of elephant ivory from East Africa through the United Arab Emirates, and on into Hong Kong in the 1980s. Africa Hydraulics had been notorious as the main mover and shaker of the international ivory trade. They were believed to be responsible for having decimated a large portion of the elephant population.

That's when another chip fell into place. The owner of Africa Hydraulics had been a man by the name of George Leung. Was it possible that the same greedy people were now involved in the shark-fin trade? Just the thought of it sent me reeling. If so, I already knew what to expect—the consequences for sharks would be no less devastating.

Leung nearly managed to wipe out elephants, not stopping until international law had finally clamped down. He'd do the same thing when it came to sharks, slaughtering them until no more were left. I blinked back tears of rage and frustration, realizing what I was possibly up against.

"Did you find anything else?" I grimly questioned.

Vinnie glanced at me, his eyebrows arching, as if wondering what was wrong.

"That's it," he responded, and then stared straight ahead.

Damn, I felt certain that he was holding something back. But there was no time to find out, as he pulled into the lot and parked next to my Explorer.

"Okay, New Yawk. This is where you get out."

"Aren't you forgetting something?" I questioned.

Vinnie looked at me with a strange expression.

"How about my gun?" I reminded him.

"Oh, yeah. Sure. Just be careful with that thing. It'll get you in big trouble. Also, remember to check out that Magic Dragon shit and get back to me pronto," he ordered.

What in hell did he think? That he'd suddenly become my personal Godfather? I bristled, but said nothing. Instead, I watched as he drove off. Then I searched for the nearest pay phone and placed a call to the local police.

"I want to report a homicide at 85 Hyacinth Street in Nanakuli," I informed the desk duty officer.

"Oh, you do, do you?" he cynically bantered, as if used to such practical jokes. "And just who is this?"

"Who is *this*?" I countered.

"Desk Sergeant Hammel," the officer brusquely responded.

"Well, Sergeant Hammel, this is no joke. I suggest you get someone over to that address pronto," I said, and immediately hung up.

Then I phoned the best animal shelter that I knew of on Oahu.

"There's a crime scene at 85 Hyacinth Street in Nanakuli, and a number of pit bulls are in need of temporary shelter. The police are already on their way over," I disclosed.

"Exactly how many dogs are you talking about?" the female voice on the other end of the line inquired.

I counted the snarling canines, one by one, in my head. "I believe there are five in total."

"All right. I think we can handle that. I'll just need your name, address and phone number, please," the woman briskly advised.

"Sorry, but I can't give that information out at this time."

There was a moment of silence before she replied.

"I understand. Thanks for letting us know about the dogs. Don't worry, we'll take care of them."

"Um, one more thing. There's also a mountain lion," I added.

"You are joking, right?" the voice sternly cross-examined.

"No. I'm afraid I'm deadly serious," I answered. "I've heard there's a big-cat specialist somewhere on the island. Do you think that she could possibly house the cougar for now?"

The woman sighed. "I know who it is. I'll contact her, if you like."

"That would be terrific. Thanks again," I said and hung up, with one less concern on my mind.

Then I slipped into my Ford and sat there for a while, not yet ready to go home, but unsure of exactly what to do next. The one thing I didn't want to think about was Yakimov, and how he'd looked lying on his bedroom floor. But the image had become permanently seared into my head.

Whoever had done the deed was frighteningly proficient with a knife. Stas had been cut to induce the maximum amount of pain. I realized I was gripping the steering wheel with all my might, the day's tension having lodged in each of my ten little fingers. Only by now, it had become night.

My thoughts drifted as I sat in the dark and watched the locals cruise in and out of the mom-and-pop shop. I was curious as to whether Sammy had ever been here. Funny, how we'd first met. I'd never have gone to the docks if it hadn't been for the body found floating near the pier that day. In a sense, Charlie Hong had set the chain of events that followed into motion. Strange what a dead man could do. I wondered if he'd been nearly as influential in life as he'd become in death.

Sammy believed that he'd been knocked off by another fin dealer. If so, Hong must have been powerful enough to present some kind of threat.

I racked my brain as I tried to remember the name of his company. I finally gave up, and simply listened to the distant sound of the Pacific Ocean at my back.

That was it! Hong's business had been called Pacific Catch Products. It was also the one spot where I hadn't yet thought to look.

The police had written off Charlie Hong's death as a suicide. As it turned out, that worked perfectly for me. It meant they wouldn't have scoured his place, and there might still be something left to find.

I picked up my cell phone, called information, and got the address. What do you know? Pacific Catch Products was located at Pier 33 on the Honolulu docks. I turned on the Ford's engine and sped there now, no longer caring about the dull pain that throbbed in my arm.

If the docks seemed like a different world during the day, at night they became downright lurid. Longliners still filled the piers, where they bobbed like toy boats in a bathtub. But the evening brought into play another type of fishing as well. Sailors were now joined by a colorful parade of hookers.

The girls trawled the wharves, flirtatiously going from boat to boat, where they serviced each man who was willing, flush, and able. Their high heels *click, click, clicked* on the wooden boards, the sharp staccato beat like that of a traveling troupe of flamenco dancers. One girl walked over to a car that idled nearby. The next moment, she disappeared inside, only to reappear again a few minutes later.

Bright lights lined the piers, giving the docks a party atmosphere, as fishermen gathered together to drink, buy drugs, and get jacked up on ice. I now realized that Caucasians resided on one side of the wharves, carousing and playing cards, while Vietnamese and Filipinos kept their boats docked on the other. It was an entire subculture where Asians chattered among themselves as they cut up fish and threw the pieces into cooking pots. Meanwhile, the boat owners resided in Diamond Head, living high on the hog.

Underlying all this was a low, steady groan that worked its way through my bones. It was the moan of boats pulling against their ropes, accompanied by the *putt, putt, putt* of bilge pumps spitting out water. The slap of the ocean lapped against their hulls in a mesmerizing fashion that seduced me. Perhaps it was to lure my attention from the fact there was no law enforcement on the docks at night. Neither the state wildlife division nor the National Marine Fisheries Service had an officer anywhere in sight. It made this the perfect time in which to smuggle illicit cargo.

I continued to cruise the docks, curious as to what I would find. It wasn't long before I managed to trip across something. Four Asian crew members had begun to haul large, black garbage bags off a longliner. Ten, fifteen, twenty sacks were tossed into the back of a pickup truck that sat parked next to their boat. I decided to mosey on over, being that I had the perfect cover—yet another *haole* tourist that had stumbled upon the docks while out for a joyride.

"Wow! You guys must have had a good trip. It looks as if you caught a lot of fish," I remarked, slowing my Explorer to a crawl.

The men glanced at me and smiled, but said nothing.

"What did you catch? Maybe I'd like to buy something," I chattered on, remaining intrepidly cheerful.

That brought a rapid response to their lips.

"No fish. No fish for sale," one of them irritably replied and waved me aside, as if my presence was cramping their style.

"Then what have you got in there?" I stubbornly persisted.

"Only our laundry," another responded, after which they all turned their backs to me.

Uh-huh. As if they weren't standing on a dingy longliner but sipping drinks on a luxurious cruise ship. That would have been the only explanation for hauling such an extensive wardrobe out to sea. Either that, or the men liked to change their clothes at least three times a day.

I watched as they drove away. The pickup didn't go very far, but stopped at a locked gate near the other end of the pier. One of the men jumped out, opened it, and guided their vehicle through. Then the enclosure was once again fastened behind them.

I waited a few minutes before following, carefully parking so that my Explorer was just out of view. Then, grabbing a flashlight, I snuck up to the gate and peered through. A warehouse area lay spread like a grimy city behind it. I quickly checked that no one was around, and pulled myself over the chain-link fence.

 *Sixteen*

My feet thudded on asphalt, the sound dully echoing in the night. It mixed with the low rumble of boat generators as I scurried toward a building that had its lights on. It was there that the pickup sat parked, like a vehicular amputee, its rear end partially consumed by the building's garage entrance.

I hastened my pace, eager to learn what was taking place, only to hear a splash and realize that my feet were sloshing through liquid. The flashlight's beam revealed a series of wastewater puddles laced with dark swirls of blood, which led me to wonder if they came from an animal or human. At the same time, an acrid aroma hit me full force, as if I'd been slapped across the face. It was the smell of ammonia; the very same odor that had clung to Kalahiki's pants.

There was no longer any question as to what was inside those black plastic garbage bags, or where Sammy had gone that night in search of more evidence. But I had little time to speculate further, having reached my destination.

No one was in the pickup, and I leaned in to examine the front seat. Damn. There wasn't a thing other than a crumpled pack of cigarettes and a couple of empty beer cans. Equally frustrating was that the truck's back end blocked any view into the warehouse. I could hear voices inside, but there were no windows through which to peek. At least, not in this section of the building. Perhaps there'd be some along the rear. I began to head there now, fully determined to check it out.

I was so focused on my mission that my heart nearly burst through my chest as a hand grabbed hold of my arm. I whirled around to find a man in his mid-forties, with a face as smooth and unlined as an eggshell. He stared at me with unblinking eyes that betrayed not the least hint of emotion. Rather, they were as vapidly cool as those of the lizard that had been on my bedroom wall.

"This is private property you're on. Would you mind telling me what it is that you're doing here?" he asked, in a tone as neutral as his expression.

It was the intensity of his grip that gave him away. That, and the fact that I caught a glimpse of something deadly in his eyes.

"I'm sorry. I didn't realize," I replied. "I'm looking for a Mr. Hong of Pacific Catch Products. Perhaps you can direct me to the proper building."

I didn't wait to be released, but jerked my arm from his grip. The man continued to study me in what quickly became a staring contest. I could deal with that. My sister and I used to play the same game years ago. Best of all, I usually won.

"Pacific Catch is out of business, and Charlie Hong's not here anymore," he finally said, ending the match. "How did you get in, anyway? The warehouse area is closed to traffic after five o'clock."

"Oh, really? That's odd. I just came in through the gate," I responded, hoping he wouldn't bother to check.

But my opponent wasn't buying my explanation.

"That's impossible," he said, his tone taking on a sinister edge. "The gate is always kept locked. I check it my-self. Especially since there was a robbery here the other night."

My mind raced, wondering if the burglar had been Sammy. And, if so, what had he discovered? The only way I'd ever know now was to find out for myself.

"That's too bad. Someone must have accidentally left it open, the same as they did tonight. People will just have to learn to be more careful," I said, and turned to leave.

But my assailant stopped me by grabbing onto my arm again. Only this time, his fingers clamped down directly over my wound.

"I suppose so. After all, accidents do happen. In fact, quite a few have taken place just recently on Oahu."

It felt as if jellyfish tentacles were burning through my skin, the pain so palpable that even my teeth began to ache. I tried to pull away, but the man refused to loosen his grip. Instead he smiled, as if aware of exactly what he was doing.

"Let go of my arm," I demanded, flinching as the pain traveled up inside my head.

"We don't appreciate trespassers around here," he warned, his voice taut and terse as a garrote.

I began to worry that the stitches in my arm would burst if he continued at this rate.

"I'm not a trespasser. I'm a federal agent, and you're about to land in deep trouble if you don't immediately re-lease me," I hissed.

"Oh, really? I suppose that depends on exactly what type of agent you are," he countered. "For all I know, you're the kind that likes to play illegal spy games."

"I'm with the U.S. Fish and Wildlife Service," I furi-ously revealed. "And this is your last warning. Let go of my arm."

He hesitated one tenth of a second too long, and I ground my heel into his foot while slamming my palm hard against his chin.

The man's head flew back, clicking his teeth together. He grunted in surprise and relaxed his grip. I pulled myself free, as he spit on the ground and angrily glared at me.

"Now see what you've done? I bit my tongue." His fingers gingerly probed its tip. "Look at that. You've made it bleed."

"What a shame. Then I guess we'll both have bruises from this evening," I responded, and checked my arm.

Unbelievable. The stitches were still all in place.

"You're going to regret this," he vowed. "It's common knowledge that Fish and Wildlife has no jurisdiction over the docks. National Marine Fisheries Service won't be very happy to learn that you've been snooping around their territory."

"I have a suggestion. Why don't you give me your name, along with that of your company, and I'll be sure to report this to them," I caustically responded. If he thought that kind of threat was going to scare me, he could join the crowd at the back of the line.

He smiled and his face glowed like a pale moon in the night.

"My company is Capital City Fish Products," he obligingly revealed.

An inner alarm warned me that the answer had come way too easily.

"But I have a better idea," he continued. "Since you seem to be so interested, why don't I take you on a personal tour right now? You know, I have the strangest feeling that not a soul knows where you are this evening."

My suspicions were confirmed as the man suddenly lunged for me. I reached for my gun, knowing I'd be in trouble if he again grabbed hold of my arm. But we both stopped cold as a figure abruptly lurched from out of the dark. He bumped into my assailant, knocking him off balance, and then swayed from side to side and back and forth like a punch-drunk fighter as he stood between us.

"Hey, Mikey! So you finally got yourself a hot date, huh? Whatsa matter? Doesn't she like your moves?"

My hero hiccuped and burped, exuding a wave of booze that came rolling toward me like a tsunami.

"Be a pal. How 'bout cuttin' me in on the action? What can I tell ya? It's been a while since I've had a woman," he slurred, and leered suggestively at me.

He stood close enough so that I saw what I'd thought was a sweater was actually his hairy chest. His pot belly flopped over shorts slung dangerously low around his hips, and a pair of yellow rubber boots reached up to his wrinkled knees.

My knight in denim cut-offs had a complexion to match his hoary breath. Broken capillaries snaked across his nose and cheeks like crooked routes on a road map, attesting to the fact that he'd been drinking for too many years. A pair of droopy lids hung heavy over bloodshot eyes that were positioned above a nose the shape and size of a rutabaga. Even his hair looked as if it was on a bender, sticking out on all sides. As for his voice, it sounded as though he'd gargled with broken glass, most of which still remained in his throat.

Mikey's gaze coldly flitted between the two of us.

"Sure, Dave. She's all yours. Have yourself a blast," he replied, clipping off the end of each word as if it had frostbite.

He pulled a wad of cash from his pocket and peeled off a ten-dollar bill. "Here. Buy another bottle of booze while you're at it, and have yourselves a really good time."

"Aw hell, Mikey. That's awful nice of ya," my booze hound said, choking up and getting all teary-eyed.

He moved in to give Mikey a hug, but Mr. Capital City shoved him aside.

"Get off me, you lousy drunk," Mikey contemptuously responded, and began to brush off his clothes.

I took the opportunity to leave while the going was good.

"I'll be seeing you," I called from over my shoulder, while heading for the gate.

"You can count on that, Agent Porter," Mr. Capital City replied.

A flurry of goosebumps instantly broke out on my skin. I'd never told him my name.

I whirled around to confront the man, but he'd already disappeared inside. Only the drunk remained, staring at me with an odd expression.

A sickening feeling took hold as I realized that everyone seemed to know more about what was going on than I did. I hurried forward, increasingly aware that I was living on the edge of a sword—one on which I didn't have a very good grip.

I'd just about reached the gate when the *squish, squish, squish* of rubber soles, pounding on pavement, swiftly came from behind, and a hand landed on my shoulder. I took no chances this time, but spun around, grabbed onto it, and twisted the offending arm behind its owner's back.

"Hey, wait a minute! We gotta talk," a raspy voice protested.

I didn't have to see a thing to know who I had in my grip. His breath provided all the clue that was needed. It was my ninety-proof, alcohol-embalmed friend Dave, with the bloodshot eyes.

"I think you'd better sleep it off," I suggested, not in the mood to deal with him.

I released the drunk and started to walk away.

"Like hell, I will. I'm trying to help you here. This is serious business. Or are you too dense to understand that?" he challenged.

I slowed my pace, having become aware there was something about him. For one thing, he no longer slurred his words.

"You're the Fish and Wildlife agent, aren't you?" he continued to address my back. "In which case, you damn well better be interested in what I have to say."

I came to a halt, turned, and looked at the man.

"I thought you were wasted back there."

He tapped his temple with his index finger and shrewdly smiled. "Nah. That was just an act to help save your ass. You can trust Sharkfin Dave. I never get more than a little wasted. It don't matter how much I drink."

"Sharkfin Dave?" I repeated.

The name rolled off my tongue, conjuring up an image as vivid as Davy Crockett or Daniel Boone. Only this was a shirtless drunk that stood before me.

"Why are you called that?" I questioned, my adrenaline kicking into action.

"Because I'm so *goooood* at catchin' sharks," he responded, with a greedy gleam in his eye. "You know what I like to call 'em?"

"No. What?" I asked, my stomach beginning to hatch butterflies.

"Wolves of the sea," he said, licking his lips as though he could taste the words.

"What made you give them that name?" I continued, half repulsed, and half mesmerized.

"Because if you listen real close, you can practically hear them howl when they're caught."

He burst into a raucous laugh, and a sour taste filled my mouth.

"So then, you still catch them?" I followed up, determined not to let the man off my hook.

He silently nodded. "At least, I did until about a week ago. But I'm not the one you want. I can help you land the real son of a bitch that's running this business."

"And why would you do that?" I promptly inquired, afraid this might only be a dream, and I'd suddenly wake up.

"Because that bastard you were playing *mano-a-mano* with a minute ago is the dirtbag that killed my boss," Sharkfin Dave disclosed.

My pulse joined my heart in a whirlwind sprint.

"And who would your boss have been?" I queried although certain I already knew.

"Charlie Hong, owner of Pacific Catch Products," Sharkfin replied. "I was his right-hand man. I just about ran this place in the good old days, when finning was legal. That's how much fin we used to bring in. Once it became banned, I turned into his cargo man, going out to sea to rendezvous with tankers. We'd pick up bags of fins off the ships and smuggle 'em back in. The money wasn't as good, but it was still a living. 'Course, even that's over, now that Charlie's dead."

He hacked up a lugie and spat on the ground.

"I'm telling you, that bastard took my livelihood away. So he threw me a tenner tonight. Big friggin' deal. It won't pay my rent, or keep me in food and booze." Sharkfin wiped the back of his hand across his lips in distaste.

"If you're not still involved in finning, then why are you hanging around the docks?" I asked, not yet ready to trust him.

"This is where I live these days. In a shack that used to be my office. Hell, I can't afford anything else. Besides, you oughta be damn grateful that I was here tonight, keeping a watch on things. Mikey would have killed you

the same as he did Hong, and thought nothing of it,"
Sharkfin attested. "Come on. We can't talk out in the
open. Let's go to my place."

My hand strayed to the butt of my gun as I followed,
assuring that I'd be safe.

Sharkfin Dave led the way past shuttered buildings,
slumbering forklifts, and sheds of corrugated steel, as my
feet slogged through water and slippery strands of fish
guts. His yellow boots reflected in pools of scum like twin
golden suns as we stealthily traveled across the warehouse lot.

He walked with a limp, and I realized that his one leg
was as deeply scarred as a cat's scratching post, its girth
much thinner than the other. I wondered what had happened, and if Mikey had something to do with it.

We arrived at a small gray shack with a plywood door
and a white plastic bucket in front. Sharkfin kicked the
pail aside and booted in the entrance.

To describe the place as a crash pad would have been to
give it too much credence. The hut was an absolute dive.
Girly calendars were plastered on the walls, and the fur-
nishings consisted of rusty filing cabinets, a three-legged
table, and a broken down chair. A mattress as old and
thin as Methuselah lay like a corpse on the floor. Sharkfin
flopped down on it and motioned for me to take the chair.
I gingerly balanced myself on the wobbly seat.

The only thing of interest in the room were two shark
jaws that hung on the wall. One had a mouthful of notched
and serrated teeth, while the other contained what could
have passed for a collection of lethal knives. Sharkfin Dave
caught my eye, and his lips curled up in a smile.

"Those belonged to a couple of badass friends of
mine—a mako and a tiger shark. I can tell you it was one
helluva job yanking those things from their mouths. I cut

the shit out of myself. They may not look lively now, but those two gave me quite the time. Yep, I've got fond memories of 'em. We'll always have Paris, isn't that right, my little beauties?" he bantered, looking up at the two deadly sets of jaws.

"The man that confronted me out there—Mikey—is he a shark-fin dealer?" I questioned.

"You betcha. Michael Leung is now the main mover and shaker of fins in Hawaii," Dave said, and then discharged a snort. "Did I say Hawaii? Who am I kidding? We're talking the whole goddamn world."

Leung. My stomach tightened, and the pain in my arm began to throb even more. My assailant had the same last name as the notorious ivory dealer in Hong Kong. Not only that, but *Leung* had also been scribbled on Sammy's drawing of a shark.

"His father wouldn't happen to be George Leung, by any chance, would he?" I asked, almost afraid to hear the answer.

Sharkfin responded with a shrug. "I couldn't tell you. All I know is that his daddy lives in Hong Kong and makes big bucks. Word has it the family's rich as shit. Daddy set Mikey up in the shark-fin trade over here. And to do that, you've gotta be plenty wealthy and have a chunk of ready change in your pocket,'cause this is purely a cash business."

Fins would naturally change hands for cash only. It was one of those gray markets in which most transactions weren't even recorded. It made me all the more curious as to how Sammy had gotten hold of those papers.

So that's what George Leung was doing with his money from the illegal ivory trade these days. He was setting up another lucrative cash business for himself and his family.

"Mikey's job is to buy and dry the fins over here,"

Sharkfin explained. "After that's done, he sends them on to his daddy's factory in Hong Kong, where they go through the final process."

Sharkfin Dave watched me with the stealth of a spider and I knew what was going on. He was waiting to see if I took the bait. Most likely, he was turning on Leung in the hope of taking his place. That would be something I'd have to deal with later on. Right now, I needed to learn all I could about Leung and the shark-fin trade.

"I saw a boat unloading about twenty garbage bags into a pickup tonight. After that, it drove into the warehouse area. Do you suppose shark fins were inside those bags?" I probed.

"You're talking about the blue pickup that's parked over at Mikey's place?" Sharkfin asked, and began to scratch the back of his head.

I nodded.

"Probably, but that's just kid stuff. Mikey usually gets anywhere from eleven to twenty tons of fins in at a time. What you saw tonight was a small haul." Dave kicked off his boots and proceeded to pick at his toes.

"Eleven to twenty tons? That would be one hell of a lot of garbage bags," I remarked. "He couldn't possibly pull it off without drawing a lot of attention. How does he manage to do it?"

"They come off his boat packed in bales and are thrown directly into containers," Sharkfin matter-of-factly stated.

I looked at him, clearly puzzled.

Sharkfin Dave sighed and sat up. "Okay. Let me lay it out for you. Mikey has an eighty-foot boat called the *Magic Dragon*. It rendezvous with those big-ass foreign mother ships about two hundred miles out at sea."

"I've never heard the term 'mother ship' before. What are they?" I asked.

Sharkfin Dave shook his head in disbelief, as if unable to

imagine such a thing. "They're the large vessels that roam the high seas, refueling and resupplying fishing boats. Think of them as sort of giant UPS platforms. These same mother ships also collect shark fins from the boats that they supply."

"Why would they do that?" I asked, curious as to the reason.

"Because eighty-foot fishing boats don't have enough space on board to store hundreds of shark fins. Not if they want to have plenty of room for all the tuna they're hoping to catch. Besides that, they also need lots of storage space for the ice that's used to keep the tuna fresh until they finally get back to port," Sharkfin explained.

That was something I hadn't thought about before.

"So the fishing boats will leave all the fins they've gathered so far on the mother ship whenever they refuel. Well, Mikey, being the shrewd businessman he is, decided to work out a deal with them. He takes pre-orders for shark fins from traders in Asia, and then guarantees the fishermen that he'll buy all the fins they're able to collect. That way, the fishing boats don't do business with anyone but him, and Mikey's able to monopolize the trade. Pretty clever, huh?"

That was putting it mildly.

"How does he go about actually collecting the fins from these boats?" I questioned, curious as to every aspect of the trade.

"As I said, the fishing boats transfer their haul of shark fins to the mother ship. Then Mikey's boat makes a five-day trip out to sea to pick them up all in one place. That's what's called trans-shipment. It's also why he wanted my boss out of the way. Now there's no other competition in Hawaii, and he's king of the hill."

"No wonder Leung makes a fortune," I exclaimed, softly whistling under my breath.

"Don't be fooled," Sharkfin corrected. "The big money isn't made just by drying and sending the fins on to other buyers in Asia. It's Daddy Leung, and his shark-fin processing factory in Hong Kong, that gives sonny boy Mikey the edge. This way, the Leungs are able to keep the entire business in the family. Hell, I heard their company made over twelve million dollars in profit last year alone."

The papers I'd found at Yakimov's had revealed the Leungs were also involved in the restaurant trade. They were clearly able to keep their customers well supplied in high-priced shark-fin soup. The Leungs were nothing less than a one-stop, one-shop shark-fin operation.

"Except that Daddy's been getting pretty mad at Mikey lately," Sharkfin dryly revealed.

"Why's that?" I inquired, always eager to hear the dirt.

"It seems that Mikey's gone and gotten himself a sideline that's taking time away from the family business. I guess he's grown tired of being under Daddy's thumb, and wants to branch out and make his own money," Dave said, idly scratching his belly.

"What kind of sideline is that?" I asked, figuring it probably involved the chameleon trade. Why else would his name and Yakimov's have been linked together on that same piece of paper inside Sammy's box?

"He's gotten hooked up in some sort of bootleg Viagra scheme. Talk about a booming business. I hear that his company's growing about six inches an hour," he joked. "Mikey's got a cousin that handles the distribution of it in Hong Kong."

Of course. Magic Dragon Medicinals. So *Leung* was the big fish that Vinnie was after. There was no question but that I needed to snag Leung before Vinnie uncovered this information and tracked him down.

"I think we can help each other out," I told Sharkfin,

figuring he could interpret it any which way he chose. "But I need proof to back all of this up."

Sharkfin looked at me, and that same greedy gleam snuck back into his eyes.

"How about if it's arranged so that you're here to see the fins off-loaded for yourself? Would that be good enough?"

My nerves stood up and gave a twenty-one-gun salute. "You can do that?"

"Sure. Why not? I know everything that goes on in this place. The *Magic Dragon* went to pick up a shipment of fins about nine days ago. They should be coming back into port any time now. I'll give you a call as soon as they dock," he promised.

I couldn't ask for better evidence than that. Sharkfin Dave seemed to feel the same way. He beamed at me like a cat that had presented its owner with a dead mouse. I realized that since he was here all the time, he might have other information as well.

"By the way, did you happen to spot a local Hawaiian guy with a hefty build, in his mid-twenties, hanging around the warehouse area a few nights ago?" I casually inquired.

Sharkfin began to nod before I'd even finished my sentence.

"Yeah. And I wasn't the only one. The kid was a turncoat National Marine Fisheries observer, right?"

"How did you know that?" I shot back.

Sharkfin Dave emitted a noise that was part bark, part laugh. "What, are you kidding? You think Hawaii is small? Try living on these docks. Nothing gets by anyone down here."

The thought made my skin crawl. It meant someone could be watching us even now. I glanced around the room to spot a small, grimy window and imagined that Leung's eyes were peering through it. But he wasn't the only one I was concerned about.

"Does that include the National Marine Fisheries Service?" I questioned.

Dave shrugged. "Maybe yes, and maybe no. People don't see much when they choose to turn a blind eye, if you know what I mean."

I stood up, suddenly eager to go.

"Here are the numbers where I can be reached," I said, handing him my business card. "You'll call me then, when the *Magic Dragon* comes in?"

Sharkfin Dave started to twitch, as if he'd caught a whopping case of fleas.

"Sure, no problem. Hey, do you think you could spot a poor drunk a couple of bucks to get by?"

I placed two twenties on the table, figuring that ought to keep him in booze for a while. Then I made my way back across the warehouse lot, nervously glancing over my shoulder.

There were no eyes to be seen, but I could feel them watching from every dark nook and corner. Oahu had begun to ever so slowly close in on me, trailing my every move, and I suddenly knew that I was no longer alone.

Seventeen

I climbed into my Ford, turned on the engine, and began to head home. The docks disappeared behind me like a bad dream. Soon the whole world was swallowed up by the blackness of night.

All the better to conceal deep, dark secrets, my dear, a menacing voice suggestively whispered in my ear.

I pressed down hard on the gas pedal, but there was no escaping my own demons.

Some find the evening to be full of solace, a time to relax and retreat from the day's ordeals. But when the sun goes down, my guard quickly rises, ever vigilant of ghouls and goblins. I firmly believe there are things that go bump in the middle of the night. I could feel them swirling around me even now.

I turned off Nimitz Boulevard, and Honolulu gradually evaporated into the distance, its lights merging with the stars. I drove toward the North Shore as I tried to focus on what I had learned so far. I was clearly pissing off a growing number of people. I took that to be a good sign. It meant that not only was I stirring things up, but also that a hornet's nest was probably close by. I could almost hear their buzzing in my ears as I continued to race through the night.

I sped past dozing pineapple fields, their plants nestled in a bed of red earth. I was tempted to stop and lie down beside them. My eyelids felt heavy, and all I wanted to do was to sleep. If nothing else, it would provide temporary solace from all the trouble that was beginning to surround me.

My head started to nod and I turned on the radio, hoping it would keep me awake. But the crappy music on each station only seemed to make matters worse. I didn't realize how badly my nerves were shot until the cell phone sprang to life and began to ring on the seat beside me. I jumped as if having been shocked by a defibrillator. With any luck it would be Santou, and he'd help out by talking me all the way home.

"Hello?" I anxiously answered, expecting to hear Jake's Cajun drawl.

"You're gambling with your soul, Porter, and you've just played your last card," intoned a male voice.

The words ended with an angry dial tone that droned in my ear. Just as frightening was that I hadn't recognized the caller. It further confirmed what Sharkfin Dave had told me this evening. Nothing slips by in Oahu. There was no longer any doubt that I was being watched.

My chest felt tight as the warning took root and insidiously began to spread. Even so, I tried to shake the fear that I was in way too deep. I'd been in tight situations before. But this one grew more convoluted with each new piece that fell into place. I no longer knew who I should trust, or who might be secretly turning against me. As for the anonymous call, that only added to the tangled web in which I now found myself.

Spam was at the door to greet me as I walked into the house. He licked my face and then sniffed my arm, as if aware that something was wrong. Even Tag-along seemed to be concerned as she rubbed against my leg.

"Hey, chere. It's about time you got home," Santou called from the living room, and I eagerly followed his voice.

He lay stretched on the couch, looking as seductively tan and toned as any Hawaiian god. Jake opened his arms and I gladly fell into them, feeling safe for the first time all night.

It felt like our own private residence until Kevin came sauntering out of his room. Old habits die hard. My guard instantly flew up. As it turned out, I had plenty of reason.

"Hey, what gives? Did you get into a rumble or something tonight?" he questioned, immediately stirring up trouble.

Damn the man. That was enough to make Jake take note of the bandage wrapped around my arm. He touched it, and I quickly pulled away from his reach.

"That seems to be one hell of a wound you've got there, chere. How did it happen?" Santou questioned, a look of worry spreading across his face.

"It's no big deal," I said, attempting to brush off his concern. "I tripped on a piece of lava rock. You know how sharp that stuff can be. I had to get a few stitches. But believe me, it's nothing serious."

Jake looked at me, and instinctively sensed that I was lying.

"Don't give me that, Rachel. I know you too well. There's something more going on. Just tell me what it is," he insisted.

"Don't be ridiculous," I denied, trying hard to maintain my innocence. "I wish it were anything other than the fact that I'm simply a klutz. But I'm afraid that's all it adds up to."

There was no question that if Santou knew the truth, he'd do whatever he could to stop me. And I had no intention of backing down now. Not when I was clearly so close.

"Your arm must hurt like hell," Jake said with a shake of his head, letting me know that he didn't buy my story.

"Yeah, it does. But I'll live," I muttered, wishing Santou would once again wrap his arms around me.

Instead I felt Kevin's eyes and irately turned to him, only to be taken by surprise as he smiled and gave the slightest nod of his head. I found that to be more disconcerting than anything else. What did the guy think? That for some unknown reason, we'd become secret compatriots?

"Well here's news that should make you feel better. I've got some information," he revealed.

Kevin was right. I instantly perked up.

"What did you find out?" I asked, dispensing with any formalities.

"Word has it that Sammy was running around complaining about his job to anyone who would listen," Kevin replied.

This was the big scoop that Mr. Secret Agent had to offer? I could have told him that much myself, a few days ago.

"Thanks for all your help," I dryly responded, suddenly wanting nothing more than to go to bed.

"Hey, I'm not done yet," Kevin retorted with a laugh that struck me as far too jovial. "As punishment, Kalahiki was ordered to report to the docks at six A.M. yesterday morning. The same tuna boat he'd just come in on was heading out again for another two-week run. He was ordered to be on it or to hand in his resignation. When Sammy didn't show, the folks at National Marine Fisheries figured that he'd made his decision. No one thought any more of it until the police called with news of his death."

His superiors had been pushing as hard as they could to make him quit. They'd surely known that Sammy wouldn't get back on a boat whose crew had threatened him just a few days ago.

"Did your source also happen to mention that Sammy complained about illegal shark finning going on?" I inquired.

Kevin thoughtfully rubbed his chin. "No. All I heard was that Kalahiki was unhappy with his accommodations and the food being served on the boat."

"And you believe that line of crap?" I asked, ready to tear into him.

Talk about your lame story. Surely, Kalahiki's bosses could have come up with a more creative tale than that. But there was something else that bothered me. Sammy hadn't said he'd been instructed to ship out again so soon. Neither had his mother, and she would surely have known. Once again, I was left to ponder if what I'd been told was true.

"To answer your question, it sounds like the typical line of bullshit to me. Which is exactly why I didn't buy it, but continued to dig deeper," Kevin revealed.

"Okay. So what else did you find out?" I asked, my body beginning to tingle.

Maybe it was the predatory look in his eyes, but I now realized why Kevin had nodded at me. The man was obviously onto something big.

"A tidbit that you're going to love. A friend of mine got hold of Kalahiki's original pathology report, as well as the police record that was later filed. The autopsy showed that while Kalahiki was slashed and killed by shark's teeth, he definitely wasn't attacked by one," Kevin now disclosed.

"You've gotta be kidding," Santou responded, with a low grunt.

"How do you explain that?" I asked, not having the slightest idea what he was talking about.

"Stop and think about it for a minute," Kevin said, squatting in front of me. "What happens when a shark bites down? That action creates a series of semi-circular patterns somewhat akin to a half moon. But the marks found on Kalahiki's body were a sequence of straight slash lines."

He leaned forward with the intensity of an animal preparing to pounce, as I wondered where this was headed.

"The thing is, a shark has both an upper and lower set of teeth, isn't that right?" Kevin asked, beginning to lead me down a logical path.

"Of course," I agreed, and then suddenly realized what he was getting at. "Are you saying that wasn't the case with Sammy?"

"No way, no how," Kevin crowed, nearly bouncing up and down on the pads of his feet. "The problem with your boy is that there was no pattern of matching teeth marks found anywhere on both sides of the body."

"But the wounds . . . I saw them," I insisted, my mind flashing back to the angry gashes that had practically torn Kalahiki's torso in two. "The damage was unbelievable. What else could have done something like that?"

"My guess is that is that it had to be a weapon studded with shark's teeth. Maybe some kind of blade. I actually saw something like it in an exhibit of ancient Hawaiian weapons at the Bishop Museum in Honolulu. One of the most popular devices was a combination knife and war club about the size of a man's palm. The thing was flat and lashed with shark's teeth, each of which was razor sharp," Kevin explained.

He was right. A weapon like that would be incredibly lethal. Especially if the teeth came from a tiger shark. They'd most likely leave a jagged mark closely resembling those made by a serrated-edge blade. Come to think of it, they'd be rather like the wounds that had been on Sammy's body—and, the one that was on my own arm.

I flashed back to the weapon that had been held above my head at Yakimov's. Though I'd only caught a glimpse, the blade had been both oval and flat, perfectly fitting Kevin's description. The more I thought about it, the more convinced I now became that my attacker had to have been Sammy's killer. Which meant that he'd also murdered Stas Yakimov. And since a ritual weapon had been used, I assumed that the assailant was probably Hawaiian.

My hand inched up, covering my wound, as the fear in my chest once again began to expand. I had no doubt that Kevin was correct. Sammy's death hadn't been an accident, but rather a deliberate act of cold-blooded murder. Given a choice, I might have preferred facing down a shark. At least, I'd have had a good idea of what to expect.

"Are the police looking into this?" I asked, struggling to keep a tremor from sneaking into my voice.

Kevin didn't help matters any by resolutely shaking his head.

"Uh-uh. Why should they? After all, the report was deliberately changed to make it appear as if Kalahiki was attacked and killed by a shark."

There was something about this that kept nipping away at me like an annoying mosquito.

"But what about the pathologist? He had to sign off on the report, didn't he?" I pressed, convinced there had to be some checks and balances left in this world.

"That's the easiest part of all," Kevin matter-of-factly replied. "His signature was simply forged."

The puzzle pieces that had begun to fit together now all came raining down upon my head.

"But how can that be? Surely the pathologist would still realize that his report had been altered," I insisted.

Kevin looked at me as though he'd stumbled upon a latter-day Pollyanna. "You've been in this business long enough to know what goes on. How can you remain so naïve?" he said.

I gritted my teeth to keep from screaming. Of course, I knew of all the underhanded maneuvers and dirty dealings that went on. I just continued to hope for something better than what was usually served up. I still had faith in those much-maligned and little-valued twin virtues, justice and decency.

I caught Kevin studying me and had the same reaction that I normally reserve for spiders—my skin began to crawl. Though I couldn't put my finger on it, I knew that something was wrong. Then it hit me.

"How can you possibly know so much about all this?" I fired at him.

Actions of this sort were always buried dark and deep, with as little muss, fuss, and paper trail as possible. The only ones privy to it were those who had been involved.

"I have my sources. Don't ask about them," he responded, and raised a hand to fend off any further questions.

How convenient. Kevin continued to use the old dodge-and-swerve technique. So far, everything I knew about the man consisted of nothing more than smoke and mirrors.

"What I can tell you is that someone pretty high up wanted the paperwork changed. But I wasn't able to find out who it was, or for exactly what reason," Kevin added.

Part of me remained suspicious, while the other half was grateful for even these few crumbs.

"I'm trying damn hard not to butt in here, chere," Jake

chimed in. "But this unauthorized case of yours is driving
me nuts. I know you don't want to hear this, but I'm going to say it anyway. You'd better back off while you still
can. If not for yourself, then at least think of me. I swear
to God, my blood pressure is about to ratchet straight
through the roof," he pretended to joke.

But I knew he was deadly serious.

"He's got a point," Kevin agreed. "There are fights
worth climbing out on a limb for, and others where you
have to use common sense and retreat. Sacrificing yourself
on this one isn't going to do any good."

I wondered if Kevin knew something more than what
he was revealing. Specifically, who was sawing off the
limb to which I was barely clinging.

"Kevin's right. This is a battle you simply can't win,"
Santou advised.

"Anybody can fight a winning battle, but it takes a real
Fish and Wildlife agent to fight a losing one," I morosely
joked.

"That's great if you don't mind getting your ass kicked
and your head handed to you. And that's the best possible
case scenario," Kevin warned. "Gut instinct tells me there
are some pretty nasty people involved in this thing."

Yeah, like that was a real hard reach on his part.

I was suddenly so exhausted that I could barely keep
my eyes open. What was wrong with me, anyway? I already knew the answer, though I'd never admit it out loud.
Eating away at me were depression, frustration, and fear.
Depression at the lack of support from within my own
agency; frustration at continually banging my head
against walls; and fear that I was barreling down a path
that would finally prove to be my undoing.

"Come on, chere. It's time to call it a night," Santou
said, and practically carried me in to bed.

I don't remember getting undressed, although I was

suddenly nude. All I wanted was to mercifully sleep. But that wasn't yet in the cards.

"Listen to me, Rach," Jake murmured, as he stroked my hair. "You asked me not to take on the big waves, and I've been keeping my end of the bargain. But you haven't lived up to yours. You were supposed to fill me in as to what's going on. Remember?"

I didn't respond, but willed myself to stay awake long enough to ask him a question.

"I don't know what Kevin's job used to be, but it turned out that he was crooked, wasn't he? That's why he's no longer working. What happened? Did he serve time in jail?" I guessed, putting Jake on the spot.

His fingers tensed in my hair, and I knew that I'd hit the mark.

"We'll talk about it another night. But no, he didn't do jail time. Let's just say he got caught up in something that he shouldn't have been. Kevin didn't listen to orders and took it upon himself to act in a manner he believed to be correct," Santou said, beginning to sound weary himself.

"What did he do?" I questioned.

"It doesn't matter right now. The upshot was that he sank his career, and nearly lost his life. He reminds me a lot of you, in that sense. That's what scares me. I never know what drives you to such lengths, or how far you'll go."

Neither did I. All I knew was that I seemed to have no choice.

Santou kissed me on the forehead, and I promptly fell asleep.

I'd just closed my eyes when a strange noise suddenly woke me. It was one that I'd heard before. Something was desperately clawing and scrambling its way up a steep cliff of rocks.

The frantic sound clutched at my heart, and tore at my soul, wrapping me in a winding sheet of fear. I kept my eyes tightly closed, hoping whatever it was would eventually go away. But no such luck. The clawing finally stopped, only to be replaced by something far worse. An arctic breeze settled upon me like a shroud. I could scarcely breathe, let alone scream, as frigid fingers danced on my skin and a ghostly breath whispered in my ear.

Rachel, it murmured over and over, until I was entombed in a thin sheet of ice.

That was all I needed to hear. I knew what to expect before I even opened my eyes. Sammy Kalahiki was standing there beside me.

His gaping wounds wept, enveloping him in a layer of blood, as he ever so sadly smiled. Then his bloody corpse slipped beneath the covers and into the bed, where he remained with me for the rest of the night.

I lay there awake, not daring to move, knowing that Sammy's ghost would never leave. We were bound together, forever and ever, as surely as if we'd been married for life.

Eighteen

I woke the next morning and rolled out of bed, relieved to find that Sammy Kalahiki had disappeared with the dawn. But I knew he'd return each night until his soul was finally able to rest.

With that in mind, I quickly showered, dressed, and got ready for work. I fed and walked Spam, played a game of "what will I eat" with Tag-along, and was nearly out the door when my cell phone rang.

"Porter here," I answered, not yet in the mood for polite conversation.

"*Here* is exactly where I don't want you," Jaba the Hut snapped. "You're giving me one hell of a massive headache, Porter. But we're about to change all that."

Uh-oh. Something told me that my morning bowl of Rice Krispies was about to snap, crackle, and pop right in my face.

"High-level calls are coming in, and they're all complaints about you," Pryor briskly broke the news.

"Are you talking about Fish and Wildlife? Or, perhaps a different federal agency whose nose is out of joint?" I countered, ever the suave diplomat.

"That's very clever, Porter," Pryor retorted. "In fact, you're so damn clever that you've finagled yourself right into a temporary duty assignment. Don't bother to come to work today, but instead start packing. Because you leave at the end of the week for two glorious months in Guam."

"Guam!" I exclaimed in dismay. That was the Pacific equivalent of being sent to Siberia. "Why? What's going on?"

"What's going on is that you'll be somewhere else other than here. You're so interested in invasive species that I've come up with a little job for you. Guam is inundated with alien brown tree snakes that are killing off all the local wildlife. There are about thirteen thousand of the suckers on every square mile of the island. The snakes are easy to identify. They're long, brown, and they bite. I want you to do something about the problem," Pryor ordered, nearly chuckling with glee.

The son of a bitch. I was obviously being shipped off to nowhere land as my own particular form of punishment.

"This will get you out of my hair until things cool down around here. Consider it a favor. D.C. isn't involved yet, which means I'm saving your neck. But unless this shark nonsense stops right now, we're both likely to lose our jobs. Who knows? Maybe prying those snakes out of trees will help you appreciate your posting in Hawaii a little more," Jaba proposed.

I got off the phone feeling more despondent and frustrated than ever. The only difference was that anger now replaced my fear. It was clear that I'd inched close enough to make some very powerful people extremely nervous. I should have known that Pryor would crumble under pressure. Still, I hadn't expected to be exiled.

"What's the matter, chere? You're looking awfully glum

this morning. And why aren't you at work yet? Do you have the day off?" Santou asked, padding into the kitchen in only his jockey shorts.

I gazed at the man and nearly burst into tears. No way did I want to leave him for two months. But it was already a done deal.

"How would you like to visit the lovely island of Guam for a while?" I dourly suggested.

"Thanks, but no thanks. You're kidding, right?" Santou responded, with a laugh.

I gave him a look that made it clear this wasn't a joke. "I'm afraid not."

"Oh, Lord. What happened now?" he asked, wrapping his arms around me.

"I'm being sent over there on temporary duty assignment to atone for my sins," I succinctly summed up.

"For how long?" Jake questioned, not seeming to be very pleased.

"A couple of months. Apparently, I'm getting too close for comfort to whatever's going on," I revealed.

If I'd been expecting sympathy, I was in for a shock.

"Pryor's doing the right thing. In fact, you're probably getting off damn easy," Jake responded.

I opened my mouth to let loose a rant, only to be stopped.

"What's more important? One lousy case that you have no business sticking your nose into in the first place? Or continuing on with your career? I mean it, chere. Be practical. Which will help you achieve your goal? You're not a one-woman show. You can't save every species that's on the planet. Remember what we talked about last night? You've got to carefully pick and choose your battles," he lectured.

Bullshit. I stewed in silence for a moment, and said

nothing. Not because I didn't want to fight, but rather because the grown-up thing to do was to think things through before I blew up and went ballistic.

Guam. Great. All I needed was a black-and-white-striped prison uniform, along with a ball and chain shackled to my leg. Jake must have been thinking along the same lines.

"Come on, chere. It's not as bad as all that. I'll fly over to see you on visiting days," he jested, by way of cheering me up.

"Very funny," I sullenly retorted.

"Don't worry. The time will go by fast. You'll see. Besides, there are other cases to be made. Ones that are probably far better. But forget about all that for now. Kevin and I are going to hit the waves this morning. Why don't you come outside and watch us for a while? You can sit on the beach and admire my physique," Jake playfully suggested.

I sulked in the house as he and Kevin got their act together and left, taking Spam along with them. My standoff lasted all of ten minutes before I became deadly bored. Grabbing a tube of sunscreen, I headed down the beach to join in the festivities.

A line of cars had already formed up and down the road, their drivers urgently searching for anything resembling a parking space. They planned to either surf the waves themselves or sit on the beach and watch the show. That was the thing about living along the North Shore. Part of me felt smugly elitist, while my other half felt as if I were hanging out with a fraternity of cool jocks.

I found Spam, already sprawled on the ground, and plopped down beside him. His tail wagged back and forth in the sand, wiping away any bird tracks and imperfections. Santou caught sight of me and waved from his slice of Shangri-la, a surfboard bobbing in the sea.

I jabbed my toes deep into the sand with the dogged determination of ten tiny spades, intent on building my own bit of paradise out of something a little more solid. I soon tired of that and followed a bird coasting along the water, like an avian surfer, before it disappeared behind a wave.

I spent most of the day sitting on the beach, stuffing myself with junk food. If this was the life of a beach bum, it didn't seem half bad. Maybe Guam would prove to be "a good thing," in the words of Martha Stewart. Yeah, right. Who was I kidding? Try as I might, I felt as if I were living under a black cloud.

I barely paid attention as Santou and Kevin coasted down one breaker after another, sometimes as graceful as a pair of dancers, sometimes as clumsy as two sloppy drunks. By late afternoon, my mind was on a more important matter: the fact that this wasn't simply a throwaway case but rather an entire species at risk.

Perhaps it was the fact that I had too much time on my hands, but the longer I sat there, the angrier I became. What was wrong with people, anyway? Why was it so difficult for them to understand, or care, about another living, breathing creature? It couldn't have been any more clear that unless something was soon done about it, sharks could very well vanish.

A breeze blew across the water, momentarily turning the waves as choppy as rippling muscles. I sat there looking at the swells and was reminded of Stas Yakimov's washboard abs.

One of the things that bothered me was that I'd found so little evidence at his place. The intruder had obviously been searching for something important when I'd walked in. But what could it have been? The question continued to haunt me nearly as much as Sammy Kalahiki's ghost.

Vinnie and I had both carefully combed through the house. There was always the chance that Vinnie had stumbled upon something more and decided to stay mum. The other possibility was that whatever evidence existed still remained hidden behind those walls.

A car backfired and tore off with a growl, catching me by surprise. Funny how such a simple thing can set off a chain reaction of thoughts. I now realized where further evidence might possibly be concealed. Why hadn't I come up with this before? Stas had been as crazy as he was clever.

I raced back to our place without waving good-bye or leaving a note. Instead, I jumped into my Ford and took off, driving straight to Stas Yakimov's house.

I arrived to find his residence neatly wrapped in yellow tape and closed up tight. It clearly announced to passersby that the house had been the scene of a crime. All was as quiet as a grave as I walked through the front gate.

There were no howls of dogs or grunting and trilling of lizards coming from the backyard. Neither were there calls of *Spartacus* to stop an attack—only the specter of puzzled chameleons bobbing their heads as they pondered their fate. I proceeded around to the back, having little interest in the house itself.

It felt as if I'd entered a cemetery the moment I set foot on the grounds. The headstones were the pens in which Yakimov's dogs had resided; the footstones, a few scattered wire cages that had been left. Even the mobile of pit bull bones sounded pitifully hollow, giving more of a whimper than a snarl, as the skeletal remains swung dejectedly in the ghost of a breeze.

I wasted no time, but headed directly to the cinderblock bunker where Yakimov's cougar had been housed. The padlock was no longer on the door, and the cat had been removed, probably clawing and screeching all the way, to a feline sanctuary. However, traces still remained of its former presence. Mounds of scat littered the floor, along with a chunk of raw meat laden with maggots. It lay like a decomposing corpse beside a heap of bones. I held my breath and walked inside hoping to find something more.

Dealers in South Florida were notorious for maintaining cougars to guard their drug stash. I figured that strategy would work equally well when it came to safeguarding anything else. After all, who in their right mind would willingly walk into a pen holding a growling, pissed-off mountain lion? That made this bunker the perfect hiding spot.

A steel bar had been driven into the concrete floor. Attached to its top was an iron ring and a chain. Stas must have somehow hooked the cat to it like a leash. I couldn't imagine that any secrets would be buried beneath the poured cement floor, unless perhaps for Jimmy Hoffa's body. Other than that, the cage was bare. All except for a large wooden perch that had been suspended off the ground.

The perch was supported by heavy metal brackets on either end, and hung like a shelf on the wall. I figured this was probably where Yakimov's cougar had slept. It was only upon closer inspection that I saw it wasn't one piece of wood. Rather, the perch had been constructed from two separate boards.

Each board had been carefully cut so that it measured the same length and width. After that, they'd been placed one on top of the other, just like a sandwich. That should have made it all the easier to dismantle the perch. However, I found myself struggling to lift off the top plank.

The wood landed on the floor with a thud. But the battle proved worthwhile as I caught sight of a manila envelope that was fastened to the bottom board.

It was an early Christmas in Hawaii as my hands anxiously tore at the tape, fending off splinters as they pried the envelope loose. They nearly tripped over each other in a ten-digit race, eager to liberate the contents and reach their goal.

I finally yanked the envelope free and ripped open the sealed flap. Then my hand impatiently dove inside, only to find there was nothing but photographs. Wouldn't you know? It was probably Yakimov's secret stash of porn. If so, the pictures could have used better lighting. The images appeared to be mostly dark and grainy.

I walked outside the bunker and into the sun, hoping to get a better view. It proved to be a smart move. There were no naked bodies, but rather something of much more interest. The pictures were of the same man that had confronted me the night before, Michael Leung, and appeared to have been taken inside a warehouse. My pulse promptly joined in the race. This could very well be the interior of Leung's dockside business, Capital City Fish Products. I swiftly began to shuffle through the rest of the photographs.

There were some in which Leung was standing beside a woman. The only problem was, I couldn't make out her face. Then it dawned on me. The shots must have been snapped with a concealed camera. Neither one seemed to be the least bit aware they were being photographed.

It wasn't until I flipped through a few more images that I began to understand what I held in my hands. I now realized why the photographs had been hidden. In the background of each were hundreds of shark fins laid out on drying racks. No wonder Leung had rushed outside to stop me from snooping around his building. But what I still didn't get was how he'd known my name.

There were still a couple of derelict photos left inside the envelope, and I pulled them out to take a quick gander. They were all pretty much the same: snapshots of Leung and the mystery woman standing in his warehouse. That is, until I reached the end of the stack. Stas had saved the best for last. He'd finally managed to get a clear shot of the woman's face.

Something about her seemed incredibly familiar. I studied the image, trying to figure out what it could be. The woman was Asian, had short dark hair, and a gaze as sharp as high-heeled stilettos, with a mouth as firmly set as the concrete floor of Rocky's bunker. It was clearly apparent that she was used to getting her own way and controlling things.

Where in the hell had I seen her before? Damn the fact that I was getting older. My memory wasn't what it used to be.

No excuses, Porter. Come on, think!

Oh shit.

A near electrical shock raced through me as I suddenly realized exactly who I was looking at. It was none other than Hawaii's representative to Washington, the honorable Senator Shirley Chang.

Dear Lord. Could this be the high-level government official that Sammy had alluded to during our one and only meeting? My head began to spin as another thought hit me. I was willing to bet that these pictures had been taken by Sammy. The images had the same poor quality as those I'd found inside the hat box.

Perhaps he'd tried to document what he'd found at the docks the night before he died. If so, this could very well be the evidence that he'd brought along to Ka'ena Point.

I suddenly felt deathly cold and glanced around, wondering if his ghost was anywhere in sight. But there was no sign of Sammy. Instead, Senator Shirley Chang's image continued to glare up at me.

It was true. Chang had her fingers deep into every facet of the Hawaiian fishing industry, and pulled whatever strings were necessary. However, these pictures implied that a U.S. senator was embroiled in the illegal shark-fin trade. It was an accusation that would be difficult to prove, regardless of photographs. I needed more concrete evidence, along with a good reason as to why she was involved.

I continued to stare at Chang's image, as if it might telepathically provide the information. A closer look revealed that her hair was stylishly coifed, and she wore makeup even when visiting a dingy warehouse. I also noticed that her clothes weren't the beat-up jeans, polo shirts, and sneakers that I normally donned, but expensively tailored and chic garments.

The senator was probably a vain woman. She also loved to see stories about herself and all her good works in print. Maybe that was her Achilles' heel. I asked myself, why bother to skulk around, trying to uncover information, when I could go straight to the source? I pulled out my cell phone and morphed into Lois Lane, girl reporter.

"Senator Chang's office," a female voice pleasantly answered the phone.

"Hello. This is Rebecca Whiting. I'm a reporter with the *Honolulu Bulletin*, and we're planning to run a feature on all the things that Senator Chang has done for the state," I said, lying through my teeth.

"Oh, how wonderful. The senator will be so pleased," the woman said, sounding truly delighted.

"However, this is also a human-interest piece. Would Senator Chang possibly have a few minutes available to answer one or two questions?" I asked.

"I'm sorry, but the senator is visiting the mainland for a couple of weeks. However, I'm her secretary, and would be happy to set up an appointment for when she returns," her employee responded.

"That's all right. I'll try her at the office in D.C." I

replied, impatient to learn whatever I could right now.

"That won't do any good. The senator is on vacation and out of reach. By the way, I know almost everyone at the paper. Your name doesn't sound familiar. What did you say was it again?" her secretary inquired.

"Rebecca," I answered, purposely leaving off the last name. "I'm new at the *Bulletin*. That's why I'm so anxious to get started on this profile. I'm sorry. I should have asked your name as well."

"It's Christy," she said, in a friendly tone.

"Well Christy, I know how much everyone appreciates what the senator has done for Hawaii. Gee, I'd love to get started on this story right away. Do you suppose you could possibly answer a few simple questions for her?" I plaintively asked.

"I don't know if I can help, but I'll certainly give it a shot," she agreed, willing to try.

"Maybe you can tell me a little about the senator's childhood," I suggested. "Such as, where did she grow up?"

"Senator Chang was raised right here in Hawaii," came the snappy response, as proudly as if it were a badge of honor.

"And what about her parents? Were they born here, also?" I prodded.

"Her mother was, but her father originally came from Hong Kong," Christy replied.

"Really? Does she still have family over there?" I asked, intrigued by her answer.

"Now that you mention it, I seem to remember hearing that her brother works for some sort of company in Hong Kong," she revealed.

My adrenaline kicked into gear, telling me that I was on the right track.

"Oops. There's another call coming in. I really need to go," Christy said.

"Just one last question," I pleaded. "Is Chang the senator's maiden name?"

"No. Her full maiden name would be Shirley Marie Ting. Sorry, but we're going to have to talk another time," she anxiously told me, and got off the phone.

I barely heard her hang up. My mind was somewhere else, furiously racing a mile a minute. Ting had been one of the three names scribbled on that piece of paper inside Sammy's shoebox, along with those of Leung and Yakimov. It had also been on the document I'd found at Stas's house. S. M. Ting and G. C. Leung had been listed as two of the officers for Magic Dragon Restaurants, Inc.

My heart sped up, keeping pace with my brain, as I now began to put two and two together. Clues were pointing to the fact that Senator Chang, formerly Shirley Marie Ting, was in business with the Leungs. Yakimov probably knew about this, and must have been blackmailing either the senator, Leung, or possibly both. Most likely, that's what had led to Stas's death.

I jumped, caught off guard when my cell phone rang. Sometimes I hated the damn thing. In addition, I wasn't yet willing to admit that last night's phone call had unnerved me.

"Hello?" I warily answered, wondering if Christy had caller ID. Perhaps she was phoning back to find out my true identity.

"I got the shit kicked out of me last night, and I want you to do something about it!" Rasta Boy irately demanded.

I was almost relieved to hear the sound of his whiny voice. But if he expected any aid, he'd have to get in line behind Pryor and his damn tree snakes. In fact, I was tempted to give Dwayne's attacker a medal of honor.

"You've got a lot of nerve asking for my help. As I recall, you almost got me killed after our last meeting," I replied.

"What are you talking about?" he shrieked in my ear. "I'm your golden boy, your informant. Remember?"

"What I remember is that you set me up to be attacked by Yakimov's dogs," I reminded him.

There was a moment of silence, during which I could almost hear Dwayne's brain cells popping as he tried to figure out his next move.

"Aw, come on. You can take a joke, can't you, Porter? I knew you'd be able to handle a couple of dogs, no sweat. No harm done, right?" he asked, attempting to smooth things over.

I sighed, knowing it was useless to expect any kind of apology.

"Do you know who attacked you?" I asked.

"Yeah. Some big-ass ugly dude from New York, with enough glop on his hair to start a grease fire. He said that Stas had been killed and I'd be next, unless I told him what he wanted to know. I've been trying to call Yakimov ever since, but the lunkhead won't answer his phone."

There was a pause, as if Dwayne was afraid to ask the question. "Is it true? Is Stas really dead?" he inquired, with a note of desperation in his voice.

"Yes. He was killed yesterday," I confirmed.

"That's it! I want federal protection right now," Dwayne wailed into the telephone.

"Calm down and tell me exactly what this man wanted," I instructed, already aware that his attacker must have been Vinnie.

"Who the hell knows? All he kept blabbering on about was Viagra. Friggin' Viagra. Shit. I told him I could get hold of a coupla hot babes who'd make him forget that he'd ever needed the stuff. But the guy's a complete drug freak," Dwayne insisted.

I figured it took one to know one.

"What did you tell him?" I pressed.

"That I didn't have any idea what the hell he was talking about. That's when he began wailing on me like his own private punching bag."

I actually felt bad Vinnie had beat him up, but was relieved to hear that Dwayne hadn't told him anything.

"Then after rearranging my face, this moron wants to know who Stas has been dealing with besides pet stores," Dwayne continued. "Like, he couldn't have asked me that in the first place? I told him the only guy I knew was some Chinese dude by the name of Michael Leung."

Damn it!

"One more thing. Do you have any idea how this guy managed to hunt you down?" I asked, having purposely made sure not to give Vinnie his name.

"Yeah. Stas had me listed as an employee in his address book. This goon must have lifted it when he went to Yakimov's house," Dwayne revealed.

So *that's* what Vinnie had found and not told me about. A searing pain shot through my stomach with the realization that he'd also be able to find Michael Leung. I needed to reach Vinnie immediately and try to steer him off track.

"We'll talk more later. I have to go now," I told him.

"Hey, wait a minute, bitch! How am I supposed to work as a beachboy with two black eyes, a broken nose, and a fat lip?" Rasta Boy angrily demanded.

It was nice to know that some things never change.

"Don't worry. It'll make you stand out from all of the other pretty boys," I said by way of consolation, and hung up.

Then I phoned Vinnie's hotel, only to be informed he'd left a message that he wasn't to be disturbed. That had to mean he was still in his room. I decided the smart thing to do was to pay him a visit. I stashed the photos in my Explorer and gunned the engine, setting course for Vinnie's digs in Honolulu.

I got as far as the freeway before slamming on my brakes and coming to a dead halt. This frigging island and it's crazy bumper-to-bumper traffic! Rush hour seemed to run from 6 A.M. until nine o'clock every night. What was with this place? I'd have taken a water buffalo over a car any day. I drummed my fingers against the steering wheel, pretending it was a Tommy gun. If nothing else, it helped take my mind off the sharp, stabbing pain that had hold of my stomach.

I finally calmed down enough to collect my thoughts. I needed to buy time. There had to be a way to convince Vinnie that Leung wasn't his Viagra connection. That would give me a chance to nab the guy myself.

My cell phone rang, momentarily taking me away from my task. It was probably Rasta Boy with another one of his demands.

"Hello?" I answered.

I was greeted by a voice that was a combination of raw gasoline, cheap booze, and gravel.

"Look at your watch and tell me what time it is," Sharkfin Dave commanded, sounding like a human cement mixer.

Great. As if the traffic weren't enough, I was now being treated like some down-and-out drunk's Gal Friday. What did this guy think? That I was his own personal timekeeper?

I held back the sarcasm, and glanced at the clock in my car.

"It's seven P.M.," I responded, all the while inching up on a Volvo's rear end.

Sharkfin Dave chuckled, as if at his own private joke. "I

just got word that the *Magic Dragon* will be coming in later on."

"At night?" I asked, in surprise.

I'd always taken it for granted that fishing boats docked during the daytime.

"Sure. Any state boys assigned to the docks always vamoose by five o'clock, and there are only three National Marine Fisheries enforcement agents for the entire Hawaiian islands. Not that it matters. They're rarely around here anyway."

No wonder shark fins were streaming into Oahu on a steady basis. There wasn't anything resembling a wall of law enforcement plaguing the smugglers.

"Yeah, night's the perfect time to do whatever you want," Sharkfin Dave continued. "What say you pick us up some Chink food and bring it out here with you? Get me some moo shu pork, beef fried rice, sweet-and-sour chicken, and a couple of eggrolls. It's been days since I've had a good meal. Oh, yeah. And make sure you grab a bottle of booze while you're at it."

The pain in my stomach not only intensified, but also grew queasy. However, I wasn't about to turn the man down. Not when I was faced with both Guam and Vinnie Bertucci as ticking time bombs.

"I'm stuck in traffic, but I'll be there as soon as I can," I responded, and hung up.

Nineteen

I turned my attention back to crawling up every car's rear end. No way was I going to be late and miss the biggest break that I might ever get in this case.

Pulling off the nearest exit, I stopped at the first Chinese restaurant that I found. Then I dashed into a grocery store for a container of Mylanta and hit a liquor store for a bottle of scotch. Soon I was back in my Explorer and battling traffic. Only now, I had some antacid to chug-a-lug.

I traveled along Nimitz Boulevard thinking about all that had taken place that day. So deep was I in thought that I nearly ran over a bum who jumped in front of my Ford. My stomach churned into action as I slammed on the brakes.

The bum was Sharkfin Dave, looking as suave as ever. Only tonight, he was wearing a T-shirt decorated with sharks. All had their jaws wide open and were chasing each other's tails. How appropriate.

"What's the matter with you? Didn't you see me waving like a goddamn lunatic for you to stop?" he demanded, opening the passenger door.

"I didn't expect to see you walking along the street," I countered in my own defense.

"With the way you're driving, no one is safe on the road," he grumbled.

Sharkfin climbed inside and closed the door.

"What are you doing out here, anyway?" I questioned. "Why aren't you waiting for me down at the docks?"

"It's just a couple of blocks from here, and I figured this was a safe place to meet. This way, we won't be seen by anyone."

Good thinking—all except for the forty or fifty other cars that were on the road.

I began to turn toward the piers, only to be stopped.

"Keep on going," Sharkfin directed. "There's a little park directly across from the docks. We can sit in the car and eat our food over there."

He didn't wait for our arrival, but dug into the bags and pulled out the scotch. Twisting off the cap, he up-ended the bottle, took a deep slug, and smacked his lips.

"Now that's what I call a before-dinner nip," he announced, and then pounced on the eggrolls.

My stomach protested, and I held my breath, trying to stave off the smell.

"Turn in here," he ordered, leading me to an isolated area.

The park was deserted, but for my Ford. What it did provide was a killer view of the waterfront. Sharkfin Dave inhaled his food as I watched container ships slip in and out of port.

"None of those are the *Magic Dragon*, are they?" I anxiously questioned him, not wanting to miss my opportunity due to a carton of moo shu pork.

"Don't get your panties all in a knot," Sharkfin admonished. "It won't be in for a while yet. Why don't you relax and help me eat some of this stuff?"

I looked at the food and took another sip of Mylanta.

"Got an upset stomach, huh?" he responded.

"Yeah, something like that," I replied, figuring it was probably the beginnings of an ulcer.

"Best thing for that is to take a nip of scotch," he instructed.

What the hell. I took his advice. I was mid-gulp when my cell phone rang.

"Why don't you turn that damn thing off?" Dave suggested, sullenly glaring at it.

Good idea. I didn't need Santou calling to inquire where I was, and what I was doing.

Over and out, I thought, and killed the phone for now.

Then I flicked on my flashlight and began to clean up Sharkfin's mess. Its beam highlighted numerous scratches and teethmarks that festooned both his arms.

"How'd you get those?" I asked, pointing to them.

"Oh, they're from handling shark fins and crap. Those fins are sharp as hell, especially when they're dry, which is why it's important to wear gloves. And that skin of theirs is tough as a mother. It's a lotta work ripping those things off, even with a machete or knife," Sharkfin divulged. "As for the teeth marks? Sharks can spin around on boat decks like damn rodeo broncos while you're trying to cut the fins off of 'em. It's just as well I'm not doing it anymore. That was fun when I was young, dumb, and full of come."

Funny. He'd told me only last night that he'd been out catching sharks just a week ago.

"Nah, I haven't been out on a finning expedition ever since it was outlawed," he reiterated, as if reading my mind. "I was just Charlie Hong's office manager."

Bullshit. Those scratches appeared to be fairly fresh. Sharkfin Dave seemed to be setting things up to take any heat off himself.

He burped and picked a sliver of beef from between his teeth. "We should probably head back about now."

I turned on the engine and pointed my Ford toward the

docks. Sharkfin guided the way to a distant pier, where we parked in the shadows. It was just about ten o'clock.

"I've never been on this pier before. Are you sure this is the right spot?" I said anxiously.

"Shh. Just take a look over there," he muttered, and intently stared ahead.

I pulled a pair of binoculars from the backseat and followed his finger to its target.

There it was: the *Magic Dragon*. The boat was illuminated by a few dim lights.

Every ghost ship needs a crew. This had one, too. I watched as a man proceeded to slide a large bale of shark fins down along a ramp. They were tightly wired together in a four-by-four-foot bundle.

"That bale represents about two hundred dead sharks," Dave related, as if narrating a film. "And it probably weighs anywhere between a hundred-twenty and two hundred pounds, depending on the size of those fins."

I could think of little else at the moment other than making my own documentary. Grabbing my camera, I rapidly began to take pictures. The entire off-loading process was witnessed through my camera's view finder and telephoto lens. The bundles were thrown onto a large wooden pallet as I proceeded to snap away.

"Are you getting a whiff of that?" Sharkfin asked, sniffing the air with the fervor of a crazed bloodhound.

"God, yes. It smells awful," I replied, my stomach rock-and-rolling to the stench.

"That's the ammonia inside them," he explained. "Sharks will devour just about any damn thing."

My shutter continued to click as a forklift raised the pallet and drove it to the back of a container. From there, a crew member grabbed hold of the bales with a gaffe and stacked them inside the truck. I watched as the procedure was repeated over and over, until the twenty-foot receptacle was finally filled and the cargo doors had slammed shut. After that, one of the men slapped on some sort of seal.

"What's he doing?" I asked, not having the slightest idea.

"Putting a Customs tag on the container," Sharkfin revealed, with a snicker.

"But tags are only supposed to be applied by a Customs agent after an official inspection has taken place," I blurted out.

"No kidding? Well, how do you like that?" Dave sarcastically responded. "Leung's a pretty smart guy, with good connections. He gets a bunch of those tags and has one put on each of his containers. That way, no one bothers to check inside if they're ever stopped while driving back to his warehouse. Everything's nice and official."

I watched as the three crew members jumped into the truck and began to drive off. I quickly turned on the Ford's ignition.

"Stay right here," Sharkfin ordered.

"But aren't we going to lose them?" I asked, in dismay.

"Don't worry. I know where they're going," he responded.

We waited about five minutes before Sharkfin gave the okay. It felt as if my Ford didn't need to be told, but drove straight to the warehouse area and parked in the same spot as last night. Then we got out and stood in front of the locked gate.

"You don't happen to have a key to this thing, do you?" I inquired.

"Nah. Mikey's hoping I'll get locked out one night and won't be able to make it back over with my bum leg."

That's what I was concerned about.

"And can you?" I asked.

"Just watch," Sharkfin said, with a wink.

He scrambled up the wire fence with the proficiency of a monkey.

"Follow me and be quiet," he instructed, as I landed with my camera on the other side.

I played hopscotch among the blood-tainted puddles as we drew closer to Leung's warehouse. The container truck sat stolidly in front, having already been unpacked.

"There aren't any windows in the building. How am I supposed to see what's going on?" I complained, sorely tempted to crash their party.

"Like I said before, just stay with me and try to keep your yap shut," Sharkfin commanded, and limped ahead.

It took all my self-control not to break into a giggle. Slap an eyepatch on him, and Sharkfin Dave would have been a real pirate.

I followed him around to the back of the warehouse.

"There's your window," he said, and pointed to one that was about ten feet off the ground.

Terrific. A lot of good that did me.

"What's the matter? You got some kind of problem?" he asked with a grin.

"Yeah. How am I supposed to get up there?"

"Well, you don't look like any kind of angel to me. So, I guess you're going to need a ladder," he astutely observed.

"And do you happen to have one handy?" I retorted cynically. I was just about ready to jump out of my skin. Who knew what was taking place in there by now?

"No. But Mikey does," he said, and pointed to a ladder that lay like a snake in the grass.

A loud buzzing from inside masked any noise as we lifted the ladder and carefully placed it against the warehouse wall. Then I swiftly climbed up, not wanting to miss a thing.

The window stood slightly ajar. I realized why as the stench of ammonia sinuously wafted through and smacked me in the nose. The opening helped to air out the building.

I peered down at the spectacle below. All three men wore respirator masks to protect them from the fumes. One crew member was busy sorting the fins into piles while another worked at a table with a large bandsaw. It looked like a scene from *The Texas Chainsaw Massacre*, only Hawaiian style, as shark body parts were fed beneath the rotating blade. The buzz of the saw severed the air, setting my nerves on edge, as excess meat was trimmed from the fins.

A third man lay the newly cleaned fins out on racks identical to those that had been in the pictures. In fact, the place looked exactly as it had in Sammy's photographs, except for one thing: Senator Chang and Michael Leung were missing.

I tried to curtail my shooting so that I didn't run out of film. But I found it hard to control myself. The men finally solved the problem for me. They stopped their work at 2 A.M. and locked up for the night. Only then did I leave my perch and climb down to find Sharkfin Dave stretched out on the ground. He was snoring up a storm, sleeping off the bottle of scotch. I was just glad that the sound hadn't tipped the men off.

"Hey, get up. Everyone's gone," I said, and roused him with my foot.

Sharkfin woke up, snorting like a startled pig.

"Great. Then I can go back to sleep. Nighty night," he said and laid his head back down again.

"Not so fast," I told him. "I want to sneak into the place."

"Aw, what the hell for?" he protested. "You've been up there for hours. Haven't you seen enough yet?"

"No. And after coming this far, it would be crazy to

leave without getting the pictures I need. But don't worry. I know how to jimmy the lock," I replied.

"A helluva lotta good that'll do you. Leung's been turning on the alarm ever since your friend broke in," Sharkfin revealed.

A tsunami of pain rushed through my insides and gave a good twist, so that I flung my arms around my waist to keep from doubling over.

"You never told me it was definitely Sammy that broke into the building," I gasped, hoping the discomfort would soon go away.

"That's 'cause you never asked," Sharkfin retorted. "All you wanted to know was if I'd spotted the kid."

So that was how this game was being played.

"Did Leung catch him?" I shot back.

The pain retreated, and I wiped a trace of sweat from my brow.

"What do you think? Of course he did. Just not right then and there," Dave answered with a sneer.

"Then *you* must have been the one who tipped off Leung," I assumed, beginning to feel sick with suspicion.

I had no doubt that Sharkfin would sell me out in a New York minute.

"Of course not," Dave demurred. "I already told you. I want to even the score for what he did to my boss. It's just that Leung knows everything that goes on in this place."

Sharkfin was definitely doing his best to scare me away. It only made me all the more determined to get inside the warehouse.

"I'll take my chances," I obstinately told him.

Sharkfin gazed at me, hacked up a spitball, and then wiped his mouth with the back of his hand. "Aw, what the hell. I know the code. I'll shut the damn thing off for you."

My own inner alarm system instantly kicked in. "Why would Leung trust you with information like that?"

"Well, I'm living here and don't have a job. So Mikey's paying me a couple of bucks to keep an eye on the place. He had to give me the code in case the damn thing went off. Pretty funny, huh? Turns out, I'm a dick just like you. And that's exactly what I intend to do, is to guard this warehouse. Which means, I'll stay out here and keep watch while you go inside and take a look around," he said, with a wink.

I pulled a twenty from my pocket and gave it to him. It was all I had after paying for food and booze. I just hoped it would be enough to keep Sharkfin happy over the course of the next few minutes.

He snatched the bill from my fingers, muttered a thanks, and hobbled around to the front of the building. I followed to where a security pad was mounted next to the door. A solid red light on its face plainly warned away intruders. Sharkfin glanced about, as if checking to see that the coast was clear. Then he swiftly punched in four numbers. The red light immediately turned green, giving the okay.

"All right, go on in. Just don't take too long," Dave advised, as he unlocked the entrance. "And if you hear a knock, try to hide damn quick."

I impatiently nodded, the words flying past me in a blur, as I stepped inside the warehouse. I barely heard the door close, so focused was my attention on the bizarre scene ahead.

A few lights had been left on, giving the place an eerie glow. However, the first thing to hit me was the stench. The interior reeked of fish guts and blood, the odor reaching so deep inside that bile rose in my throat. I held my breath and tried hard not to gag, but the desire to throw up was nearly overwhelming.

Then there was the ammonia itself. My eyes began to itch and burn, following that with a bevy of tears. It was as if I were a mourner at a dearly departed friend's funeral. I quickly looked around and spotted a respirator mask. Snatching it off its hook, I slipped the guard over my nose and mouth. Only then did I begin to examine the room.

Electric heaters glowed, their coils burning as bright red as hot coals as they hummed a monotonous tune. Giant fans assisted the process by blowing warm air all about, transforming the interior into a virtual hothouse.

A number of boxes stood stacked in one corner, and I walked over to investigate further. Each was tightly wrapped in clear plastic, and had an airbill attached on top. Their destinations were all the same: Magic Dragon Products in Hong Kong. I knew that nestled inside were dried shark fins with their whispered promise of health, wealth, and happiness.

But something far more disturbing now caught my eye. It was a close-up view of dismembered fins that had been formed into piles. There appeared to be millions of them heaped together like trophies. I was both appalled and drawn to it.

To think such magnificent creatures had been reduced to just this: five little fins that had been hacked off of their bodies. Each triangular piece of flesh was classified according to type and size. There were dorsal, pectoral, pelvic, anal, and caudal fins. Some were so small that clearly, they had been sliced off of juveniles. Their tiny piles could easily have been mistaken for a mound of shriveled Frito-Lay chips.

I stared in growing horror at the mountain of fins and realized it was nothing less than genocide.

Picking up a fin, I instantly sliced my finger—its surface was as rough as sandpaper, its edge as sharp as a knife. The membrane fell from my hand back onto the pile, where it lay like a corpse stained with a drop of my blood.

I sucked my finger dry and then went to work, turning everything I saw into pictures. While neither Fish and Wildlife nor the National Marine Fisheries Service might be interested in the case, I knew of an entity that most definitely would be. This had all the earmarks of a bombshell story to be eaten up by the press.

I was so involved in snapping photographs that I rarely lowered the camera from my eyes, but simply stepped from one pile of evidence to the next. That is until Michael Leung unexpectedly appeared in my lens. He wasn't alone, but held a knife close to his face, its blade studded with jagged teeth, each of which dripped with blood.

I didn't stop to think, but instinctively snapped the photograph. That brought a smile to Leung's lips, as if he were privy to a joke I didn't know. Then it hit me. Perhaps this had been the last image that Sammy had also viewed through his camera. And I suddenly realized where I'd seen that same weapon before, hovering above me at Stas Yakimov's house. Kevin had been correct. The murder weapon used had been a shark-tooth knife. It seemed to whisper mesmerizingly, *You're going to be next. You're going to be next.*

The camera dropped like dead weight to my side, and I began to sway, woozy from the heat, the stench of the fish, and sheer fear. All the while, my eyes remained glued to Leung's, wondering how he'd managed to sneak inside so quietly—not wanting to speculate on what might have happened to Sharkfin Dave.

My thoughts raced to the gun tucked into the back of my pants when a noise crept across the room. Perhaps that was Sharkfin even now. But it was as if Leung could read my mind, his smile growing ever more sinister.

"I'm afraid Dave won't be able to help you any more tonight. He's just become food for the fishes. Too bad. I'll miss him. But then again, he never could seem to hold on to a job."

My hand grabbed my .38 and began to pull it out when a pain, powerful as a train, slammed into the back of my head. A roar swept me off my feet, and bright lights popped in the air all around, like strands of cheap flash-bulbs. Then I began to float, carried on a billowy cloud, as everything was swallowed up by a tidal wave of darkness.

Twenty

A hard bump woke me. Something solid rammed against my arm, as if I were being jostled about on a New York subway car. My sight was blurry and my head hurt enough to explode. I swallowed some saltwater and began to cough and choke. It was then I became aware of the wet and cold. I was by myself, floating in the middle of the ocean.

My vision cleared, and I caught sight of a shadow of movement passing off to my right. A dark shape was gliding nearby, its pace as leisurely deliberate as an unhurried lover. It looked to be some kind of miniature submarine, perhaps fifteen feet in length and weighing half a ton—until the damn thing circled around and came back toward me. That's when I realized it was a steel torpedo of muscle; one with thick, broad pectorals, and a dorsal fin that slashed through the water like a knife.

I held my breath, my heart thumping wildly, as it passed by once more only to return closer and faster this time. It was then I felt another bump. I looked down to see that a wisp of blood had begun to ooze from me. I stared in disbelief. A shark had taken a bite from my arm.

Perhaps if I closed my eyes and prayed, it would simply

go away. I shut them for as long as I dared, before finally sneaking a peek. No such luck. The shark was still there, as if purposely taunting me. It clearly took pleasure in my fear, for its giant scythe of a tail now propelled it forward, rapidly approaching for the kill.

I would have screamed; I would have cried. However, I had no choice but to die as the shark's upper jaw unhinged, its lower jaw dropped open, and a pair of emotionless black eyes rolled back up in their sockets. I gaped helplessly inside a dark cavern filled with razor sharp scalpels, each notched and serrated like those on Michael Leung's knife.

I was the perfect captive, frozen in fear, as those spiked blades proceeded to slash through flesh and bone. I cried out and jumped, only to collide against something hard.

"Good. You're finally awake."

I opened my eyes and escaped my dream. Michael Leung slowly came into focus, his cold black orbs impassively watching me.

Then I remembered. Leung had caught me inside his warehouse. Or, perhaps that had also been part of my nightmare. Maybe I was dreaming even now.

My stomach clenched as the world swayed to the eerie percussion of water slapping against wood. The sound was punctuated by the grinding of an engine, and I realized this was far worse than any nightmare. I was no longer on land but fully awake and lying on the deck of a boat.

I glanced at Leung, who nodded as if in confirmation. And for the first time in a long while, I was truly afraid for my life. I did what I always do in such situations. I brazenly opened my mouth.

"I don't know what you think you're doing. But if you have any sense, you'll turn this craft around right now," I warned, trying to sound a lot tougher than I felt.

"And why would I do that?" Leung asked archly, studying me as if I were some sort of science project.

I was momentarily stymied, and then came up with the only reason I could.

"You do know I'm a federal agent, don't you? I'm not someone that's simply going to disappear. People will be searching for me," I advised.

"Do you really think so?" Leung lightly mocked. "From what I've been told, I'll be doing more than one agency a favor. I hate to break it to you, but you're not all that popular among your peers."

He'd clearly done his homework. Still, it wasn't something that I wanted to hear.

"Maybe it has to do with the company you choose to keep," he continued. "Sammy Kalahiki wasn't very popular with those in his agency, either."

"You killed him, didn't you?" I responded, more to stall for time than anything else.

I looked around, but nothing was in sight—except for the sea, which stretched and yawned as if aware that it was nearly break of day.

"It became a necessity. He was snooping into things that didn't involve him. In fact, part of the reason he died was to send you a warning," Leung revealed.

It was as if I could feel those razor-sharp teeth tearing into my flesh again. I couldn't stand the thought of being responsible for yet another death.

"What in the hell are you talking about?" I said.

"Really, Agent Porter. Don't act so dense. If you'd listened to your superiors, you wouldn't be sitting on this boat right now. You have your own stubbornness to thank for that."

I closed my eyes, wishing this would all go away, wanting nothing more than to be seduced by the waves rocking me in a watery cradle.

Ouch!

Something hot nipped my flesh and I opened my eyes to find Michael Leung standing over me, having slashed my arm with his knife. I quickly lashed out, determined to fight him off, but discovered that my wrists were tightly bound in front of me.

"Don't worry. It's just a surface wound. That won't kill you," he advised, and swiftly moved away.

I struggled to my feet, only to be struck by a stench so vile that I promptly grew ill. Turning around, I wretched off the side of the boat. The remains of my Chinese dinner joined a stinking line of chum comprising flesh, fish guts, and a dark slick of blood.

Sharks generally lurk in our nightmares, but mine now sprang to life, as a gang of dorsal fins crisscrossed the water like a nautical rally of SUVs. I didn't even want to think about what Michael Leung had planned for me.

"And what about Yakimov? It was you that attacked me at his house the other day," I stated, partially to distract myself from the feeding frenzy below.

"Guilty as accused," Leung responded, with a self-satisfied smile.

"So then, Stas was also involved in the shark-fin trade." I naturally assumed he was.

"No, not at all. I thought you knew," Leung said, appearing to be slightly puzzled. "Yakimov was my supplier for black-market Viagra."

"Then why did you kill him?" I asked, feeling somewhat confused.

"Because the man had more muscles than he did brains. Stas became greedy. He knew about my shark-finning operation and heard that Kalahiki was poking around. He decided to contact each of us and see who would pay him the best price. Yakimov got hold of your friend and offered him information about my business.

Meanwhile, he threatened to use Kalahiki against me unless I met his demands. Believe me, Yakimov got exactly what he deserved."

I wondered if Leung knew about the photographs that I'd found at Yakimov's place. This seemed as good a time as any to find out.

"Whose idea was it to kill him, then? Yours or the senator's?" I asked, anxious to gauge Leung's reaction.

My mini-bombshell hit its mark as Leung stared at me in surprise.

"I don't know what you're talking about," he softly replied.

"Of course you do. I'm referring to Senator Shirley Chang. Or maybe you know her better as Shirley Marie Ting. She's an officer of Magic Dragon Restaurants Incorporated, along with your father. In fact, her brother works for one of your family's companies in Hong Kong. Wasn't that part of the deal? He gets a job and she gets a cut of the business so that you can operate freely on Oahu?" I probed, figuring I had nothing to lose.

Leung must have thought so too, because he responded with an amused chuckle.

"Very good, Agent Porter. You know more than I had realized. However, you should also understand that it's a grave mistake to toy with a woman of Senator Chang's stature and power," he replied.

"I take that to mean she's on the payroll and keeps things running smoothly for you here in Hawaii," I sarcastically retorted.

"Yes, she does. But not for the reasons you think." Leung paused, his eyes twinkling in amusement. "Senator Chang is my aunt. We like to keep our business all in the family."

It was my turn to be astounded. No wonder he had a lock on the illegal shark-fin trade in Hawaii.

"I suggest you take what little time is left and enjoy it as best you can. Breathe in deeply. Look up at the sky, gaze down at the ocean and watch the sharks at play," he said with a snigger, and grabbed a fishing gaffe from the deck.

Leung leaned forward and jabbed at the sharks, driving them into even more of a frenzy. My nerves shrieked as their teeth furiously gnashed at the pole like a flurry of bullets raining against metal.

"What about Sharkfin Dave? Is he involved in this too?" I asked, wondering if I'd been caught in a well-constructed web.

"Dave made a fatal mistake when he helped you to-night," Leung placidly responded.

"Why is that?" I asked, almost afraid to know.

Leung nodded at the shreds of flesh that the sharks were still fighting over. "See down there? You're looking at what's left of him. But don't worry. He's just a little treat to stir up their appetite. You're going to be the main course."

I tried not to think about Dave, but tore my gaze away, damned if I'd play the helpless victim as I had in my dream. If I was going to be shark bait, I fully intended to take Leung with me.

I watched as he continued to poke at the sharks, all the while waiting for just the right moment. It came as he dropped the gaffe and turned to throw more chum into the water. Lowering my head, I began to race toward him. But my scheme backfired, as Leung heard me approach and swiftly whirled around. Picking the gaffe back up, he used it to ram me hard in the stomach.

My muscles screamed, and my breath took flight, as my feet slid out from under me. Stumbling backward, I tripped and nearly fell overboard.

"Not so fast," Leung said, grabbing hold of me. "All in good time. You're to be the entertainment for my new business associate. I want to show him how we take care of our problems here in Hawaii."

He didn't keep me in suspense as to who that might be. A familiar figure emerged from the cabin, and my eyes locked with those of Vinnie Bertucci. There wasn't an ounce of sympathy in his gaze. Rather, his eyes were as deadly blank as those of any shark. I stared in horror, finally realizing that Santou and Kevin had been right all along. It was dangerous to get caught on the wrong side of Vinnie Bertucci—except that I'd learned my lesson too late.

"Nothing personal, New Yawk, but my boss will kill me if I go back without his money. Besides, it's business. You understand," he stated in a low monotone.

"Then you've been involved in shark finning this entire time?" I asked, cursing myself for having ever been so naive.

"No, just Viagra. But you know me. I'm always looking to hook up with a profitable new scheme," Vinnie said and turned to Leung. "She's an acquaintance. Do me a favor and make it quick, will ya?" he requested, and started to head back down into the hold.

"Wait a minute. I planned a special show. Don't tell me that you're not going to stay and watch," Leung responded, with a snort of disbelief. "And here I thought all you New York wiseguys were so tough. This will make a good story for my friends back in Hong Kong."

Vinnie stopped and glowered at him. "Shut the fuck up and just do as you're told."

"No one orders me around. Remember that," Leung coldly responded.

"Does that include Daddy, too?" Vinnie taunted. "I'm sick of the smell on this shit bucket. Just clean up your mess, and let's get the hell out of here already."

What a guy, what a guy.

"Coward!" I yelled at Vinnie's retreating back, as Leung now began to approach.

I wanted to fight him off, but it would be nearly impossible without the use of my hands. That being the case, I relied on what weapons I could. I bit down hard on Leung's ear as he attempted to grab hold of me.

"You bitch!" he cried out in pain, and smacked me across the face.

That only angered me all the more, and I went to knee him in the groin. But Leung was ready for such a move and countered with a punch to my chest.

The force of the blow sent me reeling to the back of the boat, where my feet became entangled in a length of coiled rope. I lost my balance and fell against the railing. The ledge cut into my stomach, as I stared down at the bloody remains of Sharkfin Dave floating in the water.

I must have become paralyzed with fright, because I suddenly couldn't move. The sharks seemed to sense it, too. Either that or they smelled fresh blood, for they now gathered below me.

One took the lead and partially breached the water, as though unwilling to wait for his meal any longer. I stared in dread at the open jaws, abruptly aware which of us was prey and which was the hunter. I was no longer anything other than a quivering tower of red meat.

The shark drew so close that I could smell the stench of death on his breath, and I pulled back with a terrified shriek. My bloodcurdling scream must have jarred the last bit of humanity still left inside Vinnie.

"All right, screw it. That's enough. Leave her alone, Leung. We'll find some other way to deal with the problem," he ordered.

But it was as though Leung had gone stone deaf. He continued to approach. My legs buckled beneath me, and I slid on the deck futilely searching for anything with which to defend myself.

"I said that's enough," Vinnie repeated, and roughly grabbed hold of Leung.

Leung's hand slid into his pocket and pulled out the shark-tooth knife.

"Watch out!" I cried.

Only my warning came too late, as Leung whirled around and slashed Vinnie's arm.

"You son of a bitch," Vinnie snarled, and started to go for his gun.

But the blade showed no mercy, slitting Vinnie's wrist so that the gun fell from his grip. That's when I spotted the gaffe near Michael Leung's feet and lunged for it. I clutched the pole between my bound hands, and whacked him across the legs with all of my might. Leung let out an enraged howl as metal hit bone, making contact.

What I didn't expect was to have the pole ripped from my grasp. But that's exactly what Leung did, tearing it from my fingers, and flinging it across the deck. Then he stumbled toward me once more. Only this time, the shark-tooth knife was held high in his hands.

I pressed myself into the corner, trying to become as small a target as possible. But once the blade found me, nothing would help. All I could do was to cover my head with my hands and prepare for the worst.

However, rather than the sting of the blade, a loud scuffle ensued, as Leung seemed to sprout wings and fly over me. I scrambled up to find him desperately clinging to the railing, where Vinnie had hold of his legs.

"Don't throw me overboard! Please, I'm begging you! I'll pay whatever you want!" Leung cried out, pleading with Bertucci to spare his life.

"Put him down, Vinnie," I seconded. "I'll take him back to Honolulu, where he'll be prosecuted."

"What, are you crazy?" Vinnie growled, and glared at me as though I'd lost my mind. "Don't you know how scum like this works? Leung's got enough connections to walk out of jail scot free in under two hours and come gunning for us. That is, if he doesn't make a deal and hand me over to the Feds first."

"Sure, but you were going to let him kill *me*," I angrily snapped.

"Aw, come on, kiddo. I wasn't ever gonna let him do anything. You know I've got a soft spot for you. I was just testing the water, so to speak."

I didn't have any idea whether or not that was true, but I wasn't in the mood to argue. Instead I picked up Vinnie's gun between my bound hands and aimed it at him.

"Just do as I say," I instructed.

"Unbelievable. You mean, I saved your ass and now you're turning on me?" he asked in amazement.

"It's not a matter of loyalty, but of doing what's right," I responded, not all that convinced of it myself.

Vinnie released Leung, never taking his eyes off me. That was a fatal mistake, as Leung twisted around with the shark-tooth knife still in his hand. I didn't give him the chance to plunge it into Vinnie, but quickly pulled the trigger.

The bullet hit its mark, nicking Leung in the arm, so that the knife skittered across the deck, madly clattering like a prototype for shark-tooth dentures. I glanced back up to find two angry men now glaring at me. As if that weren't bad enough, none of us any longer trusted one another.

"Nice work, New Yawk. What do you plan to do next?" Vinnie asked sarcastically.

I could hear the tinge of rage simmering in his voice. That was a good question. Who knew where Vinnie's loyalty might now swerve?

"Get some rope and tie him up," I said, nodding toward a mound of braided cord on the opposite side of the deck.

I expected Vinnie to drag Leung along with him, and was surprised when he released his hold. Great. I'd never felt more like a mouse trapped by a couple of wily cats. I swung the gun back and forth while trying to run every possible scenario through my head. Even worse, I stood dangerously close to the edge, suddenly finding myself caught between the two men.

"Damn it!" Vinnie muttered, bending down for the rope.

I turned to see what he was up to when Leung made his move. He slammed head first into my side, so that I flew against the railing and the gun was knocked out of my hands. I desperately fought to hold on as I felt myself being roughly pushed overboard.

"No!" I screamed, catching sight of the sharks below.

Vinnie must have started toward us, because Leung suddenly let go. I fell back down in time to see him scramble for the knife and start to slash at Bertucci once more.

I frantically searched for the gun, knowing that Vinnie didn't stand a chance against him. I cried out in relief upon spotting it. That was enough to snag Leung's attention so that he now came racing toward me. Flinging myself across the deck, I grabbed hold of the gun. Then rolling onto my back, I pulled the trigger as Leung loomed directly above me.

The 9mm shrieked, but even a bullet couldn't deter Leung from his mission as he swayed and then came crashing down, holding the knife so that it would slit my throat. I tried to shift onto my side, only to realize that I was held in place by his legs. Instead, I twisted my head as the knife angrily raced past, grazing my cheek and slicing into my shoulder.

Leung lay like a dead weight, his warm breath slithering across my neck, when he took a last rasping gasp and whispered something into my ear. But I couldn't make out the words as Bertucci roughly jerked the man off me. I no longer fought but instead watched as Vinnie lifted Leung up and flung him overboard like a sack of unwanted garbage.

The water burst to life, intensified by the thrashing of shark fins, and teeth, until nothing was left other than blood and silence.

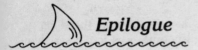

Epilogue

"**C**ome on, chere! You can do it," Santou yelled encouragingly from the beach.

I took a deep breath, aligned my hands by my ribs, and pushed up. Then I planted my feet in a wide stance, as a magical swell lifted my heart on the crest of a wave, and I was carried toward shore. For the first time, I now understood what Kevin and Santou were talking about. I'd never felt this free in all my life. It was a rush of supercharged energy and power, provided gratis of Mother Nature.

I laughed in pure delight, partly out of exhilaration and partly out of fear. Perhaps what everyone said was true. Maybe surfing really did capture a person's soul. For me, facing down a wave had become akin to confronting a predatory shark. It forced me to defy my limitations and, at the same time, accept just how vulnerable I really could be.

I jumped off the board and paddled the last few feet into shore.

"Cool bananas," Santou said, giving me a hug as Kevin flashed the hang-loose sign.

Both men realized what an important step this had been

for me. I continued to be plagued by nightmares of what might be lurking in the water below.

"I think you're well on the way to becoming a hot surfer babe," Kevin said with a wink.

"What do you mean on her way? She already is one," Jake replied, and I rewarded him with a kiss.

But I still couldn't forget what had happened only a few weeks ago. Probably because I dreamt about it every single night.

Vinnie and I had bound our wounds as best we could and then steered the boat back to shore. Once there, he'd jumped into his car and driven straight to Doc No Name's house. Vinnie had gone alone, insisting he'd be all right and didn't need any help.

"Just don't forget that you owe me big-time, New Yawk," were his parting words.

As if that was something I didn't already knew.

The last I heard, Vinnie had caught the first plane back to New York, where he said the streets were safe and he didn't have to worry about looking over his shoulder or getting whacked.

I'd stayed behind and cleaned all telltale blood off the boat, disposing of any evidence as I'd seen Vinnie do once before. Only then did I call Santou and the police, in that order.

I still wasn't sure what happened next. What I did know was that only after Kevin stepped in was my tale of abduction by Leung, and the ensuing battle, accepted without question. It was a valuable lesson. I learned that it paid to have good connections.

That prompted an investigation into Leung's illegal activities. Funny how justice sways with the prevailing wind. It was now believed Leung had been responsible for the deaths of Charlie Hong, Stas Yakimov, and Sammy

Kalahiki. In addition, a few low-level scapegoats within the Honolulu Police Department were accused of covering up evidence and receiving payoffs. But that's where the buck stopped.

Most upsetting was that the incriminating photos of Senator Shirley Chang had been taken from my Ford. I'd returned from Leung's boat to discover the Explorer had been broken into, and the documentation from Yakimov's was missing. I could only assume who the guilty party had been. Without those, there was nothing with which to tie Senator Chang to the ensuing scandal. Equally frustrating was that S. M. Ting could have been nearly any one of thousands living in Hong Kong.

Much to my surprise, I wasn't promptly shipped off to Guam, but rather asked to stay and continue my work on Oahu. Things grew even stranger than that. Norm Pryor actually suggested I investigate a few cases that he'd formerly refused to let me work on. I even had my fifteen minutes of fame when lauded by both Fish and Wildlife and the National Marine Fisheries Service for having uncovered "an isolated and highly unusual case of illegal shark finning."

The cherry on top of the poisonously sweet cake came when I received an official letter of commendation from the Hawaii state legislature. The letter was boldly signed by none other than Senator Shirley Chang herself. I was sorely tempted to return it to the sender, but dissuaded from doing so by both Kevin and Jake. I now view it as a reminder of the frustrating role that politics continues to play in my career.

I walked back to the house, leaving Santou and Kevin to surf the waves alone. Heading inside, I gave Spam and Tag-along each a treat, showered and changed, and then left a note that I'd be home in time for dinner. There was a task that I'd put it off until now, wanting to make certain of the final outcome.

Jumping in my Explorer, I drove down through the heart of Oahu and cut over to the West Coast. I didn't stop until I spotted the mountain that was deeply gouged with a skid mark. Then I turned onto the road that led to Auntie Ellen's house.

Her powder puff of a pooch materialized to yip and guide the way, much as it had before. However, there was a marked difference in its barking this time. It felt almost as if the dog had come to welcome me home.

The other disparity was that I no longer was tempted to turn and run. There was now a positive purpose for my visit.

Auntie Ellen opened the door as I pulled up, as if she had been waiting for me to arrive all along. A lavender orchid nestled in her hair, delicate as a butterfly, and a brilliant blue muumuu covered her sturdy figure. She waited in silence as I reached into my purse and pulled out a small wooden carving.

"I found this inside Sammy's box and thought you might want it," I said, and handed her the sculpted image.

Auntie Ellen clasped the wooden shark to her breast, and her eyes crinkled into a beatific smile.

"Sammy's grandfather made this for him when he was just a young boy. It represents our family's *aumakua*."

"That's why I came today. I wanted to let you know that part of the aloha has been repaid," I said, and suddenly felt painfully awkward.

"I already know," Auntie Ellen calmly told me. "I heard about what happened, and of how Michael Leung died. It was his fate for what he did to my Sammy boy."

I shifted my weight and bent down to pet the dog, hoping it would help ease my discomfort.

"The sharks would never have hurt you, you know. They'd have proteced you the same as they would have my Sammy," she staunchly insisted.

I wasn't so sure of that myself. On the other hand, I hoped I'd never have to find out.

"I just wanted to let you know that Michael Leung paid for his crime. Also that the police officially declared Sammy's death to be a homicide, rather than an accident," I divulged, wondering why I continued to remain so damned uncomfortable. Perhaps it was because I still didn't believe that I'd done quite enough.

Auntie Ellen looked at me without a word.

"Well, good-bye then," I uttered, and started to walk down the steps.

"It's not good-bye, but aloha. You do remember what that means, don't you?" she asked, by way of stopping me.

"Yes," I answered, hoping I wasn't in for another lecture.

"It's also the traditional way in which we Hawaiians part. Here, let me show you how it's done."

I waited as Auntie Ellen made her way down the steps and stood in front of me.

"First we look into each other's eyes, for that's where the soul resides. Then we lean forward until our foreheads and noses touch like this."

Auntie Ellen's skin felt cool against my own, and I finally began to relax.

"Now inhale deeply," she instructed.

I followed her lead, and unexpectedly found myself filled with an overwhelming sense of peace.

"That is what is known as sharing the *ha*, or the breath of life," she said softly. "It's the true meaning of *aloha*. Now you are one of us."

Auntie Ellen pressed the wooden shark into my hands and firmly closed my fingers around it. Then she silently walked back up the steps and into the house.

I remained standing where I was for a moment. Finally, I slipped into my Ford and started to drive home. But I could still feel Auntie Ellen's breath lingering inside me. And I instinctively knew that aloha was so much more, its meaning resonating deep in my soul.

Everything shares the breath of life in this world, and each has a purpose for its existence. Be it a culture, sharks, or little blue butterflies, nothing must ever be allowed simply to vanish.